Beyond Confusion

Sheila Simonson

Critical Praise for *An Old Chaos*
by Sheila Simonson, WILLA Award Winner

"VERDICT: Simonson packs great characters, fast-moving action, and suspense into this thought-provoking tale. This Pacific Northwest series just keeps getting better."

—*Library Journal*

"Simonson is a keen talent. Her characterization is clean and effective.... You'll be hard-pressed to find a better way to spend a few hours. You'll learn about the environment of the Pacific Northwest, you'll learn about Native American causes, about architecture and design, but the heck with all that. You will, simply, read a well-written mystery with several characters you want to spend time with."

—*Reviewing the Evidence*

"...[*An Old Chaos*] is primarily a character-driven book, deftly brought to life by Simonson, who lives in Vancouver, Washington. Her love for and appreciation of the beauty of the Pacific NW is made clear to the reader, and some arguments for and against its development are cogently set forth. The book is a fast and a good read."

—*Spinetingler*

"This book is satisfyingly convoluted, with enough subplots and red herrings to keep the most plot-minded reader happy. The setting and characters are also interesting."

—*Deadly Pleasures*

"*An Old Chaos* is an excellent character study told from multiple points of view, deftly illuminating the town's outrage when the people realize that their dishonest leaders set them up for tragedy."

—*Mystery Scene*

"The author does a good job evoking the beauty of the Washington-Oregon border area between Mount Saint Helens and Mount Hood...."

—*Publishers Weekly*

Beyond Confusion

MYSTERIES BY SHEILA SIMONSON

Beyond Confusion

A Latouche County
Library Mystery

Sheila Simonson

2013
PERSEVERANCE PRESS / DANIEL & DANIEL PUBLISHERS
PALO ALTO/MCKINLEYVILLE, CALIFORNIA

A Perseverance Press Book
Published by John Daniel & Company
A division of Daniel & Daniel, Publishers, Inc.
Post Office Box 2790
McKinleyville, California 95519
www.danielpublishing.com/perseverance

Distributed by SCB Distributors (800) 729-6423

Book design by Eric Larson,
Studio E Books, Santa Barbara, www.studio-e-books.com

Cover image: Monotype by Lillian Pitt, from the *Ancestors* series
Collaborative Master Printer: Frank Janzen, TMP
Printed at Crow's Shadow Institute of the Arts, Pendleton, Oregon
Photographed by Dennis Maxwell, Portland, Oregon

13 5 7 9 10 8 6 4 2

LIBRARY OF CONGRESS CATALOGING-IN-PUBLICATION DATA
Simonson, Sheila, (date)
Beyond confusion : a Latouche County Library mystery / by Sheila Simonson.
p. cm.
ISBN 978-1-56474-519-4 (pbk. : alk. paper)
1. Librarians—Fiction. 2. Indians of North America—Fiction. I. Title.
PS3569.I48766B49 2013
813'.54—dc23
2012014824

For my Mickey
Fifty years!

Here are your waters and your watering place,
Drink and be whole again beyond confusion.

—Robert Frost, "Directive"

Beyond Confusion

Chapter 1

November 2008

THE COLUMBIA RIVER poured west in November gloom, but light from the restaurant didn't reach the water. The mile-wide flow was visible from the dining room of the Red Hat only as streaks of reflected brightness when cars passed on Washington State Highway 14. Across the water in Oregon, sodium lamps traced the route of Interstate 84, which also paralleled the course of the river, a pink blur on the southern shore. The prevailing west wind rattled the windowpanes but threatened nothing worse than leaf-fall. Cliffs and mountains loomed, invisible. It was as good as November nights get.

Meg McLean gave a sigh of satisfaction and raised her wineglass. "To us."

Rob Neill set his salad fork down and raised his glass. "Us."

"It's been four years. *Salud.*" They drank.

"Four years and seventeen days." He smiled at her, a sweet, intimate smile without a trace of irony. "Marry me, Meg."

She kept her tone light with an effort. "'I am deeply sensible of the honour, but...'"

"No?"

"Thank you, my love, but no."

He started to say something else, gave his head a shake, and smiled again, this time with irony. "'If at first you don't succeed...'"

"'Try, try again.' Don't, Rob. I love you, but I don't love the institution of marriage." As far as Meg was concerned, marriage had turned her mother into a wuss and her father into a tyrant—all in the name of Christianity. Rob understood Meg's prejudice, or said he did.

"'Faint heart...'"

"'Never won fair lady.' Cut it out."

He laughed and turned back to his salad. Both of them enjoyed capping each other's clichés.

She said, tentatively, "'I could not love thee, dear, so much...'"

"'Loved I not honour more.'" He stabbed his salad. "'There's honour for you.'"

"Oops, you lost me."

"*Henry the Fourth, Part One*—Falstaff looking at the corpse of Sir Walter Blunt after the Battle of Shrewsbury. I identify with Sir Walter. My grandmother," he added, "took me to the Shakespeare Festival in Ashland when I was twelve."

Rob's grandmother, Hazel Guthrie, had preceded Meg as head of the Latouche Regional Library. Rob spoke of Hazel Guthrie with simple affection, whereas Meg's feeling was closer to awe.

Hazel had made the small rural library system into a national model. Meg would never have left Los Angeles for the wilds of wet Washington if the Regional Library had not been a beacon for idealistic librarians. That her own leadership had been less remarkable than Hazel's was a sore point. Meg had just passed her first tax levy after two tries, a secondary reason for their celebratory dinner.

The efficient waiter whisked her salad away as she speared the last morsel of oak leaf lettuce. He had already snatched Rob's.

"So how are things down the nick?" she asked.

"What?"

"British police procedurals. They're popular with middle-aged women, for some reason. How are things at the cop shop?" Rob was undersheriff of Latouche County, which meant he ran law enforcement while the sheriff, Beth McCormick, learned on the job. Beth was learning fast.

Though Rob lived with Meg, they had scarcely had time for greetings in the past hectic weeks, so he gave Meg an update on what was happening. Fortunately for his budget, not much in the way of serious crime. He wound up his tale with the latest wrinkles in an ongoing saga of llama-rustling. He saw the most recent episode, three prize llamas whisked from a mountain pasture in the dead of night, as a training exercise. He'd given the case to the junior deputies he had transferred from the uniform branch to Investigations. Meg was fond of Jake Sorenson, the last transfer. Jake's sister, Annie Baldwin, drove the bookmobile.

Meg launched into a mournful account of repairs to the lumbering vehicle, a rebuilt schoolbus. The waiter returned with their entrées, poached salmon for Rob, rack of lamb for Meg. With her daughter at Stanford, seven hundred miles to the south, Meg had thought it was safe to order lamb. This one was local and luscious.

"Why the smirk?" Rob tasted salmon with the air of an experienced critic.

"Luscious local lambie," Meg murmured. "I was thinking of Lucy. She still won't eat lamb. How's the fish? Farmed?"

"No, but I suspect Copper River."

He meant the salmon had been spirited down from Alaska some days earlier at a temperature just above freezing. The parlous condition of Columbia River salmon runs led restaurateurs to such shifts. Rob did not approve.

They ate awhile in silence. Then he said, "Your levy passed. Buy a new bus."

She sawed lamb with a savage knife. "A new bookmobile would cost the yearly salaries of three aides. I'm already trying to decide how to cut my staff. Whom should I throw out on the street in exchange for a Winnebago?" She jabbed a bite of lamb and chewed viciously.

"Marybeth Jackman," he said without hesitation.

Meg contemplated that. "If only."

Marybeth was a thorn, had been from day one. Unfortunately, she was a thorn with seniority.

Rob chewed salmon. "And anyway," he said at last, "you can't transfer money budgeted for capital improvements to salaries, or vice versa, so your thinking is muddled. I suppose you're thinking about the decline in tax revenues."

"Point-oh-one-percent of nothing is nothing. There are houses in foreclosure all over the county. Real estate is in free fall." Revenue depended on property taxes.

"And banks are failing left and right. True. I got an e-mail this morning from Willow. My ex-wife's husband got stung from two directions—mortgaged house and stupid investments."

"Do I detect a note of satisfaction?"

Rob grinned. "Ah, now, would I gloat?" The smile faded. "I think they're going to lose that plastic palace they built down in Malibu. Willow's upset because her mother is."

Willow was Rob's daughter, now a sophomore at Lewis and Clark College in Portland. Meg wondered whether he resented the fact that her daughter was sharper than his, at least academically. No, she thought, not Rob. But Willow might.

Meg had spent an uncomfortable week in Willow's company the previous summer, though nothing drastic had happened up there on the shores of Tyee Lake. Rob and his daughter had caught trout and cleaned them. Meg had cooked them, a division of labor she approved of. She liked to cook. She didn't much like wallowing on the lake in a rowboat, even with a good book.

Her mind drifted back to the issue of marriage. *We're not really compatible, Rob and I,* she mused. *You say tomato and I say tomahto.*

"You ought to get rid of her."

"Her? Who?"

"Jackman." Rob chewed more salmon. "She's poisonous."

Meg sniffed. "She's a bully. Did I tell you she drove a homeless man out into the rain the other day?"

"Does she make a habit of that?"

"She said he was smelly. So would she be smelly, if she slept in a cardboard box and wore all her clothes all the time to stay warm."

Rob frowned. "It's a public place. Did one of the other patrons complain?"

She liked the way he said "other." As far as she was concerned, everyone, smelly or not, was welcome in a public library. "So Marybeth said. I didn't believe her. It was a quiet morning, except for the toddlers there for story hour, and they were all herded into the children's library, miles from the regular reading room."

"One of the mothers...?"

Meg waved her fork. "Yes, yes, it's possible one of them complained. The point is, Marybeth hounded him out of there because she could, because he had no defenses." She laid the fork down. "She picks on people. On the staff, too."

"Who?"

"Annie, for one. She's always complaining about Annie's lack of credentials or her clothes or whatever. Says she isn't professional. And never mind that Annie's patrons love her. Bob Baldwin has kept that old clunker going for the last five years, too."

"Why pick on Annie?"

"Because she *can*," Meg said wearily. "I told you Marybeth is a bully."

"Get rid of her."

Easier said than done. The library was civil service. So was the sheriff's department, for that matter. "I have to show cause," Meg snapped.

They ate awhile in rueful silence.

Rob was frowning. "Bullying is cause for dismissal, Meg. Document it."

Meg's cheeks felt hot with suppressed resentment. Did he think she hadn't tried?

He took a swallow of wine and made a face—it was a local pinot noir, nice with lamb, less so maybe with salmon. "Bullying is an issue with us, too, believe it. The uniform branch dealt with a case last year. The perpetrator was persuaded to resign." His mouth eased in a smile. "Police brutality sounds worse than librarian brutality somehow."

"Marybeth has a wide range of victims." She kept her voice even and colorless.

"You included."

"Yes."

"Let me guess—pious comments about fornication and community standards?"

Meg was silent.

He swore under his breath. The waiter, who was heading their direction, veered off as Rob cut an unenthusiastic forkful of salmon.

Meg concentrated on her lamb before it could be whisked away. When she had chewed a last succulent bite, she said, "I gritted my teeth and ignored that woman's gibes for two solid years, though she did me damage with the Assembly of God folks before my first levy attempt."

"You should have said something to me."

"I did." She stared at him until he met her eyes. "I said no when you asked me to marry you."

"If that's the reason..."

"You *know* my reasons, Rob, and they have nothing to do with Marybeth Jackman."

He made an impatient noise. "You said two years."

"I cut her some slack. I felt sorry for her. She was in the running for my job, or thought she was." Meg drew a breath. "After that, I started documenting—and repairing the damage when I could."

"When you could?"

"Female bullying, especially in the workplace, is harder to pin down than the all-guys-together male variety."

"Sexist."

"It's true. Women, especially educated ones, don't sling politically incorrect labels at each other or beat each other up in the parking lot. They're subtler, but they can be as cruel."

Rob looked as if he were about to offer examples of female violence, but he restrained himself. "So what did you do?"

"I dispersed Marybeth's worst cronies to the Azimuth and Black Bluff branches, and I started courting the bystanders and the people she picked on. Gave them training opportunities, interesting assignments, praise for good work, a sympathetic ear. Some of them have hellish problems at home. I listen. Marybeth doesn't."

"Does it work?"

"Pretty well. I'm isolating her. I'm polite, of course, very very polite." She crumbled the remains of a rather dry roll. "If the levy *hadn't* passed, if I hadn't ridden Obama's coattails, I would have had open staff rebellion. I may yet, if revenues fall drastically." She raised her glass and gulped the last of her wine. On cue, the waiter materialized and took her dinner plate.

Rob held onto his and tucked into his broccoli rabe.

Meg watched his dutiful ingestion of vegetable matter. "I don't like the effect Marybeth has on my staff, but my real concern is what she does to the patrons she picks on."

"The homeless."

"And kids and undefended seniors. She really enjoys wrong-footing elderly ladies who forget to check a book out and trip the alarm, or lose a paperback they *have* checked out. And she's hell on teenagers."

"They can be trying."

"No kidding. But the library's a refuge for a lot of them, especially the shy ones. I set up a board of shy girls to review the YA novels in the collection, and Marybeth kept hushing them when they got excited—as if those kids needed to be squashed more than they already have been. I had to let them meet in my office."

"Softie." He smiled, his gray eyes warm with affection.

"Can I interest you two in dessert? Marionberry cobbler? Poached pears in wine sauce...?" The waiter sounded bored.

"Dessert?" Rob said.

She fluttered her lashes at him. "I want dessert, big boy, but not here." The waiter blushed.

Meg and Rob drove home.

Chapter 2

MEG WAS SORTING through e-mail at her office the next morning when Madeline Thomas telephoned, sounding grave, even portentous. Could she see Meg after lunch?

"Let me check my calendar, Chief Thomas." Meg didn't try to pretend she had a meeting. Had one been scheduled, she would have cancelled it. Madeline was principal chief of the Klalos, who were the most numerous tribe in the county. She lived in Two Falls where Meg had promised to build a new branch library, a promise that was now in jeopardy. "Two o'clock in my office?"

She could hear Madeline's computer keys clacking. "Yes. See you then."

"Is it about the library?"

Madeline gave a short sharp laugh, a strange sound. "In a way. Tell you when I come."

"How have you been, and how's Jack?" Meg listened to an account of Jack Redfern's arthritis. Madeline's husband was a great friend of Rob's.

Meg made noises of sympathy as she scrolled through the spam on her computer. Penis enhancers. Christian debt removal. High school reunions. Nigerian investment opportunities. Strange messages in the Cyrillic alphabet.

She was about to zap the lot when she spotted a singularity. Mary-beth had sent her an e-mail. Why? She removed the check beside the address and deleted her spam.

Madeline wound down, both women hung up, and Meg's respect-able mail loaded. Wondering how she was going to explain to Chief Thomas that there would be a delay in construction, Meg worked dutifully through her messages, interrupted only twice by phone calls. She saved Marybeth for last.

The mysterious e-mail was an invitation. Meg reread the words several times before she noticed that the message was not directed to her personally, that Marybeth had sent out a mass mailing to the entire staff of the Klalo town branch of the library. That was a relief.

Meg clicked on Reply and was about to decline with thanks but paused with her hand on the mouse. What if the invitation was an olive branch?

Meg entertained staff members frequently, sometimes at her own house, which was small, just right for committee meetings and gab sessions, and sometimes in Rob's big empty Victorian next door, which had been Hazel Guthrie's home and was suitable for larger li-brary events. Meg had included Marybeth when she couldn't avoid asking her, and Marybeth had come, gushed to her face, and stabbed behind her back. However, Meg had never seen the inside of Mary-beth's house.

She'd heard about it from the privileged. It was Marybeth's por-tion of the community property settlement when she divorced her husband, a chemist employed at the old paper mill, since closed. By McMansion standards, which had drifted north from California in the previous decade, the house was small, but everyone said it was a band-box, and it perched on a steep bluff that overlooked the river in one direction and the town of Klalo in the other, so its intrinsic value was magnified by its site. Meg's own house sat on a quiet side street with no view whatsoever.

She had driven by the Jackman place any number of times, coveted the setting, and admired the neat, seasonally appropriate flowers and mature maple trees in the front yard. Clearly Marybeth took pride in her home.

In a spirit of pure curiosity, Meg sent an acceptance for what was to be a "deck-warming" party, tea or wine, the Wednesday before Thanksgiving—eight days off. The library closed early that day.

She wondered how, in the course of deck warming, Marybeth was going to control the late autumn weather, a storm of sleet, for example, or a thundering gale. It was not until Meg headed off for lunch with a donor that it occurred to her she had sent her acceptance out to the whole staff. She had clicked Reply All.

~

MADDIE showed up at the library at two on the dot.

Madeline Thomas was hereditary chief of the Two Falls band of the Klalos and principal chief of all the Klalos by election. That made her a power in county politics, and increasingly, in the state. For one thing, she got out the vote, an achievement given the lack of interest in what the Klalos considered an imposed and alien government. More important, she had been raised by traditional grandmothers and understood Klalo culture from the inside out. She spoke both Klalo and the Chinook jargon, knew most of the teaching stories by heart, and looked the part. That she also had a sharp mind, a business degree from Portland State, and the instincts of a Tammany Hall politico made her formidable.

Chief Thomas and Rob had clashed repeatedly, but he respected her. Meg liked her enormously. All the same, she greeted the chief with the natural caution of any civil servant in the presence of any politician.

She offered coffee or tea. Madeline declined.

Proper conversation followed a ritual path, Meg had learned, so she asked after as many of Madeline's relatives as she knew by name— Maddie's cousin Bitsy, Bitsy's troublesome son, Maddie's nephew Todd who was Rob's deputy, her bereaved brother-in-law, her cousin in Flume, another cousin who was a library aide at the Azimuth branch, and young Nancy Hoover. Nancy had just been admitted to the nursing program at the community college.

Meg overlooked Lena, Maddie's niece who waited tables at Mona's, but Maddie told her about Lena anyway. Then Meg answered the chief's polite questions about Rob and Rob's daughter and her own daughter and her mother, who was ailing. Madeline didn't just ask. She was interested.

"You ought to visit her," she offered after hearing Meg's shamefaced admission of estrangement from her family.

Meg sighed. "It's a matter of principle."

Madeline nodded. "Of course it would be." That was polite, even kind.

"My father..." Meg really didn't want to explain thirty-five years of hurt and rejection so her voice trailed.

"Well, fathers are difficult sometimes, but your mother's sick."

"I'm not sure she'd welcome me." And very sure Dad wouldn't.

Madeline considered. "Your aunts?" Aunts were important in the Klalo social order, especially mother's sisters.

Meg hadn't seen her maternal aunts since she was a child. They lived back East somewhere. She wasn't even sure they were still alive. She fumbled for a response. "I was very fond of my father's sister, Margaret."

Madeline nodded, approving. "Were you named for her?"

"Yes. She left me her house."

"That was generous." Her eyes twinkled. "In Los Angeles? Profitable, too, I bet."

Meg laughed and admitted that she'd made out like a bandit on the sale of Aunt Margaret's little house several years ago.

"Real estate." Maddy's nose wrinkled. "Why I wanted to see you today."

"The new branch library."

"Yes. How long do you think it will it take you to build it?" That was blunt almost to the point of rudeness.

Meg let the silence extend, then said, "A lot depends on the economy. We haven't found the right architect or the site yet. I'll need to consult you about both." Much of the Two Falls area was Klalo trust land. Meg had been hoping the tribe would donate the library site.

Madeline waited.

"There are bound to be money problems with this current bank crisis. Maybe three years."

"A long time."

Meg sighed and said nothing. It *was* a long time. Madeline had lobbied Hazel Guthrie for a Two Falls library, and Hazel had been dead six years.

"An old friend of mine died last spring."

"I'm sorry to hear it."

"Miss Trout. Fern Trout."

"Rob went to the funeral. He said she taught him high school biology."

Madeline nodded. "Me, too." Madeline had gone through Klalo High School five or six years before Rob. "She was close friends with my Grandmother Hoover. Grandmother even showed her one of the Bear Clan huckleberry patches. Fern never told anybody where it was."

The right to harvest certain plants—native blueberries, bear grass, camas, chanterelle mushrooms, morels—passed down from mother to daughter along clan lines, and the secret of the locations was closely kept. Wars had been fought among the tribes and between clans to protect harvest rights. And strange to say, those rights were acknowledged in Anglo law, at least in the Gifford Pinchot National Forest. Private land was another matter.

Meg leaned back and looked at her visitor's beaded headband. It wasn't polite to lock eyes. She waited. Madeline would tell the story in her own good time. She came from a long line of story tellers.

She sighed and shifted on the visitor chair, which was narrow for her. "I've been talking with her lawyers off and on since then. They tell me the will's been proved."

"You're mentioned in it?" A guess.

Madeline nodded. "She left the family farm to the Klalo Nation."

"Congratulations. That's excellent news. Were you surprised?"

"No. She said she might."

"Is it large?"

"Half a section."

"Isn't a section a square mile?" Three hundred and twenty acres would be small for a ranch, big for a farm.

"Yes. It's a big place—an orchard." Most of the agricultural land northwest of Two Falls had been planted in orchard—apples, pears, peaches, and cherries—in the nineteenth century. "The trees are dying. They do eventually." Madeline didn't sound sad about the fate of alien trees. "You remember the Bjork bequest?"

"Yes, indeed."

"That was natural forest. I knew how that should be managed. I'm not sure what to do with an orchard, but I'll think of something. Organic cider maybe. Jobs for the kids." She was always looking for job opportunities for young people. Most of them left. They came back when they could, or when they had to. There was a lot of unemployment and would be more.

"Did Miss Trout manage the farm?"

Madeline smiled. "She ignored it most of her life. She was interested in native plants, not apples. Her sister ran the orchard, but she left the place to Fern. I used to visit my old friend there when she started to fail. She loved the house. Her niece pushed her to sell and move to assisted living. You know her."

Meg frowned. She'd never met the biology teacher. "The niece?"

"A Mrs. Jackman, one of your librarians."

Meg felt a jolt of surprise. "Um, yes. A senior member of the staff. An administrator." Marybeth oversaw the budget. That was the least people-intensive job Meg could find for her. "Do you know if Mrs. Jackman is going to contest the will?"

"Her lawyers advised her not to. It's a valid will, and Fern left her money. A lawsuit would just eat it up."

Meg felt a surge of hope. Money. Maybe Marybeth would move to Arizona. "A lot of money?"

"Not a lot compared to bank bailouts, but it sounded like a lot to me. The estate will pay the taxes."

Maybe she'll retire. Meg caught herself before she could utter that hopeful thought.

Madeline grinned as if reading her mind. "Why I wanted to see you. The thing is, Fern left us the farmhouse, too, and all her books. She had a lot, mostly about plants that grow in the Northwest. She wanted us to set up a library out there that would be open to anybody who wanted to study native plants."

"Sounds more like a reading room than a library."

"Yes. A good-sized room with lots of bookshelves and maybe one of those long tables."

"And a computer or two, and a photocopier."

"A desk for our librarian."

"You could furnish a small language lab, too," Meg teased.

Madeline beamed. She was deeply interested in preserving the Klalo language. There were fewer than six hundred speakers left, most of them elderly. She gave a decisive nod. "The big front bedroom would do for the reading room. Could you maybe use the rest of the house for the Two Falls branch? We could deed the house to the library district if you agreed to run Fern's book room and a room for the Klalo song-and-interview CDs."

"And the language lab?"

"And the lab. We could give you a ninety-nine-year lease on the land the house sits on."

Meg gaped. Maddie was serious. Meg's first impulse was to say no way. "It's not *in* Two Falls, is it? This farmhouse?"

"'Bout five miles northwest on County Road Three. Access road is gravel."

"We like to put our libraries where people live." Meg's mind sped into overdrive. *It was a crazy idea, wasn't it?*

Madeline cocked her head, frowning. "That's a problem, but I think it could be solved. We'd have to run a county bus out there and one of those wheelchair shuttles. I could probably horse-trade for that. The transit people owe me. It would mean building a bigger parking lot with a turnaround for buses—but there's plenty of room. There's a loading area for fruit trucks across from the house."

"We'd need fire escapes, rest rooms, wheelchair access."

"Oh, you'll have to fix the place up, and that will cost money, but if you don't have to pay a fancy architect and put up a building, you'll have plenty of cash for remodeling." Madeline had shifted from conditional to future tense. She must be sure it was going to happen. Or maybe she was making an end run.

I can buy a new bookmobile. When that thought crossed Meg's mind in present tense, she knew she would cave in. She forced herself to pause. "It's a very generous offer, Maddie, and I thank you for it, but I can't make a commitment. I need to look at the place, bring in the fire marshal and a contractor or two, talk it over with the trustees... How's the wiring?"

"It'll need work if you want Wi-Fi."

Meg groaned. Of course she wanted wireless Internet. Not to mention good lighting.

"When can you look at it?"

Meg clicked on her calendar with clumsy fingers. "Monday?" She hoped her eagerness wasn't too obvious.

Madeline stood up, and so, perforce, did Meg. "Good. Ten o'clock. Meet you there. Bet you can set the new branch up in less than a year."

"You leave me breathless." They shook hands, and both of them laughed like conspirators.

As she walked Madeline to the front entrance and saw her off in her little Toyota pickup, Meg was conscious of eyes watching them. Not just Marybeth's. Everyone's. Madeline Thomas had presence.

By Monday Meg had forgotten the invitation to the Jackman deck-warming party on Wednesday, though it lurked on her calendar.

Meg and Madeline had agreed not to make any public statements about Maddie's idea for the library branch, but Meg had had to talk to the fire department. The fire marshal said he'd send an inspector out to the farm Monday morning. She called an informal meeting with the trustees Thursday night, a work-session at which she aired the idea of recycling the Trout farmhouse, and noted their mostly intelligent objections. Also, of course, she told Rob everything and listened to his analysis.

He thought turning the Trout house into a library might trap her into having to appoint Marybeth Jackman *née* Trout to the post of branch librarian, an insight so filled with horror Meg suppressed it. It kept resurfacing at inconvenient moments like a skull at a medieval banquet.

At twenty after nine on Monday, she hopped into her faithful Accord, laid her freshly printed map and a Thermos of hot coffee on the passenger seat, drove through town with careful attention to the stop light on Main Street, and headed east on Highway 14. She even remembered to reset the trip odometer to zero.

Traffic was sparse. In Two Falls, a village composed of manufactured homes and neat but ugly government housing, an elderly Klalo woman in jeans and waterproof parka inched across the highway leaning on a walker. Behind Meg a car engine revved, impatient, but she waited until she saw the woman safe on the far curb before turning north onto the designated county road.

Meg was a little early. She hadn't seen Madeline's pickup outside the double-wide mobile home in Two Falls where Maddie and Jack lived, so the chief was even earlier. Meg wondered when the fire inspector would come.

The road cut steeply upward, away from the roaring Choteau River, and doubled back to the west in a corridor of dark conifers. She glanced at the map. Three miles to go. Was the farm completely isolated? Other than mailboxes, she saw no sign of habitation for another mile. Then the land opened up a little, prairie with groves of Douglas fir and vine maple and a scatter of houses, mostly manufactured. Finally, after a last swooping curve, Meg came out in the middle of a big orchard with the occasional barn or house roof visible in the distance amid other orchards.

She turned left at the first mailbox. Madeline had parked the Toyota Tacoma on the turnaround. Meg pulled in behind it and got out. The chief stood on the porch of the classic farmhouse. The front door was open wide.

Meg grabbed her purse and notebook, extricated herself from the car, and walked around behind it, slamming the door. Madeline still hadn't moved or spoken.

"Lovely day," Meg burbled.

Madeline didn't reply.

Meg stopped with one foot on the wide porch step. "What's the matter?"

Maddie jerked her head toward the open door. "Look."

Chapter 3

THE FARMHOUSE had been trashed.

When Meg stepped into the dim hall, she saw nothing untoward, but the stench of human waste made her gasp. She turned left at an arch that led to what must have been the family parlor and stood at the edge of the brighter room, breathing through her mouth.

Her first impression was of a chaos of ruined books. Then things began to come into focus. An ancient recliner listed against the far wall, its padding bulging from wide slashes. A pink Princess phone perched on the seat with its cord hanging loose. Ornate shade smashed, a floor lamp lay on its side near the recliner. Someone had ripped books from U-Haul boxes and left the cardboard in a heap beneath the front window. The books themselves had been wrenched apart and flung into a pile in the center of a stained square of carpet. Crumpled sheets of paper—book covers and random pages of print—lay at the edges of the rug. And someone had peed over the mountain of ruined books.

On a cracked mirror above the fireplace mantel, a stagily illiterate hand had scribbled, *The only good injun iz a ded injun* in grease pencil, but the *pièce de résistance*, a turd, lay just inside the arch. Meg would have stepped in it if she'd entered the room.

She'd seen enough. She had no doubt the kitchen would be as

bad, if not worse. She fumbled in her purse, found her cell phone, and flipped it open with trembling fingers. No service. Fuming, she made her way back to the porch. She tried to walk in her own footprints. Maybe Forensics could read the scuff marks on the floor of the entry-way.

Madeline had not moved. When she saw the telephone, however, she reached out and clamped Meg's wrist. "No cops. If it was my kids, I'll deal with them." Her fingers felt like a vise.

"That hurts." Meg pried the iron grasp loose and slipped the phone back into her handbag. "I can't phone here. No signal. It wasn't your kids, Madeline."

"Vandalism says kids." The chief's voice was dull.

"Let's go sit in my car. It's starting to rain."

Trembling or shivering, Madeline followed Meg to the Accord. When they had settled in, Meg reached for her Thermos. She poured coffee into the cap and handed it to the shaken woman. Then she started the engine and shoved the heater on high. Warm air billowed.

Madeline sipped the steaming liquid and grimaced. "No sugar?"

Meg fumbled in the glove compartment and found packets of sweetener.

Madeline doctored her coffee. "The door was open."

"When you came? Wide open?"

"No, just unlocked. I asked that woman to lock up and leave the key in the mailbox. It was there."

"What woman?"

"Mrs. Jackman, Fern's niece."

"Why was *she* here?"

Maddie heaved a sigh, but her voice, when it came, sounded less reedy. "Fern lived here until she died, so the house was furnished. I told Mrs. Jackman to take whatever she wanted. You know, family keepsakes, pictures, china. I thought she might want an old dresser or a rocking chair. She said she'd rent a truck and move the stuff last weekend. I asked her if she wanted help, but she thought her daughter's boyfriend could do the lifting."

"And she took everything." That sounded like Marybeth in a vindictive mood.

"Yeah. Well, not junky stuff like that old recliner, and not the books. We boxed them up and marked the boxes so she'd know they were ours."

"Who helped you do that?"

"My troops." She meant middle- and high-school–aged tribe members in her youth program. She and Jack were childless, and Maddie spent a lot of time working with young people. "That's why—"

"They knew what was here and how to get in, so you thought some of them had done it."

Madeline shook her head. "My brain stopped working when I saw the front room. I should have known my kids wouldn't desecrate Klalo property."

Meg thought they probably wouldn't scrawl rude remarks about Indians either.

Madeline turned, fixing Meg with a direct stare that felt like a small aggression. "Why are *you* so sure?"

"That they didn't do it? Because it looks staged. Even the crap on the floor. And because whoever did it destroyed the books." Removing a couple of hundred field guides, botany texts, and local histories from sealed boxes and ruining each of them took more than spite. It took obsession.

Madeline Thomas was not slow on the uptake. "Whoever did it had to know how things were left. Now we can't fulfill the terms of the will." Her shoulders slumped.

"Do you have a bibliography?"

"A booklist? Fern did. In order by the author's last name. The lawyers gave it to me." Madeline's mouth curved in a reluctant smile. "Author, title, publisher, date, condition—like a spread-sheet." She chuckled. "'Coffee stain on page twenty-three.'"

Meg laughed, as much from relief as amusement. "If you've got the titles and the authors' names, I can find replacements for you. I don't guarantee the coffee stains."

"That'll take forever! Some of those books were old."

"There's nothing like the Internet for finding old books. Amazon dot com, eBay, Powell's. Not to mention people's private collections."

"It'll cost a lot."

"No. They're rare books in the sense that most are out of print, but you could find a lot of them selling for a dime at garage sales. Trawl-ing garage sales and used bookstores would be a great project for your young people. Your insurance—"

"I don't think the contents of the house are covered."

"Check it out. If the books aren't insured, we'll do a fund drive. We'll find a replacement for every single title before we get the library up and running."

"You're going to open the branch here?"

"Yes, by God, I will." Meg's brain was spinning off ideas. Donations. Grants. Scholarly seminars in the parlor. Really, the wonder was, she hadn't thought of a Klalo-centered special collection for Two Falls be-fore the levy campaign. Marybeth was not the only staff member to doubt that the Klalos would use their new branch library. They would if it focused on *them*. Meanwhile, as penance, she'd do a staff workshop on racism.

Meg and Madeline waited in the Accord until the fire department inspector showed up in a radio car. He was appropriately shocked, called Dispatch, and might have rushed into the house to inspect the damage if Meg hadn't mentioned the word "evidence." Perhaps forty minutes after he got there, Rob and Jeff Fong drove in, followed by the crime scene techs in their van. When Madeline saw the van, she cheered up. She might mistrust the police, even Rob, but she liked facts.

Jeff took statements from both women while Rob set the foren-sic wheels in motion. The fireman and Chief Thomas went away. Meg waited for a word with Rob and then stopped off at Madeline's house on the way back to Klalo to get the bibliography, which was indeed thorough.

When Meg reached the double-wide in Two Falls, Maddie was making phone calls left and right and already planning a purifica-tion ceremony—after a company that specialized in cleaning crime scenes had sanitized the house. That cost the earth, and they had to come out from Portland, but they were worth it, she said. Insur-ance would cover decontamination expenses but wouldn't replace books.

She gave Meg a sketch of the farmhouse's room layout to use in planning the library. Both of them agreed to say nothing of the vandalism, though the news would leak out soon enough.

Meg had a good time scoping out the used book sites on her home computer that evening. She ordered five titles from Fern Trout's list, left queries on three sites, and was still online when Rob came home around nine. She jumped up and kissed him.

He returned the kiss with interest and led her where his heart was—the kitchen. He hadn't eaten.

"What were you doing on the computer?" Rob yawned and stretched.

Meg explained her search.

"Have a look at Gran's books. She collected local memoirs, and my grandfather bought every field guide that came out—waterfalls, trees, ferns, mushrooms, wildflowers."

Meg hadn't thought of the books next door.

Rob was tired but cheerful. Jake Sorenson and Madeline's nephew, Todd Welch, had rounded up the llama-rustlers, who turned out to be the proprietors of an exotic pet store. The business was in financial trouble. They said the theft was crime-for-hire. So far they weren't naming their employer, but Rob thought they would.

"Maybe I taught Jake a thing or two after all." He twisted the cap off a bottle of Full Sail Amber and took a long pull.

Meg was reheating stew. "I'll bet Reg and Ellen were happy." Reg and Ellen Koop owned the llamas.

"Delirious. Our predatory county prosecutor had tears in her eyes."

"I wish I'd seen that." Ellen was a lawyer with an instinct for the jugular. Reg, an organic farmer, was a milder spirit, but both of them regarded the mangy, ill-tempered llamas as pets.

Meg gave the stew a stir. When it was hot, she ladled a bowlful and cut Rob a thick slice of sourdough bread.

"Mmm, smells great." He ate with gusto, waving a spoon occasionally as he detailed his deputies' triumph.

Meg poured herself a small glass of wine, sat, and mustered patience. When he wound down, she said, "I'm happy for Jake. He needed a victory. Now, how about the vandalism at Trout Farm?"

Rob's nose wrinkled. "Lots of prints on the books and U-Haul boxes—Madeline and her kids. A woman's prints on furniture and smooth surfaces, probably Jackman's. Jeff caught up with her at the main library. She objected to having her prints taken but gave in. We'll eliminate hers. And there was blurring, as if somebody used gloves."

"Marybeth did it." Though she voiced her suspicion, Meg had a hard time envisaging Fern Trout's niece taking a dump on Fern's carpet. And somehow, despite their personal differences, she couldn't imagine a professional librarian ripping those books apart.

"She didn't hose the books," Rob said flatly. "Wrong plumbing."

Obvious. "So it was a man."

"Or a boy. With one or two collaborators. We got footprints upstairs. Sneakers."

"Not Maddie's kids!"

"No, I don't think so. I know most of them. Some have problems. One or two of them might tag a boxcar or write the girlfriend's name on an overpass, but this was calculated intimidation. You didn't see the rest of the house."

"No."

"It was a hate crime, and the Klalos were targeted."

Meg shivered. Since Obama's election, the local white supremacists had been lying low. Stunned, probably. They were bound to lash out, sooner or later. Their usual targets in the area were Hispanics and Native Americans. One hate group, who identified themselves as sports fishermen though they mainly hung out in taverns, had been vocal before the election.

"What about DNA?"

"Lot of that floating around." Rob sopped gravy with his bread. "The trouble with DNA, my sweet, is that you have to have a suspect in order to make a comparison."

"You have a suspect," Meg insisted, but her heart wasn't in it. She could picture Marybeth ordering other people to move the furniture out. Just. The woman was Miss Propriety.

Rob shook his head. "They—whoever they were—made a royal mess of that place, upstairs and down."

Meg's heart sank. "Surely it can be salvaged."

He shoved the empty bowl back and stood. "I hope the damage is superficial. It's a great location for your branch."

She finished her wine. She hadn't thought he liked the idea. Of course neither of them had seen the house before that morning. Such is the perversity of human nature, she found herself playing the devil's advocate. "It's way out in the uninhabited wilderness. Who'd be able to find it, let alone use it?"

"Provide GPS with your library cards." He flashed a grin. "Come off it, Meg. It's a great house—a comfortable house."

"The tuna fish casserole of houses."

"My point exactly. When people don't use a library, it can be because they're intimidated, and not just by officious librarians like Jackman but by the structure itself." He headed for the hall. "My grandmother said she worried about that when the central library replaced the old Carnegie building."

"She was right to worry," Meg muttered, busing but not washing the dishes. Rob could wash them in the morning.

The Klalo town library, the main branch of the two-county system, was a sore point with her, Hazel Guthrie's only mistake. It was built in the mid-sixties, and the architect had flaunted every design error peculiar to the period. Meg kept hoping for a modest earthquake to take it down some Monday. The library was closed on Mondays. She followed Rob upstairs in a pensive mood.

Later, as they lay drowsing in bed, Rob said, "Willow called me. She wants to spend Thanksgiving up on the mountain, skiing at Timberline with her friends." One of Willow's friends came from an old Portland family with a cabin on Mount Hood. "She's just sure we'll understand."

Meg could tell from the tone of his voice that he didn't understand. As a non-custodial parent, he'd got in the habit of thinking that each day he spent in his daughter's company was a victory. When Willow decided to come north to college Rob had been jubilant, but they hadn't seen much of her.

"I'm sorry," she murmured, though she wasn't.

They were scheduled for Thanksgiving dinner with the sheriff,

Beth McCormick, her five children and fifty grandchildren. Meg thought Willow's absence would not be noticed much, except by her father.

~

IN the giddy aftermath of the election—and an excess of high spirits— Meg had baked six pies. She'd frozen five of them, so she was good to go for the holiday. Breezing through her calendar Tuesday afternoon, she congratulated herself on the way her luck was running. Then she spotted the entry for Marybeth's deck-warming party. Wednesday afternoon. Five-thirty P.M. Her heart sank.

She woke in the small hours with the word "house-gift" echoing in her head. She would have to buy some doodad to "warm" Marybeth's deck. All the stores would close early.

Rob shifted and made an interrogatory noise. She gave him a pat and slid from the bed, because she knew she'd never go back to sleep. Robed and slippered, she made herself a cup of chamomile tea in the kitchen and found a raisin cookie to nibble. It was three A.M.

"The frogs!" she heard herself exclaim. Cookie crumbs flew. "Where did I put them?"

Meg had raised her daughter on the salary of a librarian, so thrift was an engrained vice. When someone gave her a gift she couldn't stand, she put it out of sight until she found a victim to bestow it on. Over the years she had probably saved two hundred whole dollars on meaningless house-gifts by this expedient.

Before Meg moved north, one of Lucy's friends had given her a set of wind chimes to commemorate Earth Day. It consisted of strips of bronzed metal from which hung tiny ceramic frogs, very green. When the wind blew, the chimes made a noise between a clatter and a tinkle. They were hideous, but Meg hadn't had the heart to toss them. The perfect gift for Marybeth. Lucy's friend would never know. Galvanized, Meg abandoned her tea and searched.

She found the frogs in the sideboard, lying in a tangle behind a stack of table linen. She filled a small gift box with Styrofoam pellets, which she loathed, and unsnarled the wires of the wind chimes from the metal strips. That took awhile, but the frogs were in excellent condition—no chips or nicks.

She tucked the *objet* in among the pellets, wrapped the box in silver paper, and found a moss-green bow. She was so delighted with her efforts, she also found a sheet of green rice-paper and folded a perfect origami frog. She inflated the frog with a single puff and stuck it to the mossy bow with double-sided tape. Perfect. She would find a gift card in the morning.

She glanced at her watch. It *was* morning. Four-fifteen. Briefly she considered making coffee and turning the computer on. No. She tip-toed upstairs, slid back into Rob's warmth, patted him again when he groaned, and fell deeply asleep. She woke at seven-thirty to the sound of Rob washing last night's dishes.

Chapter 4

HER GOOD CHEER lasted until, shortly after she arrived at work, Annie Baldwin burst into the office.

Meg leapt up. "What's the matter?"

Annie sobbed. "She's gonna fire me."

"Hey, nobody's going to fire you. Sit down, and I'll get coffee." She seated the chunky bookmobile driver in the visitor chair, handed her a box of tissues, patted her heaving shoulders, and dashed off to the staff room. Someone had brewed a fresh pot. Meg poured a mug and dashed back.

When Annie had regained her composure, Meg settled behind her desk and eyed the driver warily. "Can you tell me about it?"

Annie blew her nose. "It's that bitch Jackman."

No surprise. "You know she can't fire you. She's not your supervisor. I am."

"But I..." Annie broke down and sobbed again. "Oh, why didn't I just tell Kendra I couldn't take him?" She choked on another sob and blew her nose. "I know it's against the rules, but she couldn't find a sitter, so I said he could ride with me as far as town." Annie lived out in the hills west of Klalo. "He was real good. He didn't do anything."

Meg's stomach clenched. "Who, Annie?"

"My nephew, Pepper. Jake's ex had to take her little girl to this specialist in Portland, and Jake was on duty and couldn't mind him. So I said I'd let him ride with me to town, and Aunt Betty could take care of him. Jackman saw me take Pepper into my aunt's house."

Jake Sorenson was divorced. His former wife had custody of the two children.

Meg said slowly, "It seems to me that either Kendra or Jake should have been the one to find a sitter for the boy. How old is he?"

"Five. They couldn't. Find a sitter, I mean. And it costs." Annie sniffled. "Kendra doesn't work full-time, see, and money just falls out of her hands. It's why they broke up, that and Jake's job. I could hear them on the phone this morning. They were shouting at each other in front of the kids. Anyways, I like little Peep. Not his fault."

"Couldn't Bob do it?" Meg ventured. Annie's husband, a shy, inarticulate man, was the mechanical genius who kept the bookmobile rolling. Owing to the collapse of the new-car market, he'd been downsized from the service department of a Hood River Chevrolet dealership.

"Bob got a job clearing cross-country ski trails for the Forest Service."

"That's good."

"It's shit work, only a couple of days this week and next, and it kills his back." She gulped. "He couldn't baby-sit today. He was already gone. I can't lose *my* job. We need my benefits." The county had a medical insurance plan. Tears trickled down Annie's round pink face.

"Well, you won't lose your job," Meg said stoutly. "Don't let Marybeth get to you, Annie. But don't use the bookmobile for baby-sitting either. We're not insured for passengers."

"Oh, God, thanks, Meg. I'm sorry. Promise me you won't let Jackman change your mind?"

"I promise."

Still woebegone, Annie left to go out on her rounds.

Meg was unsurprised when Marybeth knocked on her door fifteen minutes later and entered with her latest sidekick, Wendy Resnik. Wendy worked in Circulation.

Meg drew a breath. Make nice, she told herself. "Ah, hello. I thought you were shelving books this morning, Wendy."

"I'm on break." Wendy shoved her glasses up her nose. She was a small woman, even shorter than Meg, and dressed too young for her age, which was forty.

"Early for that," Meg mused. "How are *you*, Marybeth? It looks as if the weather is going to cooperate with your party this afternoon. I hear you have a spectacular new deck. Cedar?"

Marybeth blinked. "I used a composite. It looks just like wood, and it's guaranteed not to rot. Uh, I saw Annie Baldwin leaving."

"Did you? You're observant. What can I do for you?"

Marybeth pulled the visitor chair back from its place beside the desk. "May I sit?"

"Certainly." Meg took pity on Wendy. "There's a folding chair in the closet. Do you want a cup of coffee?"

Wendy opened her mouth.

"We don't have time," Marybeth snapped. "I'll be brief. I want to make a complaint—"

"My, that sounds serious. Let me call up your file." Meg diddled with the personnel folder. "Right. A complaint." *How unusual.* "I hope the Budget Committee work is progressing in a timely fashion. With revenues falling—"

"It's not about the budget!"

"No? You're on the Safety Committee, too, aren't you?"

"It's about Annie Baldwin. Again. That woman should be dismissed. I caught her this morning taking some brat for a joyride in the bookmobile, brazen as day."

"A joyride? She was driving the bus at an excessive rate of speed? But I thought it couldn't go over forty-five—"

"I didn't say she was speeding. I mean, she was driving a very young child in that vehicle, and that, my dear Margaret, is against the rules."

Meg typed industriously. "And this joyride occurred where, on Highway 14? You caught her? Does that mean you overtook her? Did you call the state patrol?"

"She was driving in town."

Meg clucked her tongue, hit the backspacer, and resumed typing. "Speeding through an urban neighborhood."

"She was not exceeding the speed limit!" Marybeth leaned too close, the habitual signal of her aggression. Her eyes flashed. They were protuberant, hazel-green as a stagnant pool until wrath made them glow.

Meg pushed her chair back a little and said in soothing tones, "Why don't you tell me what you mean to tell me without dramatics?"

"Very well. She drove a small boy down Acacia Street and stopped the bookmobile in front of a private house. She got out and unstrapped the child from his car seat. Then she took the boy and the car seat into the house. She left the engine running. Two eleven Acacia Street. I noted the address."

Meg typed. "And?"

"That's it," Marybeth snapped. "Isn't it enough?"

"To fire her? I wouldn't say so offhand, but we'll see. I reminded her that we're not insured for passengers. What do you think, Wendy?"

Wendy gaped.

"Why are you here? Were you a witness?"

"I...no."

"So you just came along out of curiosity?"

Wendy said sullenly, "She's always breaking the rules."

The quick brown fox, Meg typed. "Which rules?"

"Well, parking the bookmobile at her house—"

"Saves on fuel." The price of diesel had skyrocketed that summer. It was still high. "Her route often takes her that direction."

"Still—"

"And her husband maintains the vehicle. I believe you applied for her job, didn't you? If you get her into trouble, that wouldn't necessarily put you in the driver's seat." She turned in her chair to smile at Wendy directly. "Not unless you have a mechanically inclined husband."

Like Meg, Wendy was unmarried. She blinked and shoved her glasses up.

"What else?" When Wendy didn't reply, Meg turned to Marybeth, eyebrows raised.

Marybeth rose without haste. "I could comment on Annie's get-up, I suppose." Her lip curled. "A purple sweatshirt with teddy bears?" Marybeth favored tailored suits. "Tschah!"

Meg admired the untranslatable epithet. She hit Delete. "Thanks for your input. See you this afternoon."

Marybeth swept from the room with Wendy trailing.

~

AT five-forty Meg rang the doorbell of the Jackman bandbox. A girl dressed in Wendy's style but twenty or twenty-five years younger opened the door. Her jeans were distressed and her navel pierced. Goose pimples dotted the flesh between her jeans and her lacy shirt. The tattoo of a screaming eagle ran down her forearm.

"Hi. I'm Carla Jackman. You must be Ms. McLean." Marybeth's daughter had a light, fluting voice, unlike her mother's.

"I am. Happy to meet you, Carla." Meg ducked in the door. She spotted a long table scattered with small wrapped gifts. She slid the frog chimes in their froggy box onto the table and shrugged out of her coat.

Carla hung it on an enviable oak coat tree. "You can go on through. They're out on the deck."

Meg took her time. She wanted to see the décor.

The living room lay a step down from the hall and boasted a cathedral ceiling, which qualified it as a Great Room. That was a term Meg didn't like. A Great Room was a big smelly chamber in a medieval keep where a baron feasted and kept his hounds at night. It ought to have a musician's gallery, rushes on the floor, and lots of fleas.

Marybeth couldn't be blamed for the verbal pomposity of architects. This Great Room was as tasteful as all get-out and sparkling clean. The carpet and walls shone, pristine, in shades of white; the furniture was vaguely Georgian, or perhaps Empire, and upholstered where it needed to be in beige—beige stripes or beige brocade. Beige watercolors of high desert scenes hung on either side of a pale stone fireplace that appeared never to have been used. An arrangement of cattails and bulrushes in an earth-colored vase stood on the hearth where a roaring fire might have cheered the November twilight.

A large mother-daughter studio portrait had pride of place in the center of the mantel. It had been Photoshopped until the edges blurred and both subjects looked airbrushed. Marybeth bared her teeth in a smile. A younger Carla looked blank.

Carla was welcoming other guests at the front door. Meg went on

through a dining area done in pale blue. The table was laden with wine
bottles, a tea urn, linen napkins, flutes, cups, and china plates heaped
with beige cookies. A French door swung open to the deck.

Meg took a deep breath and walked out to join the half dozen
members of her staff already assembled under a light pole. Meg could
see why they were there. The pole dangled an infrared lamp that cast
an infernal glow.

As Meg emerged the women fell silent.

"Hi, Wendy, Ashleigh, Nina. Ah, Tessa, I see you made good time
from Azimuth." Meg crossed to the lamp pole and shook hands in the
blast of warmth, murmuring the names of her other employees. Nina
gave her a shy smile. She liked Marybeth about as much as Meg did.
Tessa, on the other hand, was a crony.

The women made normal sounds of greeting and huddled under the heat lamp with their bone china teacups. Meg wished she'd
poured hot tea for herself or kept her coat on. A clear day in November
meant air from Alberta by way of Idaho.

Marybeth was not yet to be seen. Although it was already rather
dark and a lenticular cloud obscured much of Mount Hood, the view
of the Gorge was indeed spectacular, the river steely in the middle distance. Peach afterglow tinted the western horizon. Meg strolled to
the south edge of the expanse, grasped the railing, and looked down.

She suppressed a squawk. Marybeth's deck hung out over nothing.

Meg's hands clenched the rail. She had to force herself to remain
upright, because her impulse was to lie flat on her belly, hook both
hands to the wide composite decking, and shut her eyes. Or fling herself over the rail. She suffered mild queasiness just driving along Highway 14.

The residential area perched on the edge of a bluff composed of
basalt columns. The edge was solid bedrock, so the houses were firmly
anchored and in no danger of sliding down the two hundred or so feet
to the base. Still, they *looked* precarious. The deck looked catastrophic.

~

"VERTIGO," she told Rob that evening. "I almost passed out. It's a
deck for sadists. I might have known Marybeth would have an ulterior
motive for inviting me to her house."

Rob gave the pot of cioppino a critical stir—his turn to cook. "This is ready."

"So am I."

Rob began ladling chunky chowder into the big bowls warming on the stove. It smelled delicious. "Does she know you're acrophobic?"

Meg took a last sip of scotch and thought about it. "Probably. I told everybody how I felt when I drove the moving van up here from California. It's the sort of weakness she'd save up to use against me. Fortunately I didn't have long to suffer. The wind picked up, and we all went inside to get warm and watch her open her gifts."

"Did she gush over the frogs?" He set the bowls on the kitchen table where they almost always ate their meals.

Meg sat and unfolded her napkin. "She is phobic about frogs."

"Don't tell me. You knew she disliked them and saved them up to use against her."

"I didn't have a clue. When she pulled my origami masterpiece off the gift box, she made a face. Carla sort of giggled." A peculiar sound, high-pitched, nervous, and gleeful.

"The kid guessed what was coming?"

"I don't know." Meg sprinkled her soup with parmesan. "I thought Marybeth was just being her usual rude self, but when she opened the box and saw all those little green fellows nesting in the Styrofoam she let out a shriek."

"The frogs are that realistic?" Meg had sealed the wind chimes in their box long before Rob got up.

"I swear the shriek was genuine. And she paled. I thought she'd faint."

"What did you do?"

"Slunk off as soon as I could." Meg had been intensely embarrassed. She cringed, remembering—served her right for being cheap.

Marybeth had choked out a shrewish accusation. Meg made no reply and braced for a major assault, but the attack did not come.

Under cover of chatter from the kinder staff members, she watched Marybeth master her frog revulsion. Nina pointed out that frogs were endangered and helpful in insect control. Ashleigh, who had hitchhiked through France her junior year in college, told of a frog-leg dinner. The children's librarian, Pat, a latecomer, started a tale of family phobias that deflected the conversation into friendlier territory, and the dreadful moment passed. Carla removed the frogs. Her mother went back to opening gifts. It was all very strange.

Carla saw Meg to the door with a blank face. As Meg scooted out to her car, she heard the girl giggling.

Rob spooned a tiny Willapa Bay oyster from among the choice seafood. He'd been promising Meg the cioppino, his grandparents' traditional meal on the eve of a holiday, for several years. "You'd better watch your back, Meg. Jackman won't be able to see the frogs as a coincidence. You humiliated her in her own house in front of her allies."

Suddenly Meg's soup didn't taste all that wonderful. "I didn't even get to interrogate her about the Trout farmhouse. I meant to."

Rob's spoon clattered on the bowl. "Are you out of your mind? She's your enemy. Leave interrogation to Jeff!"

Meg bristled. She disliked taking orders. However, she was glad to know that Sgt. Fong was on the job. That meant Rob was taking the vandalism as seriously as she did.

~

THANKSGIVING dinner was wonderful in its way, because Elizabeth McCormick had just been elected sheriff of Latouche County in her own right after serving out her late husband's term. In spite of her gender—and well-financed Republican opposition—she had even out-polled Obama. Now her clan gathered to pay her homage.

Beth looked like everybody's grandmother, a white-haired dumpling of a woman. Fortunately, she also cooked like a grandmother, so the food was bound to be both traditional and tasty. Since her two daughters and three daughters-in-law were also talented chefs, Meg's pie contribution gilded the lily.

It was welcomed, nonetheless, by a procession of grandchildren charged with taking goodies to the kitchen—including pie accoutrements like vanilla bean ice cream (for the apple and pumpkin pies), whipped cream (for those who preferred their pumpkin pie conventional), and Tillamook extra-sharp cheddar (Meg's choice for apple pie). The odor of cinnamon warred with ginger and cloves. Mincemeat triumphed in the fumes of its rum.

"I could live on the scent of Thanksgiving," Beatie Potter said soulfully.

Meg was happy to see that Beatie had lost none of her wonted enthusiasm, despite transmogrifying into a blasé teenager over the last four years. Beatie was Beth's eldest granddaughter, her daughter Dany's girl.

Rob was borne into the living room in the collective embrace of Beth's other daughter, Peggy; her husband, Skip Petrakis; and their five-year-old, Sophia. As she followed the other kids to the kitchen, Meg could hear male voices shouting greetings over the noise of the requisite football game. Beth's sons had inflicted the big flat-screen television on her the first Christmas of her widowhood. She watched movies on it once in a while.

When Rob and his deputies had saved Beth, Peggy, and Sophia from the mudslide that killed Beth's husband, the McCormicks adopted him into the family. It was that simple. Never mind that Rob-the-boy had regularly slammed Mike McCormick onto the mat at the karate *dojo* both attended. Like Mike, Rob was now a son of the house—not just invited to family celebrations, of which there were many, but *expected*.

Meg was always invited as a reserve daughter-in-law. She found the McCormick adoption a bit suffocating. Though she loved Beth, she would have liked an occasional holiday *tête-à-tête* with Rob. She didn't really object, though. Rob had been very much alone growing up. He needed family. For that matter, so did she, estranged as she was from her parents and brothers who, in any case, lived in Southern California.

With a small sigh, she let herself slip into the raucous, loving crowd. It was almost dark when she and Rob arrived and seven before the feast began. So complete was her McCormick immersion, it wasn't until then that she discovered Rob had disappeared.

She was sitting at the right hand of Beth's eldest son John, who was carving the turkey at the head of the table and too preoccupied for conversation. Beth sat at the foot near the kitchen door. Meg turned to Rob's childhood victim, Mike, now a big amiable professor of American literature at an Oregon college. She liked Mike, not least because he bore Rob no ill-will for the many martial arts defeats.

"Where is he?" she asked, relaying a plate laden with turkey and dressing down the line. The grandchildren set up a shout at their rented table in the living room. Their plates had come to them already loaded with portions of the other turkey.

"Whoa, sounds like a riot in there."

"In here, too," Meg muttered. Conversation was general and loud. She raised her voice. "Where's Rob?"

"Um, I dunno." Both of them scanned the dining table. Rob's place setting at Beth's right hand had vanished. "Ask Mom."

Meg didn't get a chance to ask until everybody had toasted Beth, passed the side dishes around, and settled in to eat. When they dined *en famille*, the McCormicks had no truck with newfangled ideas like courses. A meal was served ranch-style, everything except dessert at one fell swoop.

The mashed potatoes inevitably ran out, and Beth slipped off to the kitchen. Meg followed her. The sheriff was dolloping potatoes into a serving dish. She smiled and handed Meg the warm bowl.

Meg hefted it. "Where's Rob?"

"He had a call." Beth loaded a second dish. "He said to save him a piece of mincemeat pie."

"A call about what?"

Beth met her eyes. "Unattended death."

Meg's heart sank. Rob liked his job, for the most part, though he was not a natural administrator. He had learned to delegate, but he responded in person to cases of questionable death, which was only right, he said, in a small department. Meg thought it was a form of self-torture. A nice problem of fraud or dope peddling or llama rustling intrigued, and in the case of the llamas, amused him. He was a good detective, but waste of human life cast a lingering pall of depression over him. Nearly four happy years had passed since the county had seen a murder.

"It may turn out to be an accident," Beth murmured, as if she had read Meg's mind. Maybe she had. They returned to the dining room.

The dinner was served with a choice of a local cabernet or a nice riesling, and everyone settled in to eat, booze, and talk. Despite the economic crisis, they were mostly cheerful and seemed pleased with the results of the presidential election. That surprised Meg, though it shouldn't have. Most were Democrats, including Beth, though some were rather conservative. Dany had campaigned for Hillary Clinton.

The sheriff produced coffee to go with the pies. The pies and coffee mostly disappeared, the men went off to the living room to watch a football game from Hawaii, and the women herded the younger grandchildren upstairs to the long, glassed-in sleeping porch. Meg, Beth, and Dany were sitting in the dining room, drinking coffee and loosely supervising a crew of older grandchildren with the clean-up, when Rob finally returned. He brought Jake Sorenson in with him.

"You guys must be starving!" Dany jumped to her feet. "Hi, Jake. Been rolling in the mud?"

Jake swayed on his feet. Frowning, Rob took the deputy's elbow. They had shucked their jackets, but both sported smears of mud and plant debris on face and hands.

Beth gave them a supervisory glance. "You know where the bath-room is, Rob. Wash up, and we'll feed the two of you first. Then you can tell me all about it."

Rob nodded to her and gave Meg an odd look, sad and apologetic. He led Jake off. Meg went out to the kitchen to help.

The two men ate in silence, Jake eagerly and Rob as if he were ful-filling an obligation. Jake inhaled a slice of apple pie and one of pump-kin. Rob toyed with his mincemeat. Both men drank coffee.

When Grandma Sheriff was satisfied that her boys would survive, she said, "Tell me about it."

Rob and Jake exchanged signals, and Rob drew a deep breath. He turned to Meg. "Marybeth Jackman is dead."

Meg gasped. She could not have said anything.

Beth's voice was calm and politely sad. "I'm sorry to hear that. How did it happen?"

"She fell off her deck."

Chapter 5

MEG FELT TRAPPED at the point in a story when a secondary character, usually female, clasps her hands to brow or bosom and says, "I just knew it, I had a bad feeling." She sat mute.

Beth asked the logical question. "Was it an accident?"

"Hard to tell." Rob sounded grim. The turkey in Meg's stomach churned.

Jake looked up from his last bite of pie. "The neighbor—man by the name of Frank Waltz—called 911 after three-thirty. Him and his wife had just come home from serving dinner at the Refuge." The Refuge was a community shelter for needy people. Three local churches joined together to run a meal service there Sundays and holidays.

"Go on," Beth prodded.

"Wife went to the kitchen. Waltz poured himself a glass of wine and took it onto his deck for a look at the weather. They had family coming at five. It was pretty dark by three-thirty because of the storm."

"There's a storm?" Dany squeaked.

"It's sleeting."

"I'd better warn the boys! Pete wants to drive home. I *told* him we'd have to stay the night." Pete was her husband. All of Beth's children lived in the Portland area. Dany dashed from the room.

49

Beth was used to interruptions. "Mr. Waltz went out on the deck. What then?"

"They've got one of those lights with a motion sensor. He moved farther out onto his deck. When the light came on, he saw a patch of color down on the scree."

"At the base of the cliff?" Meg shuddered. The long fall of her phobic imaginings.

Jake nodded. "What he saw was beigey-pink like those plastic grocery bags from Fred Meyer, so he just thought somebody'd tossed trash. He's a bird-watcher. He got out his binoculars and spotted the vic... Mrs. Jackman's hand. That's when he called in."

A chorus of laughter intruded from the kitchen—the grandchildren on clean-up duty, horsing around. Footsteps and muted voices overhead suggested heavy negotiation over the drive to Portland.

"Dusty rose." When the men stared at Meg, she added, "Marybeth wears...wore that color a lot." She was wearing a dress of that hue in the photograph on her mantel. Meg's numbed brain jolted. "Carla! Who's going to tell Carla? Where is she? Was she at home when it happened?"

"Who's Carla?"

"The daughter, Beth. High-school age." Rob swallowed cold coffee. "It took us a while to find her. She spends alternate Thanksgivings with her father in Camas, and this was his year. We found his number on Jackman's speed-dial." Camas was a good hour's drive west of Klalo, in Clark County. "Carla was there with him. He said he'd break the news to her, thank God. I hate doing that."

Meg felt a twinge of relief. Rob made next-of-kin calls in person when he could. Carla's father had saved him a dangerous drive.

Another burst of noise from the kitchen was followed by an ominous crash. Beth heaved a sigh of resignation, rose, and left the dining room. Silence from the kitchen, followed by grandmotherly commentary, followed by a murmur of apology.

Rob frowned at Jake. "I want you to go home."

"No, I—"

"That's an order. Call Kendra. Take an aspirin and get some sleep. My office at eight A.M. sharp."

"But the sheriff—"

"It's okay, Jake. I'll give her what she needs to know. Then I'm going home myself. We can't do anything until morning anyway."

"But I'm on call—"

"Todd can come in a couple of hours early."

Jake shoved himself to his feet and stumbled off toward the hall without a word. He looked worse than tired.

Meg stared after him. "What's going on?"

"He's not getting a lot of sleep. They think his little girl may have leukemia."

"Oh, my God, oh, poor Jake!"

Rob glanced at the door to the kitchen. "Keep it under your hat. They're not sure yet, and you know Beth. She'll smother them with advice, organize a fund drive, give Jake a year's sabbatical, offer to take care of Pepper." He made a face. "What a name."

"You called your daughter Willow."

"I did not. That was Alicia being trendy." Alicia was his ex-wife.

"I'm relieved to hear it." Meg found she was leaking tears. She wiped her eyes and wondered what was wrong with her. She didn't usually blubber at the drop of a hat. Jake's tragedy was beyond tears, and she couldn't be crying for Marybeth Jackman, could she? Or even for Carla. She didn't know Carla.

She had blown her nose and composed herself by the time Beth returned.

Beth plumped down on her chair. "Ciaran dropped a platter. Fortunately I hate that china. The girls brought it for me after the mudslide." Beth had lost most of her belongings in the mudslide that killed her husband. "I see you sent Jake home, Rob. Good idea. He looked exhausted." Her eyes narrowed. "You don't look so good yourself, so summarize, please. What's eating you?"

"The timing."

"Go on."

"The call came at three-thirty, and the medics got to her, to the body, around four. They made a stab at CPR, but she was dead, they're guessing hours."

"And nobody saw her fall?"

"We didn't find any witnesses, no. Most of the people who live up there were gone. Long gone—snowbirds—in one case. We'll catch up with the others tomorrow or Monday if they're off visiting Grandma for the holiday weekend. We'll put out a call for people who drove on Bluff Road this morning or early afternoon."

Bluff Road, steep and mostly straight, angled up from Highway 14 across the lower third of the geological formation before turning to head straight for the top. When Meg took that route, she clutched the wheel with both hands and kept her eyes on the road. Not all drivers were phobic, of course, and maybe one of them, or a passenger, had seen Marybeth fall.

"I just don't get it," Rob was saying. "When we looked at the house, we found that everything was set for a dinner for two. The oven was hot. She was roasting a big chicken or a small turkey—"

"Capon?" Meg suggested.

He smiled. "Maybe. It hadn't been cooking very long. The vegetables in the roasting pan were only half-cooked and the skin on the bird hadn't turned brown yet. The table was set. There was a fresh salad in the fridge. Soup in a crockpot. And the house was spick-and-span, I mean *nothing* out of place. No damp towels in the bathrooms. No half-empty coffee cups."

Meg choked on a laugh. That was Marybeth, compulsively tidy. "She probably cleaned the place from basement to attic a week ahead of time and erased the traces of her deck-warming party before the last guest drove away."

"Deck-warming?" Beth asked, bemused.

Meg explained.

Beth's nose wrinkled. "In November? What a doomed idea."

Neither Meg nor Rob responded. Doomed was the right word.

"Automatic oven timer," Beth said abruptly.

Rob stared. "Why didn't I think of that?"

"You've probably never used yours."

He gave a short laugh. "You're right. Okay, so she had the oven set to come on at three-thirty. Who has dinner at, what, four-thirty? Five?"

Meg said, "People who can't come at the usual times."

"Somebody on a night shift?" Beth ventured.

"Could be. Or somebody who had to catch the red-eye and wanted to digest dinner first." Rob's eyes narrowed. "I wonder who?"

Someone who shoved her off the deck, Meg thought, but she wasn't about to put the idea into words. No, it had to be an accident. *Please God*, she thought, *let it be an accident. Not murder, definitely not suicide.* Somehow suicide sounded worse than murder, because Meg would never be sure she hadn't contributed to suicide.

"If anybody shows up at the house for a late dinner, Cork's crew will call me." Corky Kononen was head of the uniform branch. Technically Rob's subordinate, he had seniority. In fact, he was set to retire in January. Being called out on Thanksgiving would not have pleased him.

"She must have set the timer early," Beth reflected, her mind on Marybeth's oven. "Midmorning."

"What about the table settings?" Rob's eyes were bright, intent.

"What do you mean?"

"Who sets a table way early?"

"Me," Beth said. "I'd set it weeks in advance if it weren't for the little problem of dust. I don't put out perishables, of course, but I do set the table early when I have company coming. Of course I always forget something and dash in with it at the last moment. What about you, Meg? You entertain a lot."

"Five minutes before the doorbell rings," Meg said firmly. "I'm a spur-of-the-moment kid."

Rob guffawed.

"What?"

"You plan ahead. What are all those dinner-sized packets of soup and stew in your freezer? The neatly labeled remains of that five-pound roast? Half pints of gravy? The cookies you trot out for passing strangers?" He stood up. "We cordoned off the area of the scree where Marybeth was found, and the house—driveway and all. A car will swing by every hour."

"City or county?" Beth asked.

Rob sighed. "County. The house is just outside the city limits. Sorry about that." The town of Klalo had two patrol cars and three full-time officers. When things got too complicated, Chief Hug paid the county for its police services. Beth was an eagle when it came to spotting sources of revenue. She needed to be.

Rob stretched and wiggled his shoulders. "We ought to leave now, if I'm going to function in the morning. Great dinner when I got around to eating it. Thanks, Beth." He dropped a kiss on the sheriff's cheek.

She gave him a pat on the arm, turning to Meg. "You'd better take some turkey home. For the freezer."

"For breakfast," Rob corrected.

~

HE must have had a nightmare. Meg woke at three to find herself alone in her queen-sized bed. That happened once in a while. When the dreams were really bad, Rob got up and went downstairs so as not to wake her. Shuffling sounds from the kitchen below reassured her. She snuggled back into her nest and let her mind drift.

It drifted, as it had to, to the death of Marybeth Jackman. Meg thought of Carla, glad the girl was with her father, of Madeline Thomas free to open a Klalo language lab at Trout Farm without danger of a lawsuit and racist sniping, and of Annie, no longer the perpetual target. Ever the administrator, she wondered whether she could rehabilitate Jackman's cronies. Tessa and Wendy had both given Meg fish-eyed stares at the deck warming. Enablers, both of them. Wendy was a schemer. They would probably blame Meg for Marybeth's demise. Certainly she was going to benefit.

It would be a relief not to have to engage in constant rearguard action. Not replacing Marybeth, who drew the salary of a senior librarian, would save the jobs of at least two of the newer aides, and open the way to fresh talent. Maybe I won't have to cut staff at all, Meg mused, dollar signs dancing through her head.

Her crassness jolted her wide awake. What am I thinking? The woman has not been dead twenty-four hours. I should be planning a memorial. She squirmed in the rankness of her hypocrisy. Not a memorial *service*, God help me. I couldn't think of anything positive to say. A memorial. We could plant a tree.

Planting a tree in Israel, in Brooklyn, or even in Los Angeles, had robust symbolism. But Latouche County nestled among orchards at the confluence of two major national forests. Disgusted with herself, Meg sat up, yanked her robe over her nightgown, and scuffed into her slippers.

Rob had plenty of warning she was coming. She stumbled on the stairs, caught herself on the banister, and swore. When she entered the kitchen, he was bending over the stove to turn off the flame under the kettle.

He stared at her. "You're what?" He let the kettle sit. It emitted a last sad whistle.

"I was planning an appropriate rite of recognition. What do you say to the Marybeth Jackman Memorial Cactus?"

Rob looked like hell. Stubble, two shades darker than his sandy hair, shadowed the lower half of his face, and his red-rimmed eyes were set in bruises. He stared at her, blank with incomprehension, then his eyes lit, and he grinned and held out his arms. "Come here."

She was crying again by then, with shame and relief. He sat by the table and held her, soothing, stroking. Maybe they were both crying. She thought he had been.

"You're the only person on earth I could say that to," she choked. "About the cactus."

"Hey, it's all right."

"I love you."

He didn't reply, just hugged her tighter.

"You had a nightmare." When he didn't say anything, she prodded. "Tell me about it."

He cleared his throat. "It was just, you know, this afternoon..."

"Tell me, Rob. You got up and came down here because you couldn't go back to sleep."

His arm tightened on her shoulders, and he was silent for a long time. "I had to identify Jackman. The others didn't have a clue who she was, but I guessed. I'd seen her a couple of times, and I knew where she lived. So I hiked up with Jake. He warned me she was...banged up. The talus there is unstable. I kept stumbling, and it was cold, sleeting. I dreamed about all that."

"And?"

"They'd covered her. The EMTs." His voice shook. "In my dream, when they pulled back the tarp, it was your face I saw." He buried his head on her shoulder. "God, Meg, I couldn't stand it. Promise me you won't go."

Meg was chilled to the bone. It was her turn to murmur soothing noises that had no meaning. She couldn't promise him not to die, nobody could. The best she could promise was not to walk out on him.

They had chamomile tea and went up to bed. Strange to say, both of them fell into dreamless sleep.

Chapter 6

As SOON AS Meg got up for good, she sent out an e-mail announcing Marybeth's death to the staff at all branches of the library system. She mentioned Carla's loss with sympathy and gave the father's postal address for messages of condolence. She suggested donations to the adult literacy fund in Marybeth's name. She refrained from speculation. And she made Rob read the message before clicking on Send.

Hair still damp from the shower, he sat in her ergonomic office chair, nursing a cup of coffee and squinting at the screen. "Tasteful and vague, the way it should be. Will you add a sentence?"

"Of course. No, you add it."

He set the cup down and typed, *As with all unattended deaths, Ms. Jackman's accident will be investigated.* "That okay?"

"It sounds bald. Use her first name. 'Marybeth's accident.'"

Rob made the correction.

"Do you want to appeal for witnesses?"

"We need to know who was coming to dinner, for sure." He scowled at the computer screen and added, *Anyone with information relevant to this tragic death should contact Sergeant Jeffrey Fong of the Latouche County Sheriff's Department.* He appended Jeff's courthouse phone number and e-mail address.

Meg was bewildered. "Jeff? I thought Jake would investigate."

Rob wheeled around in the office chair and looked up at her. "He'll work with Jeff, of course, but Jake's a little short on experience."

"Training exercise?"

He didn't smile. "Besides, his sister had an open confrontation with Jackman."

Meg stared.

He touched her hand. "Try not to worry too much. The fall was probably an accident."

"But you don't think so."

He picked up his coffee and rose. "I don't *know*, Meg. And I won't know until the M.E. looks at her, which will be a while because of the holiday. I'd take on the case myself, but..."

"But what?"

He gave a crooked smile. "But I'm your alibi, speaking of open confrontation. Probably your alibi. We still don't know when she fell."

A frisson of alarm was succeeded by relief, and inevitably, anger. "If it comes to that, Robert, I am *your* alibi." That was true. On the other hand, not having had to consort with Marybeth, Rob had no motive to cause her harm, other than loyalty to Meg.

He nodded, unperturbed. "So you see why I can't head the investigation, if it turns out she was pushed. Best to hand it over to Jeff now. I'll take on the vandalism at Trout Farm."

"Shouldn't Linda do that?" Linda Ramos was the county's other sergeant of detectives. Unfortunately, she was still only an acting sergeant. She hadn't passed the exam owing to motherhood and other real-life intrusions. She'd pass it eventually. Linda was smart, and she had far more investigative experience than Jake Sorenson. So Meg's question was valid.

Rob shrugged. "She can take it and take credit for it, but I want to supervise. Closely. It interests me—all kinds of puzzles. And of course, there's Madeline to keep in mind." Rob had reason to be wary of Chief Thomas.

For once Meg scooped the chief. She called as soon as she got to the library. Madeline hadn't heard the news. She drew her breath in audibly. "Tell me."

Meg gave her what was known, adding, "Keep it under your hat for now. The sheriff will send out a press release in a couple of hours."

"Okay. I need to see you."

"Anytime."

"Can you meet me at Trout Farm in the morning? They finish de-contamination this afternoon, and I have to inspect the place first. We can look at the rooms upstairs tomorrow and make some decisions."

Meg scrolled through her calendar. "What time?"

"Nine-thirty? We can talk out there."

"Okay." They couldn't talk elsewhere? What bug of paranoia had bitten Maddie?

"See you then." Madeline hung up with no ceremony at all. Meg wondered what was wrong. What else was wrong.

The library was wrong.

Everybody knew, of course. Someone had seen to it that the flag flew at half staff. Meg hadn't thought of that. She hoped the branch librarians had. The wide-open 1960s spaces of the main library looked deserted, though she could see patrons and staff moving about, heads down. Rain sheeted the dreary acres of windows. Carts of books, the weekday of their return displayed on stiff cards, clumped in the gap between Fiction and Nonfiction like a herd of mechanical sheep, but no one was moving the books off to be shelved. Where were her aides? Where were the volunteers?

Wendy had not come to work, but Tessa had, all the way from Azimuth—Meg spotted her at a checkout station whispering to Nina, who looked uncomfortable. When the two of them noticed Meg, they got busy. Tessa stalked off with an armload of books, a woman with a mission. Right.

"Meg! Just the one I want to see." Pat Kohler dashed up. "Is it true, well, I guess it has to be, but what happened?"

"Marybeth fell off her deck."

Pat shook her head and said a perfunctory phrase or two of regret. Then she got down to business. "Dibs on her office."

"Patricia!"

Pat gave a sheepish grin. "It wasn't my first thought when I read your message, but it came to mind quickly. Did I get in an early bid?"

Meg sighed. "Too early. We'll have to leave the office as is for a while."

Pat's brown eyes narrowed. "As a gesture of respect, or because she was pushed?" If kindhearted Pat was speculating about that question, everybody was.

Meg opened her mouth, closed it, shook her head. "I won't make a decision about the office until next week, but I'll keep your request in mind."

"Thanks. Gotta run." Pat bounced off. Story hour began in ten minutes.

Meg checked her watch. Muttering, "The hell with it," she grabbed her master keys, marched down the hall, around the corner to Marybeth's office, opened the door as if she had every right to be there, which she did, and went in.

The room was oppressively tidy, oppressively beige. Still, Meg could see why Pat wanted it. It overlooked a lush rhododendron, the tree-lined street beyond, and way beyond, the bluff on which Marybeth's house stood. When the weather was clear, she must have had a sidewise glimpse of Mount Hood. That is, she would have if she'd turned her desk around and looked out. By contrast, Meg's office overlooked the parking lot.

She shut the door and went to the big filing cabinet—beige, of course. It was locked, but one of the small keys opened the top drawer. Though Meg wasn't hiding her presence in the office, she avoided slopping fingerprints over everything. She slid the drawer open and removed the thick folder marked BUDGET with her fingertips. Legitimate prey.

Nothing in the top drawer looked even remotely interesting— meeting notices, files for lesser committees like Safety that Marybeth also served on, publicity brochures for the many public events the library hosted, and so on. The other two drawers were locked, and none of Meg's small keys opened them.

For a moment she stood, perplexed. She sat in the office chair and tried to think like Marybeth. Everything neat, tidy. Messes out of sight. Oddities out of sight. Where would she hide a key? The center drawer of the desk was locked, and there was nothing under the blotter.

Speaking of oddities, where were the books? Now that Meg thought of it, she realized there had been no visible books in Marybeth's house either, at least not in the rooms Meg had seen. At Meg's place, books stood in columns, in piles on the stairway, and in two layers on each bookshelf. What kind of librarian was Marybeth anyway?

Well, there were books atop the file cabinet: an outdated edition of *Books in Print* and discarded red volumes of the *Library of Congress Subject Heading Index*. An old *LOC* made sense because official subject headings didn't change all that often. Marybeth could have got the information online, but if she was already online for something else, grabbing a book and flipping to the right page would be easier than opening another website and going back and forth. The 2004 edition of *Books in Print* didn't make sense, however.

Aha!

Meg jumped up, opened *BIP*, and *voilà*—the secret cache. If the edition had been current, she wouldn't have bothered to check it out.

Marybeth had hollowed out a space in the center of the volume, glued the edges and lined them with paper. In this nook reposed an old-fashioned address book, a couple of folded printouts, several small keys, and an audiotape. One of the keys opened the file drawers.

Meg lost herself for a time among the files, exploring Marybeth's mentality. They were all personnel folders, though there was nothing official about them. Meg's, the thickest, contained countless dated observations, shrewd, always negative, mostly petty. It was as if Marybeth had no way of sifting the serious from the trivial.

Bored, Meg turned to Annie Baldwin's, where the same pattern—or lack of pattern—prevailed. Marybeth disliked Annie, therefore everything Annie did was charged with insult. Wendy's folder, much slimmer, surprised Meg by showing the same small-minded negativity. Marybeth was keeping track of perceived faults, even those of her friends, but why? Meg pulled a couple of folders at random and added them to the stack. Enough.

She closed the file drawers, locked them, and returned to the desk. Another key opened the central drawer and two deep drawers to the right of the knee space. The left-hand drawers contained supplies ranging from stationery and envelopes to Tampax and Advil. The other drawers contained hard-backed journals, handwritten.

At that point, Meg surfaced. She was five minutes late to an Acquisitions meeting. She took the top three journals, slammed the drawers shut, grabbed the stack of files and the keys, and beat a retreat. She hadn't even got around to turning the computer on.

As Rob had predicted, no new information came through that day from the medical examiner or from the state's forensic lab. Nobody official said anything about sealing Marybeth's office—and neither did Meg. She chunked her loot into her own office and went about her business, which was both long- and short-term. Yes, the libraries' holiday displays could be set up. No, nobody should buy new books, not yet.

At lunchtime, she holed up in her office with a cup of tea and a turkey sandwich and took a look at Marybeth's secrets. She tracked down an old tape player and listened to the audiotape first.

It was disturbing, a stream of invective in a hoarse whisper, male, she thought. Then "Answer it, bitch. Answer the fucking phone." A burst of interference, heavy breathing and something like a sob. "Answer it. You won't get away with this. I fucking promise you won't. I'm watching you, cunt." Then Marybeth's cold alto. "Recorded from my landline answering machine, November third. The message was timed at nine-fourteen P.M."

Meg listened to the message three times before it occurred to her that it could have been aimed at either Marybeth or Carla. Meg rewound the tape. She set it on her blotter and returned the player to the storage cabinet in the basement. Her tea was cold when she got back.

The printouts baffled her. They seemed to be photocopies of random pages from two different books, neither of which she recognized, though she had a good memory. The prose in both cases was undistinguished, and both passages were exposition rather than dialogue. One referred to events leading to World War I, and the other, vaguely meditative, dealt with the psychology of loss. Both broke off in midsentence. After a baffled rereading, she set them aside, too.

The journals were a disappointment. They were in code. Feeling more than a little foolish, she held a mirror to one of the pages. Not mirror writing. Take that, Dan Brown. At least she was brighter than Brown's dim-bulb heroine. She set the journals atop the printouts and picked up the little address book.

It was the real disappointment. It contained addresses, all right, on about half the pages under each letter—probably old addresses. The rest of the entries were straightforward. Marybeth had written down her PIN numbers and passwords, and done so without subterfuge. Her Visa PIN lay there under *V*, after a phone number for somebody named Violet. Her computer passwords sat smugly under *C*, set up in outline form, one each for her home, laptop, and office machines, with the names of the protected files neatly alphabetized.

Whether that was arrogant stupidity or stupid arrogance, Meg didn't know. Or care. She decided she was not going to waste any more of her life plumbing the depths of Marybeth Jackman's mind. Marybeth had had no depths.

Meg took out her passkeys, walked down to Marybeth's office, and replaced everything except the Budget file—she needed that. When she returned to her own office, her turkey sandwich had dried out. Served her right.

She photocopied the entire Budget file and replaced it, too. Then she sent Rob an e-mail, explaining what she had done and where Jeff could find the computer passwords. She didn't apologize.

~

MEG forced herself to think hard about the Two Falls branch library. She wanted to be ready for Madeline, and she wanted to be able to face the library board and defend her decision to use the farmhouse, so she had plenty to occupy her mind. All day long, staff members slid in shyly to ask her for Marybeth's office.

Meg went home early, did some housework, called her daughter for a good long talk, and consoled herself with cookery. She made a huge pot of her famous chili, which was a good thing because Rob brought Jake home for a feed. He had spent a cold afternoon combing the scree at Jeff's direction, looking for evidence—of what they did not know. Jake's life had been put on hold, in the most horrible possible way, so the evening passed under a cloud of gloom. Probably because Jake was there, Rob didn't bawl Meg out for messing with Marybeth's office.

~

MEG reached Trout Farm ten minutes early Saturday morning. No sign of the Toyota pickup. Portland's all-classical radio station had

recently boosted its signal, so she sat with the engine running, watching the rain and listening to a Rachmaninoff concerto. She did not immediately notice the front door of the farmhouse opening.

"Who the fuck are you?" A baritone roar.

Meg jumped. The piano banged to a crescendo. She shut the engine
off. In the ensuing silence, she got out and made her way to the bottom
step.

A large Klalo man glowered down at her, a fact that would have
been awesome had he been wearing more than just a pair of fashion-
ably faded jeans. He looked young.

"Your fly's unzipped," she said crisply.

She wondered why guys so often felt they had to project intimidation. All four of her brothers had gone through that phase. Meg was
not a big woman. Her Accord did not sport a gun rack. She had driven
to the front door and hadn't even honked her horn. So why the bullying demeanor? Defensive, she supposed. Somebody had scared him,
sometime, somewhere.

He turned aside, fumbling and mumbling. His hair was chopped
off, not hanging in sleek braids. Perhaps he was in mourning.

He turned back, his face set in a scowl. At least he hadn't zipped
flesh. "What do you want?"

"I have an appointment with Chief Thomas. I want to come in.
Who are you?"

He mumbled a name.

"Is there coffee?"

He jerked his head toward the house. "You could make some."

"*You* can't?" *Ball-breaker*, she thought remorsefully. *Now Margaret, be
kind.* The voice in her head sounded like her mother. She trudged up
the steps past him and went where she supposed the kitchen ought to
be. She heard the slap-slap of his bare feet behind her.

"Hoover, you said." The kitchen was clean and empty, and someone
had brought in a table and four chairs. Coffee makings lay untouched
on the counter. *Maybe he couldn't make coffee.* Meg grabbed a conical paper filter, stuffed it in the coffeemaker, and threw in three scoops from
the bag of coffee on the counter. "Any relation to Nancy Hoover?" She
filled the carafe with water from the tap.

"My sister. Baby sister, cute but dumb."

Meg's budding sympathy evaporated. She poured water and pressed the button, and the coffeemaker groaned to life. "Since Nancy made it into the Clark nursing program after only a year on the waiting list, she's not in any way dumb. Have a little respect."

Nancy Hoover was dyslexic. Beth McCormick, in her earlier incarnation as a remedial English teacher, had taught Nancy to read at the age of fourteen, so Nancy's achievement was all the more remarkable. And she had an ebullient personality. He's jealous, Meg thought, staring at the heavy sullen face. Rude of her to stare.

His eyes dropped first. "Yeah, yeah."

"Go put on a shirt. You'll catch your death."

As he slid from the kitchen, Meg heard Madeline's truck drive in. Meg listened to the coffeemaker burble and tried to calm down. Eight years of Texan butt-kicking at the national level; two wars, one of them pointless; Hurricane Katrina; Rush Limbaugh; Pat Robertson; four years of Marybeth Jackman, and now this bully. Enough was enough.

On the other hand, she told herself, forcing her jaw muscles to relax, no point in offending Madeline by blowing off futile steam.

The chief entered with a big smile and a box of fattening pastries. "Where's Harley?"

"Your pit bull? Upstairs putting on a shirt."

Madeline's smile faded. She made a clucking sound. "I hope he wasn't rude. I thought it might be a good idea to have a caretaker in the house, and Harley needed a place to stay. He just got out of the army."

"Iraq?"

"Both. Iraq and Afghanistan. He's a little mixed up."

No kidding. The thought of thousands of young people coming home "mixed up" chilled Meg to the bone. At least this one had come home.

She poured coffee into two of the mugs on the counter. Madeline doctored hers with sugar and milk. Meg sat across from her and took a hot black sip.

"He's not a bad kid." Madeline sounded defensive.

"Not a pit bull?"

"More like one of those big English sheepdogs, all bark and no bite."

"I'll take your word for it."

"Have a pastry." Madeline selected something large and gooey for herself.

Meg chose a muffin she didn't really want. She didn't for a moment believe in Harley Hoover the cuddly puppy. However, he might well scare off vandals.

Madeline was telling her about the decontamination, which had gone faster than expected. Her Danish disappeared along with the sweet coffee. Meg crumbled her muffin.

"...and the purification ceremony is set for Sunday afternoon. You can come, can't you?"

"Uh, yes, uh, is there something I should bring?"

"Clean underwear and a pure heart."

Meg gaped.

Madeline roared with laughter. "C'mon, let's take a look upstairs."

Chapter 7

"I SAVED YOU A Danish."

Harley mumbled what might have been thanks and sidled past on his way downstairs. He'd put on sneakers and a T-shirt. Madeline turned to watch him go.

"Somehow I don't see him as our receptionist," Meg murmured. He'd play the role better than Marybeth would have, come to think of it. She didn't say that aloud. She'd always resisted criticizing staff to outsiders.

Madeline gave her head a shake and went upstairs.

Meg followed. A glance told her the master bedroom would make a good reading room. A big blank space directly above the living room, it had two elements of charm—what looked like a functional fireplace and a window seat in a dormer with a wide view to the south. Ancient wiring, of course—the whole house would have to be rewired.

Meg took her cell phone from her purse and turned it on.

"Hey! Who are you calling?" Madeline looked up from inspecting the spotless hearth.

Meg clicked the phone shut. "Nobody. I wanted to see whether there's a signal at all. And there is—up here, but not down in front of the house. I wonder if we could install a receiver." Meg's understanding of Wi-Fi was primitive.

"Bring the signal in on the landline," Maddie said absently. "You can block it. If you leave it unblocked, anybody can use it."

"Hmmm." Meg tried to sound as if she were meditating about the wisdom of freely accessible Wi-Fi. In fact, she was just confused. What was wrong with Madeline that she was hypersensitive to phone calls? *She* used a cell phone all the time.

"Do you like it?"

"The room? Of course!"

They talked about how they should do it up, but didn't discuss why the rose-patterned paper had had to be ripped from the walls. The stench of disinfectant faded on the air.

The reading room would shrink with furniture in it, but Meg had fun moving things around it in her mind. There were three other smaller bedrooms on the second floor and a bathroom that gave both women the giggles. As Meg had discovered in the course of renovating her own place, something about bathrooms brought out the bizarre and experimental in people. This one had been modernized sometime in the 1950s. Chunky and heavy in the style of that era, the fixtures were a strange peach color which was exaggerated by walls enameled puke green.

The once super-modern room was now worn and battered, though someone had seen to plumbing maintenance. Meg supposed the toilets—the peach one and the one downstairs—were the kind that used too much water to flush. The peach fixtures would have to go, or would they?

"How would it be if we kept the place as much like an old farmhouse as we could and asked for historical site designation?" she blurted.

Madeline had no interest in setting up a pioneer museum, but she was willing to listen as they checked out the rest of the second floor. Maybe it couldn't be done. Changes had to happen. A fire escape and some kind of elevator, compliant toilets in unisex bathrooms, at least one with a baby-changing table, a wheelchair ramp to the porch, parking. Meg ticked off the alterations.

One small room upstairs was out of bounds—Harley's. It couldn't have been his quarters for long, only since last night. Madeline did not enter it, and Meg didn't push. The sight of the closed door did raise the issue of a resident caretaker, however.

She thought about Harley as Madeline staked out the larger of the remaining bedrooms for her language lab and oral history archive. The roar of an engine snapped Meg from her trance. It sounded like a motorcycle. Out front.

She ducked back into the master bedroom and looked down. Harley had gone onto the porch to greet the biker. He stood on the top step, or Meg would not have been able to see him for the porch roof.

Bubble helmet and black leathers protected the visitor's identity, at least from above. Meg couldn't even tell gender. She watched the interchange. Wind ruffled Harley's black hair. His left arm shot out in an ambiguous gesture. The engine revved. Harley took a step down. The biker's shoulders bunched, the engine blasted, and the cycle squirreled around, spraying gravel. Harley watched it leave, his hands on his hips. When it reached the open gate, he turned and went back into the house.

"I wonder what that was about."

Meg jumped, startled. For a stocky woman Madeline moved quietly. "I don't know."

"Ready to explore downstairs?" Maddie didn't await a reply. She led the way to the kitchen and Meg followed, though she'd wanted another look at the peach bathroom. She wondered when the chief was going to bring up the question of Marybeth's death.

They found Harley drooping over a cup of coffee. He had eaten the Danish and a muffin. Crumbs strewed the table.

"Who was that?" Madeline, blunt and direct.

Harley didn't look up from his cup. "Friend of mine."

Meg was scrabbling in her purse for a pen. She jotted what she remembered of the cycle's license number on the back of an old receipt. I really ought to clean my purse, she reflected.

"Klalo?" Maddie's voice had an edge.

Harley ducked his head. "Uh, no. Just a friend."

Meg thought he was lying. The conversation had not been all that friendly. She poked the receipt into her wallet.

Madeline said nothing.

"Get off my back!" Harley shouted.

Madeline went to the sink, dampened a sponge, and wiped the crumbs from the table.

"Won't come again, okay? I heard what you said about visitors." He went back to mumbling. "I didn't know anybody'd show up, did I?"

Maddie said nothing. She rinsed her sponge, and then leaned against the sink, arms across her chest, her face calm.

Harley set his cup down with evident care. "I'm sorry, Chief. I don't mean to yell. It just happens."

"It's okay," Maddie said gently. "If you don't want to do this, you can move in with Jack and me. You know that, but I think you can handle it." What she meant by *it* was not at all clear.

Meg looked from her friend to the young man. They were exchanging unspoken messages. She grabbed her purse and left the room as unobtrusively as she could.

Which put her in the other bathroom. In the olden days people used to take their Saturday bath in a galvanized tub in the kitchen, next to the wood stove. Logical enough. The wood stove was long gone, but the association of kitchens with bathing had led many farm families to construct the house's first designated bath right next door, and never mind that the bedrooms were upstairs. Meg's house was like that, and so was this one.

The bathroom was large, much larger than the library branch would need for its rest room. A washer, a drier, a deep laundry sink, several metal cabinets, a built-in ironing board, and a battered vanity, complete with chair and triptych mirrors, crowded a capacious toilet with a wooden seat, a claw-footed tub, and a pedestal sink. Total clutter. It would all have to go, Meg realized. She sighed. She liked clutter.

She wondered why Marybeth had not stolen the vanity table along with the other antiques—or, for that matter, removed the tub. It would fetch a good price in Portland. Meg made a mental note to tell Madeline that.

She cocked her head, listening. Maddie's voice, calm and kind, and an occasional baritone rumble—they were still at it, whatever it was. Not my business, Meg told herself, and whisked out the bathroom's second door into the hallway.

A dining room lay in front of the kitchen, opposite the living room, so the other room on the west side of the house, the one separated from the bathroom by hall and stairwell, must have been the estate office, or perhaps a second parlor or music room. It was about the size of the bathroom, with windows to the north and west. Meg stood there, eyes half-closed, reveling in all that space.

When she'd planned her levy, Meg had budgeted for a very modest branch at Two Falls—two big rooms, a rest room, and a couple of small offices. Concrete block. Nothing fancy, nor she saw now, interesting. The farmhouse was more than twice as large as the building Meg had envisaged, even if she subtracted the Trout reading room and the Klalo lab and archives. If the renovation were well done, the farmhouse shouldn't be much more expensive to heat and would definitely seem friendlier. All to the good. The extra space also meant she could set aside a room for electronic media—films, videos, games, e-books, audio books, and of course computers, for both Internet access and word processing.

Sometimes it saddened Meg to see people lining up to use the computers when the stacks were empty of patrons. She was a book person. Her new hires were all book lovers, and their weekly "staff picks" were popular. Even so, each branch of the library had its ranks of computers, and each computer had an eager user with two or three others waiting for their turn.

The number of computer users increased daily—patrons checking the "card" catalogue, tourists checking their e-mail, retirees, the unemployed, kids doing homework after school hours, little ones playing games, homeless men and women, sales reps and campaign workers checking in with the home office, immigrants far from their families, ski bums in winter, windsurfers in summer, professionals scanning obscure databases.

Children under sixteen were guided to stations with filtered Internet access. Meg supposed patrons at the unfiltered terminals sometimes accessed porn or hooked up with Russian hookers, but the very public nature of the computer setup necessarily limited the grosser abuses.

If they liked, patrons could access nothing but sermons. As far as

Meg was concerned, that was their business, and each library branch had a cadre of computer-savvy volunteers who could help them do it. One young preacher with a storefront church wrote all his sermons in sixty-minute stints at the main branch computers. He always printed out an extra copy of the finished product for Meg, and she always read it.

Madeline jolted Meg out of her smug ecumenical musing. "There you are! I was afraid you'd give up on me."

She made a polite noise.

"Tell me about Fern's niece. She fell off her deck?"

Meg gave her the story of Rob's ruined holiday, laying on colorful incidentals like the roasting capon and avoiding any suggestion of foul play.

"Was she murdered?"

So much for putting a spin on the news. "I don't know. I hope not." And Meg did hope not. So, she supposed, must Madeline. Both of them had strong motives for wishing Marybeth ill.

"Tell me about her. Did you like her?

Meg hesitated. *Nil nisi bonum.* Madeline was not being very open, and Marybeth, obnoxious as she might have been, had been staff. "I disliked her. She believed she should have had my job, and she was qualified, at least technically, but she would have been a disaster."

"How so?"

"She enjoyed setting people at each other's throats, and she picked on anyone she saw as vulnerable, including library patrons."

Madeline clucked her tongue.

"At first I felt sorry for her and tried to be accommodating. I gave her significant work, sent her to regional conferences, praised her efficiency."

"You like to be liked."

"I do. It's a failing." Meg drew a breath. "And it didn't work at all." Then it all tumbled out, all the time-consuming pettiness of Marybeth's sneak attacks, which like most guerrilla warfare had victories. "I've spent the last two years isolating her, with some success, but we were heading for a major dustup, and there's no guarantee I would have come out on top. Even if I had, that kind of conflict always demoralizes the bystanders. I hated that," Meg took a breath, "and I hated her."

"So you benefit from her death."

"Not if the rumor mills cast me as a villain. Marybeth lived here a long time. She had cronies, in and out of the system, and she made alliances, or tried to. There's a segment of the community that sees public libraries as cesspits of evil."

"Church people."

"Not all of them, just some." The same people who believed that public schools were in league with the devil, and that people who got sick or lost their jobs were being punished for their sins. It was a mind-set, right now an angry one, or angrier than usual.

"Looking for weaknesses."

Like Marybeth. Meg shivered. She wondered how anyone could live in a state of perpetual outrage.

"Did she do this?" Madeline made a large gesture to encompass the whole farmhouse.

Meg thought about what she should or should not say. "Rob's puzzled. He's going to take over the investigation."

"Of her death?"

"No. Of the vandalism." She glanced at Maddie's face in time to catch her surprise.

"That's interesting." The taut lines around the chief's mouth eased in a smile. "A good thing, too. I was afraid I'd have to hire a private detective. Tell Rob we'll help him any way we can."

"I will." She wanted to ask Madeline whether *we* included Harley Hoover. But she didn't. She excused herself, pleading a fictional lunch appointment, and drove back to Klalo in a pensive mood.

Just outside the town it occurred to her that she could probably use her cell phone. She pulled over at a rest stop and read her messages. Rob had called nearly an hour earlier. She used the speed-dial and reached him after only two rings.

"Hi. You called."

"Uh, Meg. Uh, I'm sorry. The M.E. is pretty sure she was pushed."

He was saying something about preliminary findings, but Meg scarcely heard his voice through the ringing in her ears. She had ob-

served two murder investigations at close quarters. Unless Marybeth
had died much earlier than they thought, Meg could not be considered
a suspect, but the light of a murder investigation shone coldly on the
just and the unjust.

Who knew what garbage lay in Marybeth's coded journals and
the protected files on her computer? Whatever was there would not
reflect well on either Meg or the Latouche Regional Library. As she
put the car in drive and squealed out onto Highway 14 with a savage
push on the accelerator, she cursed herself for not destroying those
demented scrapbooks of grievance.

Chapter 8

J EFF FONG HAD INVADED the library. Nina, who was still at the check-out desk, warned Meg as she entered the building, which might be a sign that her staff was rallying around. Or not.

Meg stuck her head in Marybeth's office to let Jeff know she was back. He was sitting at the desk, disassembling the computer. He looked up, smiling, and stood. A short man with a wrestler's build and an engaging grin, Jeff was always polite. Meg liked him but didn't know him well. He'd brought a uniformed deputy, a young blond man Meg didn't recognize.

"Sad business," Jeff murmured.

She shook hands with him. "Let me know what we can do to help you."

"Thanks. I need to interview you."

"I'll be in my office all afternoon, except for a four-o'clock meeting."

"Okay. In an hour?" He did not invite her to sit.

She took the hint. "I'll send out a notice asking the staff to cooperate with your investigation." She left without further ado.

She worked through her e-mail—mostly spam, but some messages of support from Friends of the Library. A co-worker from California days wrote to ask whether she could stop by in January. She and a friend wanted to ski Mount Hood. Meg clicked Reply and said sure.

All the while she skimmed her messages, she was conscious of the coming interview.

Jeff was five minutes late. He brought the deputy and a recorder with him. When Meg had asked after Jeff's wife and son and been assured that they were fine, he introduced the young deputy as Henry Perkins, a good old-fashioned name, and asked whether Meg objected to the recorder. She said no and offered Perkins the folding chair from her closet. He opened it and plunked down on it, knees up. He was rather tall.

"Ms. McLean's a reserve deputy." Jeff seated himself on her client chair. "She knows the procedure."

The deputy nodded, wide-eyed. Meg wondered whether people called him Harry or Hank or Hal or Hen. Henry was one of the few names with as many nicknames as Margaret.

Jeff turned the recorder on and made the usual introductory remarks. When he finished, he asked her if she was ready.

"Yes. Have you found out who was supposed to eat Thanksgiving dinner with Marybeth?"

Jeff hesitated.

"I'll just ask Rob tonight, so you might as well tell me. Besides, she probably works here."

"She?"

"It's Wendy Resnik, right?"

Jeff let out his breath on a bark of laughter. "Madam detective."

"Am I right?"

"Yeah, she called me this morning in response to the e-mail you sent Friday—yesterday. Said she went over around three forty-five Thursday. She'd been invited for four o'clock. Rang the bell. Nobody came to the door. Since she was early, she hung around for a while, rang the bell again, and peeked in the windows. Called on her cell phone and heard the house phone ring, but nobody answered. Went away a little after four." About the time the EMTs reached Marybeth's body from Bluff Road.

Meg wondered whether Wendy had seen the ambulance below. Probably not. Would she have had access to the deck? "Do you believe her?"

Jeff's dark eyes narrowed. "That's what she said happened. I called her back, just before you returned from Two Falls, and made an appointment to interview her at the courthouse when we're finished here." The sheriff's department offices were in the courthouse annex, which also housed the county jail. "She doesn't want to do it here. She lawyered up."

"That was fast."

"The announcement went out on the radio about three hours ago."

"Still."

"Yes, she was quick off the mark. Who is she?"

"A senior library aide, an English major with ten credits in library science. She works in Circulation—supervises the volunteers and two aides. She came to Klalo from The Dalles eight years ago, and she wants to drive the bookmobile. Fat chance."

"She can't drive?"

"She's not good with people. For the bookmobile, you have to be. So she has a grievance with the system, and Marybeth capitalized on it. She made Wendy her henchman."

Jeff looked blank.

Meg controlled her impatience. Jeff had never met Marybeth. "You'll want to know why anyone would push a nice librarian to her death on Thanksgiving Day in the middle of a sleet storm, right?"

"Well, yeah."

"So you need to know how Marybeth operated. She was a tinpot tyrant in the workplace. I imagine she was also a bully in her private life, but I don't know that from observation. Bullies always attract sidekicks, people who also enjoy watching victims squirm but don't have the power or personality to dominate. Marybeth did. Wendy stood at her elbow and gloated." Meg had made up her mind to be blunt. Even so, she felt a twinge of guilt for exposing Wendy's failings.

"So how would she react to being stood up, so to speak, for Thanksgiving dinner?" That was shrewd.

"Hurt and angry, I suppose. And worried about Marybeth when she got around to thinking, but the hurt feelings would come first. I expect Wendy stomped off home, made herself an omelette, and cried into her beer. That's a guess."

"By that time Jackman was long dead."

"Yes, if that's what happened."

"Ms. Resnik's a liar?"

"Not compulsive, but she does cover her butt."

Henry Perkins snorted.

Jeff shot him a quelling look. "Okay. Thanks. That's helpful. Any other, er, henchmen?"

"Cronies. The only other active one at the moment is Tessa Muller. Tessa works at the Azimuth branch." Meg frowned. "She's not a likely suspect, though. She's married with three kids and lots of relatives in the area."

Jeff was nodding. "So she must have been caught up in the Thanksgiving feeding frenzy."

"I assume so."

"You've been thinking."

"Wouldn't you?"

"Probably." Jeff sighed. "All right, Ms. McLean. Let's get down to business. Where were you between eight A.M. and three P.M. Thursday?" And he took her through her movements, noted with a straight face that her alibi for the crucial hours was supplied by the undersheriff of Latouche County, and that she had dined with the sheriff. Friends in high places. Then he went on the attack.

"You told Robert Neill you entered Ms. Jackman's office yesterday and removed some documents."

"That's right. I needed the Budget Committee file. Marybeth chaired that committee. I was curious, too." Meg resisted the urge to apologize. After a moment, she added, "At that point the assumption was that she'd had an accident. The office wasn't sealed."

"Why?"

Meg didn't pretend to misunderstand. "I was looking for time bombs. Marybeth and I clashed repeatedly over the past four years. I wanted to know the extent of her malice."

"Against you?"

"And against any other library employee." Like Annie. "Against the system itself. I think she tried to undermine the levy campaign."

"That's a serious accusation."

"A levy failure would not have displeased her—no skin off her nose, just off mine. It would have hurt a lot of her colleagues, but she probably thought her own position was protected by seniority."

"You're guessing."

Meg shrugged. "And I didn't find much. Her personal journals were in code. I assume that's what the hardcover notebooks are. She kept unofficial files on most of the senior employees of the library system—collections of petty faults and slipups."

"Did she ever blackmail her victims?"

That hadn't occurred to Meg. She frowned. "I don't know. I guess it's possible."

"You?"

"No."

They stared at each other.

After a moment, Meg said, "As I indicated in my e-mail to the undersheriff, she recorded her passwords and PIN numbers in that address book she hid in *Books in Print*. I didn't access her computer. If there's evidence that she was working against the levy, it will be in the journals or on the computer."

"Saves us time." Jeff sounded only mildly gratified. He was good with computers, one reason Rob had hired him, and he probably would have enjoyed figuring out Marybeth's passwords. The department would have to have her lawyer's permission to access financial records. Meg didn't think Carla would object. As far as Meg knew, Carla was her mother's heir. *Have to make a condolence call to Carla and ask about funeral arrangements.*

Jeff leaned forward a little. "I understand Ms. Jackman had a lawsuit going against the Klalos."

"You'll have to ask Chief Thomas about that."

"But it involves the library indirectly."

"Yes."

"C'mon, Meg. Give."

"Look, I'm willing to talk about the library and about my own problems with Marybeth, but I'm not going to say anything about Marybeth's relations with the larger community, and that includes the Klalo Nation." She sighed. "What I know for a fact is a matter of public record. There was a will. It left a property to the Klalos. The will was contested."

"By Ms. Jackman."

"Yes." Meg added reluctantly, "I believe her lawyers advised her to drop the case."

Jeff's eyes gleamed. "What about the vandalism?"

"What about it?"

"Do you think Ms. Jackman was behind it?"

"I do not know. You'll have to ask Rob."

"Did Chief Thomas believe she was behind it?"

"For that you'll have to ask Chief Thomas."

He dropped the subject. Once more he took her through her movements during the window of time in which the murder had been committed, and he asked her to clarify her own relationship with Marybeth—from the beginning. Meg repeated herself without self-contradiction, or hoped she did.

At that, he rose, thanked her formally, and took his leave. She felt wrung out and hung up to dry. Henry Perkins hadn't said a word.

It was well past the lunch hour, and Meg was hungry. She found a power bar in her desk, made herself a cup of tea, and munched and sipped. What now? Carla. Putting the call off another day wasn't in the cards. Resigned but apprehensive, she poked out the number for Edwin Jackman in Camas. On the third ring, a woman's voice answered. She didn't sound like Carla.

Meg took a guess. "Mrs. Jackman?"

"Yes, this is Phyllis Jackman. What do you want? I don't do surveys on the phone."

Meg could hear a television or radio in the background, some kind of commercial. "This is Margaret McLean at the Latouche Regional Library. May I speak to Carla, please?"

"She and her father are out together. I don't know when she'll be in." She sounded marginally friendlier.

"I see. I was her mother's supervisor. Has Carla set a time for the funeral?"

"Carla doesn't want a funeral. Marybeth will be cremated whenever the police release the body."

No funeral? "Er, what about a memorial service?"

"I don't know, Ms. McLean. I guess that would be up to the library. You say you were her boss?"

Meg cleared her throat. "I'm head of the library system."

"I see. Well, you should make your own arrangements. I'm sorry, but I don't think Carla will cooperate. She's very hostile. Very difficult. She refuses to talk to the police, though of course she'll have to eventually. Her father is trying to calm her down, but he's not having much luck. He always indulged her, and the last two years she's been out of control. Thank God she turns eighteen next week. She'll be old enough to live on her own." The woman heaved a sigh. "That sounds awful, I know, but she's so hard to deal with. Always has been. I have two boys, Ms. McLean—eight and ten. She's a bad influence on them. Ed doesn't see that, but it's true. And that boyfriend of hers..."

Meg made what she hoped was a sympathetic sound.

"Well, I'm sorry, but he scares me. And he's older, maybe twenty-two or -three, with a motorcycle and these awful tattoos. Ed checked him out. He went into the army right out of high school, and they let him go after one tour in Iraq. That was suspicious, I thought."

"Suspicious?" Meg didn't have to feign confusion.

"They're keeping those poor kids in for two or three tours, unless there's something really, really wrong with them. Ed tried to find out what it was, but he couldn't get to first base. Privacy laws." She clucked her tongue. "He could be a rapist or a murderer, and they just let him loose on the unsuspecting public."

"What's the boyfriend's name?" Meg tried to keep her voice mild, uninterested, as if she were oozing mere sympathy. She held her breath.

"Pascoe. Aidan Pascoe. She's going to marry him, she says, and stay in her mother's house. There's nothing to stop her when she turns eighteen." Another sigh. "And that's fine with me." Perhaps Mrs. Jackman thought she'd said too much, for she excused herself almost at once, promising to let Carla know that Meg had called.

Meg wrote the name of the boyfriend down phonetically and tried a couple of plausible spellings. There was a town in eastern Washington called Pasco.

Something to tell Rob. Something to distract Rob. Jeff's question about blackmail made Meg very uneasy. What if she hadn't been open about her relationship with Rob, about her unwed motherhood? Would Marybeth have threatened her with exposure?

It was hard to envisage Jackman blackmailing for money. She had thought about contesting her great-aunt's will, so she was capable of greed, but trying to wring large sums from the library aides who were her probable victims seemed like an exercise in futility.

Meg glanced at her watch. It was almost four, and she hadn't yet read Marybeth's Budget Committee file. Well, she'd read her own. Pit stop. She used the loo, splashed cold water on her face, combed her hair, and took several long, calming breaths. The Budget Committee meeting was her first encounter with senior staff in a clump since Marybeth's death.

Pat, Nina, and Tessa were waiting for her, subdued and silent. Tessa looked sick. The other survivor of the five-member committee was Wendy Resnik. Meg had time to wonder how she had been so dim as to permit Marybeth a majority of allies on a crucial committee.

Each library department created its own budget. The Budget Committee did a reality check and negotiated differences—or was supposed to—though with Marybeth, negotiation was apt to feel like a sharp blow from a hammer. Fortunately, the procedures were designed to make the group's decisions transparent, and neither Pat nor Nina was easily squashed.

Feeling hypocritical, Meg uttered funereal platitudes and said something vague about how difficult it would be to replace Marybeth, but that she intended to ask Abby Torres, the Middleton branch librarian, to join the committee. She herself would sit in until the members could choose another chair. "You can't do that today. Wendy won't be back until Tuesday."

"What's wrong with her?" Pat, innocent as a babe.

"She's upset," Tessa snapped. "She was supposed to have dinner with Marybeth on Thanksgiving."

"How awful," Pat murmured.

"Is it true Marybeth was murdered?" Nina, avid.

Tessa's hands flew to her throat.

Meg said, "I'm sorry, Tessa. Didn't you know? There was an announcement on the radio this morning from the sheriff's office. The medical examiner believes she was pushed."

Tessa burst into tears.

Meg jumped to her feet. "Somebody get her a glass of water." She fumbled in her handbag for a tissue.

It took a while to calm Tessa down. Meg's e-mail to the staff had gone out too late to reach Tessa before she left home. She had driven in from Azimuth after lunch, listening to an audio book rather than the radio during the hour-long journey, and when she got to the library no one had told her anything, just that a deputy might want to talk to her before she went home. All of this came out in incoherent bursts.

Apparently Meg's strategy of isolating Marybeth's cronies from the rest of the librarians had worked a little too well. She felt sad and guilty. The distraught woman had lost a friend and was clearly in shock. She was making accusations left and right, of course, most of them directed at Meg, but some at the other members of the committee.

"You hated her," Tessa sobbed. "All of you."

"Oh, put a sock in it," Pat snarled. "We didn't hate her. She hated us. She's been a bitch to work with ever since Meg got the top job, and she wasn't a peach before Meg came. If you have an ounce of honesty in you, Tessa, you'll admit it."

Tessa sniffed and blew her nose hard.

Pat's voice softened. "We didn't want her dead. Since she is, we'll have to take up the slack. Marybeth was a pro. She got the job done. We're going to miss that, even if we don't miss her snide remarks and nasty little schemes."

"Uh, Pat," Meg said.

Pat scowled. She was wearing a red sweater and a cheery reindeer pin. "I'm tired of tiptoeing around the truth, Meg. You should have fired her ass after your first levy failed. She undermined you every way she could. We all knew that. She bragged about it."

"Not to me," Meg said mildly, though she wanted to scream. "Let it go, Pat." She wondered what other dark secrets her staff cherished. "Would you like to postpone this meeting, Tessa? We can convene again next week. I know you intend to make changes at Azimuth."

Tessa nodded, her face in a damp Kleenex.

"All right. I have a couple of things to tell you all before you leave. First, I talked to Carla Jackman's stepmother. Apparently Carla does not want to hold a public funeral for her mother."

That provoked gasps and startled looks. Tessa peered at her over the tissue.

"If that's the case, we'll want to plan some kind of memorial for Marybeth here at the library. I welcome suggestions, but perhaps we should wait until the police investigation clarifies things." *Such a euphemism. Until Jeff makes an arrest.* Meg did not feel optimistic. "In the meantime, contributions to the adult literacy program seem appropriate, if patrons should ask."

She cleared her throat. "The other announcement concerns the budget. Chief Thomas and I are working on a proposal to the board that may free up some of the levy money. We'll see. I'm also going to look into whether we can redistribute Marybeth's duties among the senior staff in order to avoid Reduction in Force later."

"Not replace her?" Nina's mouth formed an O.

Meg nodded. "As you know, the economy is in a tailspin. That's already affecting our revenues. I do not want to have to cut staff next year. Marybeth did a lot of hard work for the library system. That work will still have to be done. I'll take on some of the tasks myself, and I know I can count on all of you." She cringed at the hypocrisy. All of them had full loads. She was asking a lot and knew it.

To her surprise, everyone looked more cheerful, even Tessa, if cheerful was the word. At least she was no longer spewing accusations.

It was nearly five. The library stayed open until nine, but Meg had had enough. She drove home and started cooking, which is to say she boiled a pot of water and threw in a couple of vacuum-sealed portions of venison stew. She also made a crisp salad and thawed a loaf of artisanal bread. That would have to do for dinner.

While she waited for Rob to appear, she checked her e-mail and zapped the spam. Then she listened to her phone messages. There were six, five from reporters wanting comments on the murder of one of her staff. The sixth was from her brother Duncan.

"Meg, it's Dunc. Give me a call, will you?" Her youngest brother's voice sounded tired. "It's about Mom." He left a number.

Chapter 9

ROB DROPPED MEG OFF at Portland Departures before five A.M. for a seven o'clock flight to Los Angeles.

She needed some time alone, she said. When she had checked in, she'd eat a croissant at their favorite bakery and read a little before subjecting herself to Security. Wasn't it lucky she'd got a seat, what with the holiday traffic? Lucy would drive down from Palo Alto and join her later that afternoon. Meg would stay at a motel while Lucy bunked with friends at UCLA, and she'd call him when she knew more. All very polite and fragile.

Meg's mother was in the hospital, suffering from congestive heart failure, a diagnosis that covered a multitude of possibilities. Rob's grandmother had died of congestive heart failure. But not immediately. It wasn't necessarily that kind of problem. People lived for years with congestive heart failure.

Rob pulled into the left lane of I-84 and surged past a two-trailer rig that was billowing water from every orifice. Sleet and road-scum spattered the windshield of his pickup. The wipers cleared the windows every third pass. He sprayed wiper fluid. There was no other traffic on the road, though a long line of rigs had pulled over onto the shoulder eastbound. Maybe they knew something he didn't. Apart from their red reflectors, it was as black out as the inside of a cow, as black as his mood.

Rob was a loner. At least, he'd always thought of himself as a loner. Aside from his brief unsuccessful marriage to Alicia and two short-term relationships, he'd lived alone his whole adult life—until Meg moved into the house next door.

Four years ago, when he found he was living with her and visiting his own house, he asked her if she minded. She said no, she loved it. She loved him. God knew, he loved her. He felt lost without her, but she wouldn't marry him. That much was clear, and it was also clear that her objection to marriage had to do with estrangement from her family.

Maybe this crisis would lead to reconciliation. Maybe she would change her mind. He didn't think so, but he was usually a little inclined to pessimism.

He pressed the accelerator, discovered he was doing eighty, and fell back to the legal speed limit. Why hurry? He could do nothing at five-thirty in the morning. The windshield wipers swished. The Oregon State Patrol had closed the Bridge of the Gods because of high wind, so he chugged past Cascade Locks. East of town the sleet eased a little.

His mind drifted to Madeline Thomas and the vandalism at Trout Farm, the hate crime. The damage had been superficial but nasty, and definitely directed at the Klalos. But why the torn books and why Trout Farm?

An oncoming car flashed its lights, and he dimmed.

Meg had already found thirty or so titles from Miss Trout's book list. Fern Trout. Sophomore biology. Rob's sophomore year at Klalo High School had been unhappy. His hormones flowed like the Columbia at flood crest, he kept falling in love with Older Women (juniors and seniors), his voice fluctuated between alto and baritone, and he was five feet four inches tall. As a teacher of biology, it was likely Miss Trout had known all that. She had been kinder than he deserved, at any rate.

He remembered little of what she taught. She was probably fifty at the time, so he thought she was older than God, but he liked her. She'd taken the class on a field trip in the spring to see the wildflowers at Catherine Creek, not a destination at the top of his adolescent list. He still drove out to Catherine Creek every spring. He'd never taken Meg. Next year...

A big rig passed, spraying him with gunk. He turned the wipers to the fast setting and squirted fluid onto the windshield again.

His mind slid back to Trout Farm. He'd gone out to have another look the previous afternoon. The crime scene cleaners had done a good job. He thought the house would make a fine library. Since few of the lab results had come in, the investigation was stalled.

As he'd driven up in front of the house, Harley Hoover had leapt onto the porch, yelling a challenge. He calmed down when Rob identified himself. Volatile. Meg hadn't liked him. When Rob asked Harley who he thought had trashed the place, he mumbled and looked shifty, but Rob couldn't imagine any reason why the kid would have been involved in the vandalism, so he wrote the reaction off as cop aversion. All the same, Harley knew something. He'd hunkered down in the kitchen while Rob looked things over.

Rob had a soft spot for young Nancy Hoover, Beth McCormick's protégée, who had been a crucial witness in a murder case. The Hoovers were a vast matriarchy, and he remembered Harley as a big dozy teenager, never in serious trouble. The boy's forthright grandmother had been horrified when he joined the army. After all, she said, he didn't have to. Here he was, home again. Rob was inclined to cut veterans a little slack, so he didn't push.

That evening, though, when Meg was packing for the California trip, she'd told him about the biker who had showed up during her own encounter with Harley. She even found the receipt on which she'd written the partial license number. Rob put that and her tale about Carla Jackman's biker boyfriend together. Unlike Hoover, the name Pascoe meant nothing to Rob, but he asked Todd Welch, who was on nights that week, to check out the bike and the boyfriend and to give the boyfriend's name to Jeff, who probably already had it.

The vandalism. Could it be Harley's rejection of matriarchy? Strictly speaking, the Klalos were matrilinear rather than matriarchal, but the young man had just stepped out of a heavy-duty patriarchy and was bound to be confused by military ideas, above and beyond the horrors of combat. On the other hand, the Klalos had always had male war chiefs. Rob thought he'd have another talk with Harley. Or maybe with Jack Redfern, Madeline's husband. Jack was a Vietnam veteran and must have experienced a similar confusion of values. Rob wanted to talk to Jack anyway.

As the Starvation Creek Trailhead neared, Rob's cell phone rang. From that point east, there was service most of the time. He pulled into the parking lot at the rest area and checked caller I.D. Todd Welch. The phone stopped ringing before Rob set the brake. He called the number.

"I've been trying to reach you, sir. You need to know somebody fire-bombed Aunt Maddie's house. The call came at four thirty-two A.M." Todd was Madeline Thomas's nephew.

"Jesus. Are they okay?"

"Maddie's coughing. They took Uncle Jack to the hospital—smoke inhalation, burns on his hands from fighting the fire with his extin-guisher. Neighbors and the fire department saved most of the house. The lodge wasn't touched." The lodge, a big attached room where Maddie met with the tribal elders, was full of priceless Klalo artifacts. Whoever tossed the bomb didn't know much.

"Who's on it?" Rob meant which deputies.

"Just about everybody. Linda took the lead."

"Okay. Tell her to use whatever she needs. I'll warn Corky."

"He's already in Two Falls."

"Good. You at the courthouse?"

"Yes."

"Tell Dispatch I'm back in range, but I'll go over to the hospital before I come in."

"Okay. Uh, where are you?"

"Coming up on Hood River." Rob put the pickup in gear. "Maddie is at the hospital with Jack." Not a question.

"Yes. She's pretty upset."

"Tell her I'll come straight to her."

Todd agreed, sounding more like his usual self. Rob signed off, wheeled the pickup to the on-ramp, and roared back onto the freeway ahead of a truck pulling a huge metal cylinder, part of a wind turbine.

Wind farms were springing up all over central Oregon and Washing-ton in response to the rise in oil prices.

He made it across the long Hood River toll bridge going forty-five, twenty miles over the limit. He avoided that bridge whenever pos-sible, but his mind was on Madeline and Jack. Only as he approached the span over the ship channel did he flash on the day, nearly four years ago now, when he had watched a woman plunge her car off the road-bed into the river.

At the stoplight, he slapped his light onto the roof of the pickup and headed west on Highway 14 with his foot to the floor. He figured the road would be blocked at Two Falls by fire department rigs and cop cars, so he turned onto County Road 3, which bypassed the town in a slightly longer route. Despite the detour, he cut ten minutes off the time it usually took to reach the Latouche County Hospital from the bridge.

Already, only a little after six, the lot near Emergency was full of cars and pickups—Maddie's friends and relatives, and Jack's. Rob parked in a doctor slot, not wanting to block ambulance traffic, scrib-bled the word UNDERSHERIFF on an old envelope, and left it on the dash. Then he sprinted for the Emergency entrance.

He found Madeline in the lobby, surrounded by tribe members. She was standing with her cousin Bitsy Thomas. As he watched her, she hunched over with a rattling cough. Bitsy, a large woman with a chronic scowl, hugged her cousin's shoulders, glowered around the room, and spotted Rob. She said something, and Maddie looked up.

She strode to him, bent over in another coughing fit, and straight-ened when it eased. "About time," she wheezed. "Where have you been?"

"I drove Meg to Portland Airport. Her mother's in the hospital."

Cough, choke. "Are you going to do something?"

"I hope so. How's Jack?"

Tears brimmed in her snapping black eyes. "Hurting. He'll be all right, no thanks to you." She went into another convulsive cough.

Rob waited.

"Well?"

He raised an eyebrow.

"If you can't think of anything better to do than harass Harley..." Tears streamed down her face.

He got out a handkerchief and mopped. It was okay for a chief to cry but not in public. "C'mon, Maddie, let's get a cup of coffee in the cafeteria. You can tell me what happened this morning." He herded her down the long corridor to the main lobby of the hospital, conscious of the thirty or so pairs of angry eyes that watched them leave. "Have they admitted Jack yet?"

"No." She sniffed. "They kicked me out. Doctor's listening to his lungs. Why don't they give him something for pain? His hands are awful, all black and oozing, and he's groaning. Shit, Rob."

"I know. They stand around and wait for each other while the patient twitches. It's a crime." He was just making soothing noises. He was sure the ER team was running necessary tests. He was also sure Maddie knew that. She was venting.

By the time they reached the basement cafeteria, Chief Thomas was back in control, and never mind that she was wearing somebody's plaid lumber jacket over a vast flannel nightgown and Ugg boots. Her black hair flowed over her shoulders, and her face was smeared with soot and tears. She smelled of smoke. She had stopped coughing.

Rob settled her at a table out of the view of the sleepy woman at the counter and the cooks, who were busy preparing cholesterol for the breakfast hordes. He brought a tray with water, two coffees, sugar packets, and a big sticky pastry. Also a large stack of paper napkins. "Eat. Sugar's good for shock."

"They already dosed me with some kind of glucose in the ambulance." She dipped a napkin in the water glass and scrubbed it over her face.

"Good. Try the coffee." He sat and took a sip of his own coffee, which tasted like all hospital coffee.

She wadded the wet napkin, doctored her brew with sugar, and pulled off a bite of pastry. "Meg's mother's pretty sick, huh?"

"Congestive heart failure."

"That's not good." She picked up the pastry and took a healthy bite.

"No," he agreed.

"Tell her I'm sorry."

He took a look at his watch. "I will when she gets to Los Angeles. She just took off."

Maddie ate the pastry with neat fingers, drank a swallow of coffee, and leaned back with a sigh. "I guess I was hungry after all. Sorry I blasted you. I lost it."

"It's okay. You said what I was thinking."

She shivered. "Guilt and blame—a waste of spirit."

"Yes. Do you want my house?"

"What?"

"After the mudslide, Beth McCormick and her family stayed there a couple of weeks. I don't use it. It's convenient and big enough so you could see people. You and Jack will need a place while your house is cleaned."

She smiled at him. "Thanks. Bitsy wants us to stay at the B and B." The bed-and-breakfast was a mansion on the Bjork estate that the Klalos ran as a small convention center. It was successful and lucrative. Bitsy, who had worked cleaning guest rooms at several big Portland hotels, was now the concierge. "It's closer to Two Falls."

"True." That was important. Madeline had hereditary ties to Two Falls. He took another sip. "Tell me what happened."

She shut her eyes. For a moment he thought she would lose it again, but she was just clearing her mind. The wheeze in her breathing worried him. "We went to bed early, around ten, because I have that purification ceremony to... Shit! I forgot about it."

"Ceremony. At the farm?" Rob ventured.

"Yes! At noon. Oh, it's okay. My robes are in the lodge. They'll smell smoky, but Bits can air them...." Her voice trailed.

"Maybe you should postpone it."

"I'll think about it." Her face had a set, stubborn look he recognized. She would perform the ceremony.

Rob waited.

Madeline gave herself a shake, and went on, "I always sleep like a log. We went to bed. Next thing I knew, Jack was yelling at me to get up and get out, that the house was on fire. Well, I could see and smell it. The bedroom window was broke and flames caught the curtains. I rolled out of bed and ran, bumped into Jack at the door."

"The door?"

"He got the extinguisher from the hall. I tried to stop him, but he ran in and started spraying the flames. It wasn't going to work, I could see that, but he wouldn't give up." Her voice went ragged. "Finally, I grabbed him around the waist and dragged him into the hall. He was really coughing. Me, too. We made it out the back door, but the smoke was bad. From the chemicals, I guess. That's a problem with manufactured homes."

Rob nodded, thinking. "So it started there, by the bedroom?"

"I think so."

Rob wondered if that meant the arsonists knew Jack and Maddie slept in that room, or if they were just mopes who didn't give a damn instead of dedicated killers. Either way, arson was a felony. Killing someone in the commission of a felony was classified as murder. In this case, attempted murder.

So now he had two homicide investigations on his hands, except that he was pretty sure they were the same investigation. Or would be.

His turn to sigh. "Tell me about Harley Hoover."

"Iraq and Afghanistan. Head injury."

If exposure to Agent Orange was an unforeseen consequence for troops in Vietnam, traumatic head injury from roadside bombs seemed to be the corresponding problem in the Middle East.

"He's been discharged?"

"Honorably."

"And you decided he'd make a good caretaker for the farmhouse."

"That's right. He needs a job." She sipped coffee and made a face. "Jack wants to take Harley fishing. I think he should go to college."

"But he's having trouble concentrating."

"Yes. And he shouts."

"That would spook the fish."

"It's not funny."

"I know it's not funny, Madeline." He met her eyes. She looked down. "Tell me about his friends."

"I don't know them..."

"The biker who showed up at the farmhouse."

She shook her head. "No idea. Harley wouldn't say. Just a friend from the army, I guess. Probably Iraq. Harley was only in Afghanistan a few days."

"Okay. We'll track the biker down. I need to talk to Jack, too."

"Later."

"When he's ready," Rob said gently. "I need his advice."

"About Harley?"

He watched her. "Hey, I lean on reserve deputies. Meg and Jack." Jack had refused a badge, said he was a fisherman, not a cop. To Rob's relief Maddie laughed. And coughed.

They went back then to see what was happening with Jack Redfern.

Chapter 10

SMOKE STILL HUNG on the air. The fire chief was consulting with Sgt. Ramos and an unhappy insurance agent by the time Rob got to Two Falls after a delay at the courthouse. Corky Kononen had set up a three-block detour for through traffic on Highway 14. For all the good it would do, crime scene tape encircled the corner lot where the double-wide manufactured home stood. Neighbors and fire fighters had trampled the area when they put the fire out.

A cursory look at the house suggested the structural damage was superficial. The emotional damage to the community was something else. Clumps of residents stood in the sleety dawn, staring at the house and talking in low voices. Rob could feel the heat of their anger.

Linda Ramos spotted him and trotted over to the pickup. "Good thing the arsonists took off when they threw the bomb." She waved an arm at an immense cottonwood that overhung the side street. "They'd be strung from the nearest limb."

He raised his eyebrows. "There was more than one torch?"

"I don't know yet."

"What did they use?"

"A Molotov cocktail, according to the fire chief."

"Not very sophisticated."

"No. If it had caught, though..."

94

"If it had caught, Jack and Maddie would be dead. Who's working with you, Linda?"

"Captain Kononen assigned Henry Perkins. The other uniforms are directing traffic. The crime scene crew finished with the Jackman house yesterday evening, so they're around the corner, setting lights up for a good look at the yard and alley, and Sorenson will be here in ten minutes. He had to find somebody to take care of his son."

"We need a drop-in nursery."

She didn't smile. A light rain misted her glasses. "That would be nice. I told Jake my *abuela* would sit with Pepper. She already has Mickey." Mickey was Linda's son, a third-grader. Her grandmother was a faithful nanny. "I caught her before she left for Mass."

"Good of her to baby-sit Pepper," Rob said awkwardly. Lack of day care was a staff issue. "Are there witnesses?"

"Nobody came forward."

"Do we have a bullhorn?"

"Maybe in the evidence van."

"Take a look, will you? I feel a speech coming on."

"That might speed things up."

Rob did his best. He stood in the middle of the blocked-off intersection and gave anybody who wanted to listen an update on Jack and Madeline, including the number of Jack's room and the hospital's visiting hours.

Rob explained that the chief's house was off-limits while the evidence crew worked and asked somebody to check on Jack's boat, which was moored at the mouth of the Choteau. That was unnecessary, but he thought it might soften up the fishermen in the crowd. A couple of men sloped off toward the river. The rest of the watchers drew nearer, maybe twenty adults and a raft of children. Elderly adults and young children. A lot of Two Falls residents were at the hospital.

Rob kept talking. He told them he needed witnesses—anybody awake between four and six who noticed anything at all unusual in the streets of Two Falls. It was a tiny village—one convenience store/bait shop/gas station, a souvenir shop, and a café with four booths and a counter. Strangers would stand out.

The problem was getting people to open up. To say they didn't trust the police was gross understatement. He wished he could bring Todd in to do the questioning, but Linda was already at the scene, and she didn't deserve a slap in the face. He could get Todd to relieve her at noon and do a house-to-house round. No, the purification rite at Trout Farm was set for noon. Todd could talk to Two Falls people out there, if he could stay awake that long.

Rob introduced Linda and invited witnesses to talk to her in her patrol unit, pointed out where it sat skewed behind the fire chief's car, and sent her there with Henry Perkins to take statements. Rob remembered to thank the crowd for the good work they'd done with their hoses before the fire department arrived.

Rather than hang around Two Falls, he drove to his office in the courthouse annex. He called Meg on her cell phone—she'd just arrived at LAX and was about to take a taxi to the hospital. She'd check into her motel when Lucy got there. Meg was very upset because of the fire, and because she'd forgotten to phone Maddie to apologize for missing the rite. Unreasonably upset, Rob thought. He promised to attend the ceremony as Meg's proxy and to convey her regrets.

After he hung up, it occurred to him that some Klalo rituals were closed to outsiders. When he checked with Todd, the deputy assured him even a cop could come to a house purification. Todd didn't look tired after his all-nighter. He looked supercharged. Ah, to be twenty-nine.

"We usually bring gifts." He gave Rob a sidelong glance. "Blankets, baskets, bentwood boxes, that kind of thing—but you'll be a guest, and guests get in free." He grinned.

"Tell me it's not a potlatch!" Rob found the custom of competitive gift-giving rather shocking, to tell the truth. He liked giving gifts, but the idea that the recipient might feel obliged to outdo him in return, and so *ad infinitum*, made him queasy.

Todd laughed. "Ma says it's a recent custom—like Anglo house-gifts." His mother was Madeline's sister. "Do you want to ride to the farm with me?" He meant to take a department vehicle.

House-gifts. Rob thought of Meg's ill-fated frogs and suppressed a smile. He had an idea. He checked his watch—his office had a clock, but he always checked his watch anyway. It was after eleven. *Anglo ritual*, he thought, amused. *You cannot conquer time.*

"No, I need to swing by the house first. I ought to change into something else." He was wearing jeans and a sweatshirt that had seen better days. He'd expected to have an hour at home when he returned from the airport before he had to go to work.

When he finally reached Trout Farm, dressed respectably in twill pants and a tweed jacket over a sweater, the drummers had already started pounding away. He left the pickup beside Todd's patrol car and walked over to the nearest clump of watchers. They were all women, and they shooed him over to the men, who were dancing in street clothes in the light rain that had succeeded the sleet storm— Todd, too. Nobody greeted Rob. He did not see Harley Hoover.

Rob was not incapable of line dancing or jerking in place to a basic disco beat, so he slid to the back of the male contingent amid curious looks and moved his feet the way the drums suggested. All the windows in the house were open, and Rob heard chanting inside. Eventually Madeline and Bitsy Thomas came out onto the porch, both of them dressed in elkskin robes and beaded headbands. As usual, Madeline looked splendid, but when she began to sing in Klalo her voice rang hoarse. She held a long feather and lit it, trailing the sharp-smelling smoke in wide benevolent circles. Twice she broke off, coughing, but she completed her blessing, or Rob supposed she did. The drumming stopped, as it sometimes did at powwows, without warning. Afterwards, the air trembled.

Then everyone entered the house with gifts. Rob went back to the pickup, pulled his bundle from behind the seat, and trailed into the big bare living room that still smelled faintly of burnt feather. He felt foolish but determined. Meg wasn't the only one who could recycle gifts.

Madeline took her time getting to him, but she was pleasant enough when she finally acknowledged him.

"Your grandmother's?" She stroked the cheerful green-and-light-blue plaid fabric. She set the cloth on a long folding table already strewn with gifts, including two rare Hudson's Bay blankets.

Rob's grandmother had bought the five-yard bolt for her husband on her one trip to Britain, made a side trip to Angus to find it. Robert Guthrie had laughed heartily at the idea of himself in a kilt, so Hazel stashed the cloth in her ancient hope chest. It smelled faintly of cedar.

"It's the Guthrie tartan." Rob wondered whether Maddie knew the significance.

"Family." She smiled. "Thank you."

"I thought your library should have it."

"*My* library?"

"You've made it yours."

Madeline looked troubled. "Does Meg mind?"

"Probably not. She's an in-comer. She's not territorial, and she wants the people of Two Falls to use the library. Now they will."

"I hope so."

"They will when we've got these yahoos behind bars."

"I wish I knew what it meant." She was being cryptic again. *It:* The fire? The vandalism at the farm? The malice behind those acts?

"I need to have a long talk with Jack."

Her mouth set. "He didn't see anything. I asked."

Rob persisted. "I need his advice."

She couldn't very well object to that and didn't.

"Do you know a better tracker than your husband?"

Her eyes met his, then cut away, but she was smiling. Both of them knew it was not Jack's tracking skills, sharp as they were, that Rob needed.

Having achieved a temporary truce with the Klalos, Rob went back to work.

He did not visit Jack Redfern. Jack was still doped up, by all accounts, and sleeping. Instead, Rob took the time to sort out his thoughts. There was very little to sort by way of evidence.

Two cases. Homicide and attempted homicide. Or to be exact, a possible homicide that might be an accident, a hate crime that might be simple vandalism, and a singularly inept case of arson. Three cases, two cases, or one?

Ordinarily Rob had no difficulty keeping multiple inquiries separate in his mind. In fact, there were several others ongoing. But these three kept swimming together, and the library, or the library system, was at the center. He wished Meg would come home for a lot of reasons. Just now he wanted to pick her brain.

He needed to know everything there was to know about Marybeth Jackman, librarian. Someone had killed her. Someone had damaged the proposed Two Falls library—before the proposal was accepted, true enough—destroying a book collection. The attack on Chief Thomas's house seemed unrelated, yet the Klalos had inherited the Trout family farm, and at some point Marybeth had wanted to contest the will.

There were other connections. Marybeth had a daughter whose boyfriend was close enough to Harley Hoover to visit him at the farm. Aidan and Carla had helped Marybeth remove the furnishings from the farm, so they had to be suspects in the vandalism. At the very least, they should be questioned in case they'd noticed anyone hanging around as they left the farm the day it was trashed.

He was about to send out an order to locate Aidan Pascoe when Todd called in. The deputy was still out at the farm, talking to people from Two Falls who had attended the ceremony.

Todd said without preamble, "They're claiming they heard a motorcycle revving after the fire started."

"They? Who?"

"Leon Redfern, for one. Uncle Jack's brother."

"How did I miss seeing him?" Rob knew Leon.

"He was with Uncle Jack," Todd said. Electronic interference produced a burst of static. "He came out here after you left. The other witnesses are Tillie Hoover, Harley's aunt, and my cousin, Jason Thomas. He's only fifteen, but he's a sharp kid."

"Did they see anything?"

"No."

"Okay, thank them all for me when they've signed their statements. I'm going to put out a BOLO for Aidan Pascoe." To be on the lookout, to all counties on both sides of the river as far as Biggs Junction east and Astoria west, but mainly Latouche and Clark counties. Carla's father lived in Camas.

"Did that help, about the motorcycle?"

"A lot. Thanks, Todd. Good work. And keep at it. See if some other poor soul was up looking out a window between four and six."

"Right, sir." And Todd signed off.

It occurred to Rob that he and Meg had driven through Two Falls on their way to the bridge perhaps fifteen minutes before the arsonist struck.

"Christ, what a day," he muttered, and went out to talk to Jane Schmidt on Dispatch. Thanks to Todd, he had enough to bring Pascoe in for questioning. When Rob had sent out his bulletin, he went back to the office and telephoned Edwin Jackman in Camas. It was past time to interview Marybeth's daughter.

"She went back to Klalo last night. They finished with the house, except for the deck, so she's allowed to enter it. I guess she stayed there." Jackman sounded tired. "She says she wants to go to school tomorrow."

Rob digested that. "Is she a good student?" Have to contact the high school.

"Erratic. Carla's smart enough, but she doesn't work up to her potential. It drove Marybeth crazy. Crazier." He let out a long sigh. "Sorry. What did you want?"

"To talk to her about her mother's state of mind. I know Carla is underage."

"She turns eighteen Wednesday. I told her she should stay with us, finish out her senior year here in Camas. It's a good high school. Frankly, I'd like to wean her away from her friends in Klalo. Fat chance. She wants to live in her mother's house. Since the house is now hers, or will be when the will is proved, and she comes of age this week, I don't see how I can stop her. She promised me she'll graduate."

"Tell me about her boyfriend."

Silence. At last Jackman said, in a tight voice, "He's not a boy."

Rob didn't press him. "Do you want to sit in on the interview?"

"I suppose I ought to."

"When I find her, I'll call you to set up an appointment. Can I have her cell phone number?"

Jackman gave it to him, adding, "You'll have to leave a message. The phone isn't turned on at the moment. I just tried. When are you going to interview her?"

"Maybe this evening. Is that okay?"

Mr. Jackman agreed. When he talked about Carla, he sounded helpless. Not in control. As another non-custodial parent, Rob had a certain fellow feeling. He bore his ex-wife no ill will, but she had made decisions about their daughter he did not approve of, and they had had consequences in Willow's behavior and attitudes. He suspected Jackman had had the same experience in spades. A motive for murder? Possibly. He hung up and asked Dispatch to put him through to Linda Ramos.

She was home eating lunch. He could hear Mickey and Pepper rioting in the background. Linda sounded tired.

The fire department had brought in a state investigator as a formality, so the crime scene team would be packing it in, too. They'd had a busy few days. Rob asked Linda to help him interview Carla when he found her, and she agreed. He told her to take the afternoon off. Then he went home to make himself a sandwich, having skipped breakfast and missed lunch.

However fraught she might be, it was not in Meg to leave her lover an empty refrigerator. She was scornful of fictional detectives, whether male or female, who came home to a fridge with naught but moldy cheese and one withered olive on the shelves alongside a six-pack of Coors Lite. This trope was supposed to indicate intense dedication to The Job. To Meg it indicated lack of forethought. It took her out of the fiction, she said. She didn't believe feckless detectives were capable of ratiocination. It was hell being hooked up to a librarian.

He reached for his cell phone to call her again and forced himself to reach for the ham slices instead. They were freshly thawed beside a loaf of good bread and a half-frozen container of homemade navy bean soup. He zapped the soup in the microwave, constructed a massive sandwich (the lettuce was crisp), and poured a glass of Full Sail IPA. He ate as single-mindedly as Meg's rejected detectives slurped Coors.

Leftover Thanksgiving turkey lay neatly wrapped in the meat tray. Rob was reaching for it to make another sandwich when the turkey came into focus. *Turkey—Beth. Beth—sheriff.* He slammed the refrigerator door shut and grabbed his cell phone.

She answered on the first ring. "Robert. How kind of you to call."

He mumbled an excuse.

"Corky reported in five *hours* ago."

"I'm sorry, Elizabeth. I'm an idiot."

She wasn't listening. "Am I or am I not sheriff of Latouche County? Duly elected."

"You are. I apologize. I'm a little distracted. Meg's mother is in the hospital. I drove Meg to the airport at three forty-five this morning."

Beth sniffed. "Well, report now. Everything, starting at three forty-five."

Rob walked to the counter and began to make a pot of coffee one-handed. "Where are you?" She usually didn't go to the office on Sundays.

"The hospital parking lot. I paid a visit to Jack Redfern."

She had a true politician's instincts. He suppressed the unworthy thought. Beth was just tenderhearted. She liked Jack. Rob stuck a filter in the coffeemaker and tossed in three heaping scoops of French Roast. "How's he doing?"

"He could barely speak, poor man. Very doped up. Madeline wasn't there."

"She's out at Trout Farm blessing the house."

"Oh. I brought Jack a fruitcake."

Rob couldn't help laughing.

"What!" Beth sounded offended.

"You've got to be the only sheriff in America to bribe a voter with fruitcake." He filled the pot with tap water and poured it into the coffeemaker, screwed the lid on the pot, and pressed the On button. The machine began to gargle.

"Are you going to report?"

"Yes, ma'am." While the coffee brewed, Rob summarized his day. He didn't think he left anything significant out.

Beth was a good listener. She asked only a few questions, but they clarified things he knew or pointed to things he needed to know.

When he wound down, she said, "What can I do for you?" And she meant it.

He had been talking about Carla Jackman and her boyfriend. "You still have good contacts at the high school, right?"

"Yes. I didn't teach Carla. She was a freshman the year after I left. I do remember Harley and Aidan, however."

"Harley's dyslexic?"

"No, that's his sister. Odd, because boys are more likely to suffer from dyslexia than girls. Nancy's doing very well."

"So I heard." He waited.

"I'll get in touch with Ruth Reno. She's the head counselor. She won't give me details, like grades or behavior problems in class, or personal matters like abortion, but she'll probably be willing to share her impressions."

"Okay. That'll help. I have Meg's opinion of Marybeth Jackman," he said, feeling his way, "but I don't know how the woman came across outside the workplace, or what kind of parent she was. Can you ask Ruth if she had any dealings with Carla's mother?"

"Yes. Good idea. I'll call Ruth right now. I haven't seen her in months. If you're going to interview the girl tonight or tomorrow you'll probably need something to go on as soon as possible."

"I definitely need help. Of any kind. If I had cause for a warrant, I could throw my weight around with the principal, but I don't. And I don't want to come on heavy anyway. I also don't think the counselors or the teachers will have anything dire to say about either Marybeth or Carla. I just need a bridge to this kid."

"A bridge." Beth sounded pensive. "I'll tell Ruth you're mainly interested in the mother. That should distract her from the student privacy issue, and maybe she'll let something drop about Carla, too. Is that fair?"

He chuckled. "I think so—fair but probably not admissible as evidence. Right now, I don't need admissible. I need to know who I'm dealing with."

"And after all, it *is* a murder investigation."

"We're not sure it is, but we should be fairly soon."

Beth allowed him to hang up without berating him further. He had reported. She never belabored a point.

He took a Thermos of fresh coffee back to the office with him and started phoning again. He left a message on Carla Jackman's cell, called her mother's landline and left another message, looked for a number for Aidan Pascoe without success, and checked for Pascoes in the local phone book. There was one, but no Aidan. Rob left a message anyway. He called the army and the V.A. and left messages. Finally, in a moment of inspiration, he called the Frank Waltz residence, home of the man who had notified 911 Thanksgiving Day of the body lying at the base of the basalt cliff. Rob asked whether Mr. Waltz had seen Carla Jackman recently.

"Yes, my wife saw the girl and her young man ride up on the motorcycle this morning. Laura took them a pie. She said Carla was rude and might've been drinking. They didn't stay long—took off in Mrs. Jackman's car. I guess they left the motorcycle in the garage."

Rob felt as if he'd been jolted with a cattle prod. He spent some time listening to Mr. Waltz and making soothing sounds. Waltz was fearful that wild teenage orgies were going to happen next door if Carla lived there without supervision, an apprehension that was probably not unfounded.

While Rob listened, he was already onto the DMV website calling up data on Marybeth's vehicle. By the time he hung up, police in eight counties were alerted to be on the lookout for a three-year-old bronze Camry with Washington plates. He had no reason to think the kids were trying to evade the law, and Carla probably thought of the car as hers. Innocent or not, Rob needed to talk to her.

Meanwhile, Jack Redfern.

Chapter 11

MADELINE THOMAS was feeding her husband salmon, bit by bit. Not hospital food. Jack's hands reposed on the sheet in gauze cages. They had eyes only for each other.

Rob didn't interrupt. He checked his watch. How could he not have noticed it was dinnertime? He backed out of the room into the hall, where he bumped into Leon Redfern, Jack's brother. The two men shook hands.

"How have you been, Leon?"

Leon shrugged. He wasn't much of a talker. "Fine. Wife left."

"I'm sorry."

"She'll come back. She wanted to think." Leon cleared his throat. "Hard on her."

"And on you." Their son had been a murder victim four years ago, but what were four years to that kind of grief? "And your girls, how are they?"

"Ah, fine. Say, Rob, this fire, it's a bad business. Got to find out who done it."

"I hope so. Todd says you heard a motorcycle this morning."

"Woke me up. I don't sleep a lot. They sat there and revved the engine right outside my window. And they was laughing, both of 'em. I didn't say that to Todd, about the laughing." He pointed his chin at the hospital room. "The chief was there at the interview. Didn't seem respectful."

Rob digested that. "Both of them, you said?"

"Both. Girl and a boy. Ridin' one of them Honda cycles."

That was another thing Leon hadn't told Todd. "Could you see their faces?"

Leon looked at him as if he were demented. "Helmets. Had their backs to me."

"Sorry. They revved the engine, and then you saw the fire?"

"Right. Out of the corner of my eye. I turned to it to see what was happening and heard them roar off. I called 911."

Rob was almost afraid to say anything else, as if Leon were a wild creature he might scare off. He cleared his throat. "That's very helpful, Leon. Thank you."

"Hey, no problem."

Suddenly Rob needed to be elsewhere. He knew he would have to get a fuller statement, but now was not the time, and he didn't want to antagonize Leon. "Will you tell your brother I'd like to talk to him, but I'll come by tomorrow?"

"He's going home tomorrow. To the B and B, I mean. That's what he says anyways."

"Okay. Thanks. I'll go out there when he's settled in. Say hello to Madeline for me."

They shook hands again, and Rob fled. When he reached his pickup, he called Dispatch and asked Jane to upgrade the BOLO alert to an All Points Bulletin. He was pretty sure he knew who the arsonists were, and he was not happy to know. He sat awhile, thinking, and called Linda to keep her in the loop, and to ask her to double-check the area near Leon Redfern's bedroom window for tire prints. He hoped the bedroom lay on an unpaved alley. He also asked Judge Rosen for arrest warrants and called the prosecutor to let her know what was happening. Then he phoned Jeff Fong, who was about to go off duty.

Jeff had been interviewing the library staff, focusing on Annie Baldwin, Wendy Resnik, and Tessa Muller, and finding nothing much. Marybeth had been widely unpopular, except for her two allies. Of the two, Muller was still very emotional, Resnik uptight. Jeff thought

Resnik was hiding something. Rob told him to keep at it, and filled
him in on Linda's investigation.

Everyone agreed there was bad blood between Marybeth and
Annie, as there was between the victim and Meg. The bookmobile
driver was lying low. Jeff thought she was scared. He said he was sorry
to hear about Meg's mother, and when did Rob say Meg was coming
back? Very sympathetic, very polite. It made Rob uneasy. He said he
didn't know.

He had just disconnected when the cell phone rang. Chirped.
Bloody phone. "Neill," he snarled.

"Come to dinner, Rob," Beth said. "I have a lot to tell you."

"I'm not hungry, thanks. I ate a sandwich about the time I called
you."

"I boiled the turkey bones. My world-famous turkey carcass soup."

"Hmmm."

"Noodles," she wheedled. Beth made her own noodles.

"You're on." He had to wonder how he'd managed to connect with
two women who loved to cook. He resisted the impulse to call Meg. If
she didn't call him, he would call her at eight, he told himself. He left
messages for Carla Jackman again—on the landline and on her cell.

Beth's noodles were worth waiting for. By unspoken mutual consent, they talked about their kids while they ate. Beth told him Peggy
was pregnant, and they both worried about that a little. Peggy's skull
had been fractured in the mudslide that killed her father, and she still
suffered an occasional *grand mal* seizure. However, she was in good
health otherwise, and Skip was very supportive. Sophia wanted a sister. When that topic ran dry, Rob said he supposed he would have
heard if Willow had broken her leg up on Mount Hood. Beth agreed.
Only over the last of the pumpkin pie and the coffee did they get to the
purpose of the meeting.

"Marybeth Jackman was the parent from hell, according to Ruth
Reno," Beth said at last. "Ruth is tolerant of parental whimsy, but she
said Jackman bullied Carla's junior English teacher into giving the girl
a passing grade. When Jackman found out Carla was sexually active,
she also tried to bully Ruth, because Carla talked things over with
a counselor and not Mother. Mind you, Ruth did not give medical

advice. She wouldn't do that, but she could and did refer Carla to the county mental health clinic."

"Mental health?"

"Believe me, anxiety about choice, or ignorance about choice, is serious stress for a seventeen-year-old girl."

"Not to mention a seventeen-year-old boy."

"Boys do not get pregnant." Beth glared.

"Was she?"

"Carla? No, and she didn't want to be. You can bet Mrs. Jackman tried to keep Carla ignorant. In any case, the clinic can provide information about birth control. That's all Carla wanted. Information. And before you ask, yes, she was advised to abstain. After the fact, I assume."

Rob wondered if he could lock Willow up until she turned thirty.

Beth sipped coffee. "Ruth's impression was that Mrs. Jackman didn't just bully teachers, she bullied Carla."

"Evidence?"

"Oh, nothing physical, but Ruth watched Carla closely for three years. When she entered high school, the girl was very timid. Afraid of authority figures. Lacking in self-esteem, as we say in the ed biz. All of her teachers noticed that."

"You're not in the ed biz anymore."

Beth smiled. "Oh yes I am. In fact, that may be my primary function, since you fill the other so well."

He felt his face go hot at the compliment. When she'd agreed to serve out her husband's term, Beth had begged Rob to take over the law enforcement duties associated with the county's chief executive. She would learn, she said, and she would back him up, but she wanted him there as undersheriff. He had agreed with reluctance. He'd been content as the county's chief investigator, and he disliked administrative chores.

But he didn't regret the deal, and he was glad to know she didn't either.

"You said Carla was timid when Ruth first saw her."

"Very. She barely spoke in class and had no friends."

"I gather she changed."

"She met Aidan Pascoe. Last year."

"How, if she was that shy?"

"Ruth didn't say."

Rob swallowed cold coffee. "And Aidan transformed her?"

"Swept her off her feet?" Beth shook her head. "I don't think so. The Aidan I remember was not exactly a stud-muffin."

"Kids change, boys especially."

"As you know."

"Low blow," he said without rancor.

Rob was a senior before he reached the glorious altitude of five feet eight. A late bloomer, everybody said, especially his grandmother. He was now five eleven, having shot up three painful inches in his eighteenth year, but there were still moments when he was a shrimp. The experience gave him a soft spot for kids who were miserable in high school, whatever the reason. He would have to back off from that befuddling empathy.

Beth watched him.

He sighed. "Tell me everything you know about Aidan Pascoe."

Beth took their cups to the kitchen and returned with them, emptied, and the coffeepot. "Another coffee?"

"I guess so. Might as well pull an all-nighter."

She poured two cups and set the empty pot on a trivet. "Tell me something first. You had a rough time the first years of high school, or so I imagine."

"I did."

"How did you get through the anger?"

"Jokes and judo."

"Come on, be serious. It's a grossly intrusive question, but it has a bearing on both of these young people."

He rubbed the back of his neck. "I *was* serious."

"Go on." She busied herself sugaring her coffee.

"When I was a first grader my dad noticed I was the smallest kid on the block. He did something about it."

She sipped.

"He taught me a few simple self-defense moves, so the big guys would think twice about shoving me around, and he lectured me about not misusing judo and turning myself into a bully, too. That was good, I guess, but the main thing was the jokes."

"A soft answer turneth away wrath?"

"With bullies, a soft answer doesn't work. A joke, the right kind of joke, can distract them, or their hangers-on."

"So you and your father practiced jokes?"

"Joke-of-the-day club. Knock, knock." Rob grinned. "That's about it."

"He was a smart man."

"Not smart enough to avoid being sent to a combat zone." He made a face. He did not like to talk about his parents. His father, Staff Sgt. Charles Neill, who characterized himself as a glorified file clerk, was killed in a random rocket attack on Saigon during the Tet Offensive of 1968. Within the year, Rob's mother had died in an unnecessary wreck on the River Road.

Beth waited, her eyes dark with too much sympathy.

"I lost my sense of humor."

Her eyes brimmed but she had the wit to wait.

"You remember my grandfather?" Dumb question.

She blinked and sniffed. "You're kidding. Robert Guthrie presided over my adolescence."

"At the soda fountain." His grandfather had owned a small traditional drugstore in downtown Klalo. The Guthrie soda fountain was a teen hangout.

"Cherry Cokes."

"French fries and ketchup."

"For you maybe. I had to watch my waistline. It was a great place to flirt with boys."

"And girls. Not that I was flirting at the age of nine. Mostly I picked fights. Granddad could see I was in trouble. So he found the *dojo* and persuaded me my father would want me to be a warrior."

"He lied?"

"He lied," Rob said with affection. "It's a good thing *Sensei* was a strict traditionalist." The master, an ancient Okinawan, had had almost no English, but he had conveyed his disdain for colored sashes and other Japanese corruptions of the art of the empty hand. He would have been horrified to see karate turning into an Olympic sport.

Beth nodded. "Mike quit when he realized he was never going to be a black belt at that *dojo*."

"I remember." Rob's mouth twitched. "I have news for Mike."

"Whoever the teacher was, Mike was never going to be a black belt." Beth laughed, a relieved sound.

Rob thought it was time to get down to business. "My anger was diverted into karate."

"And computers."

"Science fiction first, where Lucky Starr, space ranger, saves the galaxy."

"Not Stephen King?"

"Him I found later. Then computers. That was Gran's contribution. When the jokes started coming back, I was armed for adolescence."

"So you had an easy time?"

"No, but I survived more or less intact."

"And got out of town the day after you graduated from high school."

"I hope," Rob said, "that I didn't break my grandfather's heart. I didn't mean to." He had run off to California, then the center of the computer industry. Nowadays he would have just run to The Dalles.

Beth smiled. "No. Robert missed his fishing partner, but he bragged about your independence."

Rob felt a surprising degree of relief. If anyone living knew what his grandfather had felt, it was Beth. "So tell me about Aidan Pascoe."

"On the face of it, he should have been all right, but he wasn't. His parents were divorced, but lots of parents are. The father had custody of Aidan and his brother. The mother kept the daughter and lives in Hood River. Dad's a carpenter and a sports fisherman."

"Is that code for right-wing Republican?"

"It's not code. He likes to fish. Steelhead mostly. But he talks like Rush Limbaugh's mean cousin. He's also a sports fanatic. The older boy, Seth, was on the football and basketball teams, and Dad was a loud supporter, too loud sometimes. Aidan was the kind who tried out and never made the team. His father didn't forgive him."

"Aidan should have gone to live with his mother."

"She didn't ask for custody of the boys. That's all I know about her. I never met her."

"But you did meet the father?"

"Once. I met him when Seth's grades threatened to bump him from the football team. Seth wasn't dyslexic, just didn't concentrate. I guess his father scared him into working enough to get by. He stayed on the teams, and he graduated. I haven't heard anything about him since he left school."

"He probably moved away." Most young people did, at least for a while.

"Probably. He wasn't good enough for an athletic scholarship though, pardon me, scholarship is the wrong word. I think colleges that recruit athletes should cut the comedy and just hand out cash. Save the scholarships for the scholars."

"Beth—"

"I know. Stick to the subject. Aidan. Well, it's hard to pin down. He had trouble concentrating, like his brother, and rarely finished his homework. I didn't call his father in, but I threatened to, and it worked. Sort of. He drifted along, Cs and Ds. No hobbies, no friends. But he graduated. And then he joined the army."

"And that surprised you?"

"No, not completely. There was this superheated atmosphere of patriotism around that time. Kids are vulnerable to it, and Aidan was vulnerable every which way. Also, the military structure may have attracted him. He was a strange rootless, shapeless personality. Maybe he thought the army would give him meaning. It works for some kids. I know that's not a fashionable sentiment, but it's true. And in Aidan's case, it worked, at least for a while. This was five years ago, the year before...you know."

The mudslide. Before Beth survived her husband's death and quit teaching. Before she became sheriff of Latouche County.

"He came home the next September on what they used to call embarkation leave, meaning he was about to be sent off to Iraq with his unit, and he looked great. He came by the high school, in uniform, mind you, and thanked me for being an important influence." She sounded agitated.

"Well, that's nice. A lot of us forget to thank our teachers—"

"I didn't know where to look," Beth hissed. "I was embarrassed. I hadn't done a thing for that child, *couldn't*. He was spouting a lot of platitudes I wanted to believe. I wished him luck and didn't see him again."

"Ever?"

"Ever. The rest of this is from Ruth."

"Understood. He went off with his unit...."

"And came back too soon."

"What do you mean?"

"He was back within six months, back and out of the army. No more parading around in uniform. Ruth heard a lot of speculation, that he'd been wounded, that he was AWOL, that he'd been involved in an atrocity and booted out in a cover-up. You'd have to get on to the army to find out why he was discharged."

"I'll do that. You said speculation. Who was doing the speculating?"

"The older girls and a couple of the aides. Aidan had made quite a hit with the ladies on his embarkation leave, between the uniform and the new motorcycle."

"You didn't say anything about a motorcycle."

"Ah, well, there you are. My memory isn't what it should be. When Aidan came home from basic training, his father was proud of him all of a sudden, so proud he bought Aidan a bike. It was probably the first sign of approval the old man ever gave him."

"Dad was interested. The girls were interested. Aidan got a lot of attention, for the first time in his life." Rob turned that over in his mind. "And then it was over."

"Yes. Ruth has seen him around since on the motorcycle, but she doesn't know where he works or where he's living. She was surprised when Carla Jackman started hanging out with him. He's a good four years older than Carla, for one thing. And Carla's mother is...was fastidious."

"What did Ruth say about Carla? What else, that is."

Beth hesitated. "She said Aidan was good for Carla."

"In what way?"

"She started to assert herself. Over small things, at first. Her mother had chosen her clothes and hairdo, which meant Carla was really out of it—dresses and pantsuits and fluffy curls, like she was forty years old. Her junior year, though, Carla experimented. All black at first, including black lipstick, but Goth is boring these days. Now she's into low-slung jeans and little skimpy tops with bits of lace and temporary tattoos."

"Temporary?"

"They keep changing, so they must be transfers. Ruth said the piercings were even more dramatic."

"They tend to be." So far Willow had only pierced her ears—four times. Her mother had agonized over that.

Beth's mouth twitched in a suppressed smile. "Apparently, when Marybeth objected to the navel piercing, Carla threatened to have her tongue pierced."

Rob laughed.

So did Beth. "The biter bit."

Beth didn't have much to say about Harley Hoover, who sounded dead-center normal and depressingly well-adjusted in contrast to Aidan. She was sorry to hear Harley had suffered a head injury and glad to know he was back with friends and family. She liked him. Everybody did. Except Meg.

On the drive home, Rob thought about Marybeth's daughter. How far had the revolt against her mother gone? The change must have run deeper than mere experimentation with fads. Beth said the girl had started speaking up in class, though not necessarily in a way that pleased her teachers. If anything, her grades had gone downhill, but she had made a few friends among the rebels and outcasts at the high school. She cut class a lot. From what Rob had observed in his conversation with Mr. Jackman, and from what Meg had told him of her talk with the stepmother, Carla's rebellion extended to her father.

How all that, and what he'd learned of Aidan Pascoe, connected with the likelihood that Carla and Aidan had trashed Trout Farm and tried to burn Jack and Maddie out, Rob did not know.

He got home about nine-fifteen and found a message from Meg on the landline.

Chapter 12

"I'M STILL AT the hospital." Meg's voice sounded dull.

Rob cleared his throat. "It's bad, then?"

"Yes. I don't think she recognized me."

Very bad. "I'm sorry, Meg."

"I shouldn't be using a cell phone here. Thanks for calling. I'll phone in the morning."

"Okay. I love you."

"You, too." She sounded as if she were crying or wanting to cry. Male voices rumbled in the background. "Bye."

Rob set the receiver down and stared at Meg's whiteboard with its multi-colored phone numbers, dissociated names, and forgotten dental appointments. When she'd called earlier, why had she used the landline instead of his cell phone?

Because she'd known he wouldn't be home yet, and she hadn't wanted to speak to him. It was a desolating thought. He went upstairs, changed into his karate *gi*, and began a slow-form exercise that demanded total concentration.

When his cell rang the first time, he let it go, thinking the caller would record a message, but it was a hang-up. All the same, it broke his concentration. The caller couldn't be Meg—if she phoned, she would leave a message. He calmed, centered, sank back into mindfulness. Some time later, the cell rang again, startling him. He jumped sideways, caught up the phone from the top of the dresser, and pressed Talk. "Robert Neill."

It was Madeline Thomas. "You sound out of breath. What are you doing?" Her voice crackled. Bad reception.

"Kata." His breathing steadied. "Karate. What can I do for you, Chief Thomas?"

"Harley's missing."

"You're reporting a missing person?" He groped for civility.

"I know you don't do a search until the person is missing twenty-four hours." Her patience was exaggerated.

"True for adults."

"He's gone. He wasn't here for the ceremony...."

"Are you at Trout Farm?"

"Yes. I can get a signal upstairs. His car's missing and some of his stuff. He left the house unlocked. No, I'm lying. He was gone when Bitsy and I got here this morning for the purification, and the house was locked then. When I came out tonight, it was unlocked, like he came back and left again in a hurry."

"What are you doing out there at, what is it, midnight?"

"I had a bad feeling." She didn't elaborate. Rob knew about Madeline's bad feelings and didn't ask for an explanation. When something was wrong she felt it.

"Soon as they settled Jack down for the night," she went on through a burst of static, "I drove out here. Harley's gone. I've been calling around. His mom. His grandmother. Nancy. The kids who were out here when we boxed the books. Nobody's seen him. He's missing."

Rob fumbled in the pockets of the jacket he'd hung on the back of a chair for a notebook and pen, juggling the telephone. The sleeves of his *gi* flopped. "Okay. His grandmother lives in Flume, right?"

"Yes, but he wasn't with her. And he isn't with his mother. He doesn't get along with his stepfather."

"What's Harley driving?" He sat at Meg's dressing table.

"Nancy's old Corolla. Blue. I don't know the license number, but I think it's still registered to her. He gave it to her when he joined the army. Her roommate's taking her to the college these days."

Nancy Hoover, he wrote. Toyota Corolla. Old. Blue. "I'm going to send a patrol car to you." A welfare check, so-called. "The deputy can secure the house." And look for evidence of foul play. "Can you stick around until he gets there?"

"Okay. He didn't come to see Jack at the hospital." She meant Harley didn't.

"And you were surprised?"

"I was when I got to thinking about it. Harley and Jack are close."

Rob turned that over in his mind without result. He was too tired to think. "Tell me what you're afraid of."

"Suicide?"

Suicide would be a real fear. Harley was disturbed, and the rate of suicide among Klalos was higher than in the population as a whole. But Madeline didn't sound sure.

After a moment, she added, "Maybe revenge. He has a lot of anger. If he knows who set the fire..."

Rob hesitated. "Aidan Pascoe."

"Who's that?" She sounded perfectly blank.

"Carla Jackman's boyfriend." The bedroom was chilly and getting colder. He shivered.

"The kid who helped Fern's grandniece clear the house? You sure he did it?"

"I have a warrant for Pascoe's arrest." He didn't mention the girl.

"Fast work."

"Leon gave me what I needed. How would Harley know who torched your house?"

"Kids hear things. Harley has a lot of friends. I think the Pascoe boy came out to the farm while Meg was here. Harley talked to him. I don't think they were on good terms. Carla Jackman's boyfriend?"

"That's right."

She let out her breath with a *whoosh*. "Is that why they trashed the farmhouse? Mama told them to?"

"I didn't say they did that. I don't have the evidence yet."

"But you're looking."

"Yes."

A long pause. "It doesn't make sense." There was nothing slow about Madeline Thomas.

"No," he said, exhausted. "Nothing makes sense."

After he sent out the patrol car and heard a preliminary report from the deputy, Rob tried to resume the exercise, but he was too tired to focus. He fell on the empty bed and slept without moving for five solid hours. And woke to the telephone. Again.

It was Teresa at Dispatch, telling him the Hood River Sheriff's Department had taken Aidan Pascoe and Carla Jackman into custody at the site of a noisy all-night kegger, and what did he want done with them?

Rob thought stewing in their own juices in the Hood River lockup would do them good. Ordinarily the paperwork involved in an interstate transfer of prisoners exasperated him. Now it seemed like an excellent idea. The two arsonists would make their way across the river sometime that day, but he wasn't in a hurry to see the little shits.

He asked Teresa to let Linda know about the fugitives when Linda came on duty, but not to call her at home. He thought about phoning Edwin Jackman, but the girl was safe enough, and a five-thirty wake-up would be sadistic in the circumstances. He gave Jackman's number to Teresa and told her to relay it to the Hood River people. Rebellion or no rebellion, Rob was willing to bet Carla would call her father herself when she found out what she was up against.

There was no point in trying to go back to sleep. He felt reasonably refreshed, though it was not yet six. Meg was going to phone sometime soon. So he got up, took a long hot shower, shaved, and threw on clothes that would look semi-professional. Then he went down to the kitchen for coffee.

He was sipping at his third cup and thinking about toasting a bagel when the back door rattled. Annie Baldwin's pink face peered at him from the porch.

He yanked the door open. "Come in, Annie. What's the matter?" He poured coffee into one of the mugs that hung in a rack on the counter.

"I need to talk to Meg." She looked big-eyed, scared. Also cold. It wasn't sleeting or snowing yet but looked as if it might.

"Have a chair." He placed the steaming mug on the table and returned to his own seat.

She perched on the chair like a nervous bird, shedding gloves. "Is she home yet?"

"Still in Los Angeles. Her mother's worse. Can I help?"

Annie frowned into the mug, took a sip, and mumbled something about library business.

But the library system closed down on Mondays. "Bookmobile still running?"

"What? Oh, yeah, sort of. Bob replaced the starter."

"Good man." Rob looked with sudden longing at the bagel. Maybe he should offer it to Annie. There was only one left.

"They were quarreling."

He snapped awake.

She was looking at him with a mixture of embarrassment and determination.

"They?"

"Marybeth and Wendy."

"When?"

"Couple of times that last week." She looked as much like a teenager trapped in the principal's office as a middle-aged woman could. "I don't like telling on people I work with. Marybeth wanted me fired, and Wendy wanted my job. Meg knows that."

"And she knows you wouldn't say something out of spite."

Her flush deepened, but she seemed pleased. "That's it. You'd find out sooner or later from somebody else."

"Sooner is better."

"That Chinese guy—"

"Actually, Jeff was born in San Francisco and so were his parents."

"Oh. Yeah. I just meant, you know, Sergeant Fong. He doesn't know us."

"He's pretty smart, Annie." Rob's coffee was cold but he took a swallow anyway. "What did they quarrel about?"

"Well, Nina told me Marybeth wanted Wendy to do something for her, and Wendy was dragging her heels. But it doesn't really matter. I figure Marybeth was looking to dump Wendy. She did that. It was kind of a pattern. She'd be all friendly for a while, and then it was like she had to pick a quarrel. She did that to Nina, and to Abby Torres when she found out Abby's husband was Mexican." A rueful smile touched her mouth. "She didn't like Mexicans. In fact, she didn't like a lot of people. Me, she was never friendly with. Maybe she didn't like Norwegians."

"Okay. Thanks, Annie. I'll tell Jeff to have another talk with Nina."

"And Pat Kohler. Pat hears everything."

He thanked her again. She sent messages of sympathy and affection to Meg, but nothing about "library business," and went off, looking almost calm. She remembered her gloves. Rob toasted the bagel.

When he left for the office in the pickup—he preferred to walk but thought he might need the truck later—Meg still hadn't phoned. It was only eight, so he didn't call her in case she'd stayed all night at the hospital and was sleeping in.

The first order of business was to sort out the ongoing investigations. He started Linda on the paperwork Hood River would need and delegated Jake to bring the prisoners to Klalo when Linda had organized the arson evidence. They would have to seize the motorcycle and helmets, and the gloves and leathers the suspects wore when they tossed a gasoline cocktail at Chief Thomas's house. He set that in motion. There was no word yet on Harley Hoover.

Jeff came in around eight-thirty, and they had a useful talk about the murder. Jeff was grateful for Annie's input. He admitted he hadn't got much on the first round of interviews with the library staff, but he was scheduled to attend the autopsy, so he wouldn't be interviewing anyone that morning. However, he would check out Nina and Pat and talk to Wendy again, and when was Meg coming home?

Soon, Rob said. Jeff left, full of good cheer. Rob checked his watch. Nine. No, he was not going to phone her. She would call when she could.

He turned to his computer and opened a new file which he labeled *Fog*, but he might as well have labeled it *Why*. These cases had large patches of fog when it came to understanding motivation. Harley Hoover, for one. The arson, for another. Rob didn't buy simple racism, certainly not if the vandalism were tied to the firebomb, and he thought it had to be. And despite Marybeth Jackman's revolting personality, he didn't understand the murder at all.

Every one of the people who might be considered suspects, including Meg, had had reason to dislike the woman, but all of them, relatives, co-workers, even Chief Thomas, had been dealing with her for some time without resorting to murder. Why kill her on Thanksgiving, shortly after she set her oven timer for a jolly dinner with a friend? It didn't make sense.

What Beth had told him of the daughter indicated that the girl was beginning to take independent action—finding a life of her own, however questionable her choices—and that she was almost of an age to walk away from her mother without looking back.

He was staring at the still-blank file, fingers poised on the keyboard, when Reese Howell, the desk sergeant, stuck his head around the corner.

"What is it?"

"There's a Mrs. Muller here, asking to see the detective in charge of the Jackman murder."

"Right." Rob shoved the keyboard aside. "I'd better talk to her, since Jeff is otherwise occupied. Does she have her lawyer with her?"

"She's all by her lonesome."

"Show her in." He stood up. "Is there any coffee?" A cup of department coffee would send Tessa Muller straight to her lawyer.

"Gotcha." Howell ushered in a woman with a slight overbite who looked to be about Meg's age.

Rob had probably seen Mrs. Muller at library functions, but he had no recollection of talking to her, so he introduced himself and shook hands. "You were Mrs. Jackman's friend. I'm sorry for your loss."

"Um, thanks." Her hand was cold. She sat in the guest chair.

"Sergeant Fong, the deputy in charge of the investigation, is attending the autopsy this morning," Rob said with calculated bluntness.

Her eyes dilated, but she gave a nod.

"How can I help you? You realize *I'm* not in charge, don't you?" He wanted to underline that.

"Yes."

"And that we don't yet know whether Mrs. Jackman was the victim of foul play."

"But you *think* she was murdered."

"Yes."

An intern brought in a plastic tray with two coffees and appurtenances. Sorting that took awhile.

With Mrs. Muller's permission, Rob activated his recorder and

made the necessary introductory comments. It was nine-fifteen. Meg
hadn't called.

Tessa Muller squirmed as he said her name. When he finished, she
blurted, "He kept asking me where I was Thursday morning."

"Sergeant Fong asked you?"

"Yes. He was wasting time. He should have been looking into the
people who hated Marybeth. I was her friend!"

Rob waited.

She gave him what Meg had characterized as a fish-eyed stare. He
met her gaze without blinking. She looked down at her clasped hands.
"Marybeth devoted her life to the library. She should have had Meg
McLean's job, but of course *you* won't admit that."

He waited.

She grumbled and mumbled, spewing secondhand malice to which
he made no reply. The recorder ticked away. Rob listened without
comment until she burst into tears. He handed her a tissue.

"And it's just not fair. Everyone was against her. That Indian woman, the so-called chief, even her own daughter. The things I could tell
you..."

That was marginally more interesting. Rob sat up.

"Marybeth did everything for that girl, lavished money on her
clothes, read to her every night when she was little, gave her ballet
lessons, music, painting, took her to Disney World, you name it. She
was saving for Carla's education, every dime she could put aside, even
when it meant driving an old car. And was Carla grateful? Oh, no. First
chance she got, she took up with a biker, covered herself with tattoos,
mutilated herself...."

What? Oh, the pierced navel.

Tessa ranted on, channeling her friend. "Marybeth told me she'd
had enough. Carla was going to be eighteen this week, out of control,
but Marybeth meant to do something before that, believe you me." She
hiccupped on a sob. "She even talked to her lawyer."

"Her lawyer," Rob repeated. He had talked to Jackman's lawyer
about the will, which left everything to Carla, and about the abor-
tive lawsuit against the Klalos. The man had said nothing of a recent
conference.

"She was going to have him charged. Today! Before Carla turned eighteen."

"Him. Who?"

"The Pascoe boy. Aidan Pascoe. He's twenty-two. Carla's still underage."

"The age of consent in Washington is sixteen."

"A lot you know." Her lip curled. "He probably thought he was safe, but he was in for a big surprise."

Rob stared.

"Any sexual partner four years or more older than a young person can be prosecuted for rape if she's less than *eighteen*. That's the law, and Marybeth was going to take him to court. She was not going to let her little girl throw herself away on a loser like Aidan Pascoe." Her eyes glinted with what looked like vicarious triumph. Then her hands went to her mouth. "I wasn't supposed to tell."

"She was saving it up." Rob's mind raced. Surely the law couldn't be that idiotic. He would ask the prosecutor.

Tessa Muller stiffened. "I don't know what you mean by saving it up. She gave them every chance to back off voluntarily. She reasoned with them."

"She warned Pascoe she was going to have him charged?"

"Well, no. When they told her they were going to get married, she warned both of them that she wouldn't stand for it, that she'd find a way to stop them. She was going to have another talk with them."

"When?"

"When Carla came home from her father's on Sunday, I suppose. It was Edwin's turn to have Carla for Thanksgiving." Tears stood in her eyes. "She was supposed to spend Christmas with Marybeth."

"Did Mrs. Jackman tell Carla's father what she intended to do?"

Tessa blotted her eyes. "I don't know. Edwin always sides with Carla—well, he would, wouldn't he, just to spite Marybeth. It wasn't *Romeo and Juliet*, you know. Marybeth was right, the boy is dreadful. I wouldn't let my daughter near him. A motorcycle, so dangerous, and those bikers, the ones who swarm at Stonehenge every summer, well, Marybeth wasn't about to put up with people like that hanging around her daughter."

Motorcycle enthusiasts made a pilgrimage every Summer Solstice to a concrete replica of Stonehenge, a nineteenth-century folly near Goldendale. Biker weddings had been known to happen at Stonehenge-on-the-Columbia. Rob tried hard not to smile at the thought of Carla's ingenuity.

"It isn't funny! Even the army wouldn't have Aidan Pascoe. He's been home more than two years, and he still hasn't found a decent job. He's a loser."

"There aren't a lot of jobs out there right now," Rob offered. Why was he defending Pascoe?

"My husband says there are always jobs for people who really want to work." An article of faith. She glared at him. "Are you going to check Aidan Pascoe out?"

"Yes. Was there anything else you wanted to discuss with Sergeant Fong, Mrs. Muller?"

She gave Rob much the same story Annie had told him about Jackman and Resnik quarreling Thanksgiving week.

He did his best to exude skepticism. "They must have reconciled. Wendy Resnik was slated to eat the holiday dinner with your friend."

"They would have discussed it again. Marybeth didn't give up, she wasn't a quitter."

"What was it she wanted Ms. Resnik to do?"

"Something about meeting with church people in Flume to discuss bookmobile service. Wendy didn't want to do it. She's not easy with strangers."

"What *about* the bookmobile?" Surely Annie would be the one to talk about rural book services.

She opened her mouth, teeth briefly bared, and shut it. "Heavens, I don't know. Ask Wendy, she's the one who wants Annie's job. I can't imagine why."

He gave her his best imitation of a fish-eyed stare, but it was no use. She was gathering herself to leave and didn't meet his eyes.

His cell phone rang. It was Meg. Rob excused himself and went out into the noisy reception area with its booking desk, phones and desks for the deputies, the dispatch cubicle, and chairs along the wall for witnesses and depressed relatives of people charged with crimes. "Meg, how are you? How's your mother?"

"She died." Her voice was without affect. "At two A.M."

His throat closed. He cleared it. "My dear..."

"I'm coming home. I'm at the airport. They found a seat for me on Alaskan Flight 572. It arrives at six-seventeen. Can you meet me?" In the background the public address system said something significant.

"I...yes, of course. But what about..."

"I can't talk about it, not here." She sounded as if she were on the ragged edge of a scream. "Good-bye."

He stared at the phone. Should he ring back? He grabbed a piece of scrap paper from Reese's wastebasket and jotted down the flight number and time. When he stepped back into his office, Tessa Muller took one look at his face and gabbled farewells.

He shut the door after her and hit the speed-dial, but Meg didn't answer. She had turned her phone off. Lucy. He could call Lucy. He didn't have her number. His cell rang.

"Robert Neill," he said, expecting Meg to answer, but it was Jeff. The autopsy was finished. Rob told him to come over to the office.

Chapter 13

"I THREW UP." Jeff must have gone into his first autopsy overconfident. The deputy's air of bright cheer had dissipated. He looked both sheepish and green around the gills, if such were possible.

"Have a seat and tell me what you learned." Rob held out his hand.

Jeff gave him a printout of the M.E.'s notes and perched on the guest chair. "It's one thing to see a dead body, but watching that cold bugger disassemble a human being was..."

Rob waited while his protégé groped for words. "The ultimate indignity?" he offered after a pause.

"That's it." Jeff sounded grateful. "I used to think Native Americans were nuts to object to scientific examination of historic remains. Now I understand. It's a desecration."

"A necessary one, I'm afraid, in the case of murder."

"Sure, for murder." Jeff sounded doubtful.

"Next-of-kin sometimes object to autopsies. It's not just squeamishness. I've met relatives who say, what does it matter? The victims are dead, and nothing will bring them back. They're right, of course, but I still come away wanting to know what happened, and if possible, why. That's true, even if I think the dead person was a skunk." Time to get to work. Rob drew a breath. "So was it murder?"

"Yes, or manslaughter." Jeff half closed his eyes. His hands clenched, visualizing. "Somebody grabbed her by both arms, shook her, the M.E. thinks, and shoved her off the deck backwards."

Rob nodded. "Bruising on the upper arms."

"And elsewhere. When she fell, there was nothing to slow her down, no tree branches or rock ledges. From her deck it was straight down."

"Did she somersault?"

"No." Jeff curled forward, reaching with his arms, caught himself miming the victim's defensive posture, and gave a rueful smile that faded immediately. "The back of her head hit hard, bashing the skull, but the area between her shoulder blades impaled on a sharp rock, and that severed her spine. A quick death."

Quick but full of terror. Rob shivered. "Time of death?"

Jeff made a face. "You know how cagey they are. He says earlier than we assumed. Morning. Around ten, give or take."

"Okay, Jeff. Thanks for attending. Consider yourself initiated."

"I passed the test?"

Rob frowned. "It wasn't a test. More a plunge into icy water. We deal with a lot of bad things, but murder is the worst. Murder is a damned insult."

Jeff nodded, sober. Both men were silent. At last Jeff said, "I guess I'll go back to the library at this point. That house was clean as a whistle, by the way."

"I heard you allowed the girl back in."

"I kept tape around the deck in case the techies can bring up shoe prints or hand prints or something, but it was awfully clean, too. I think the library's the key."

"It's closed today, you know."

"Yeah, but some of the personnel are there, and I'm still working on the code to those journals. I have an idea...." His voice trailed.

Rob didn't push it. He told Jeff to look into Wendy Resnik's quarrel with the victim. "See if you can find out what they were planning to do about the bookmobile. Jackman persecuted Annie Baldwin. And if you can find anything that reflects badly on Tessa Muller."

"Jackman's friend?" Jeff nodded and took his leave. As he rose to go, he said, casually, "How's Meg?"

"Christ." For a good half hour Rob had forgotten Meg's plight. "She'll be home tonight." He checked his watch. One-thirty. "I'll have to leave around four or four-fifteen to pick her up."

"Her mother's better?

"Her mother died."

"Oh shit, I'm sorry. I didn't know that. Meg's on her way home already? I want to talk to her, but she doesn't imagine I have to see her immediately, does she? Won't she...I mean, what about the funeral?" Jeff sounded appalled.

So was Rob appalled. He rubbed his forehead where a headache threatened. "I can't say I understand either, and she's turned off her cell phone, so I can't ask. It's a big family, lots of children and grand-children. Maybe they're going to do a cremation now, then hold a memorial service some time when everybody can come. I don't know, Jeff. Meg's plane arrives in Portland around six-fifteen."

"I don't need to see her today at all. Tell her I can wait." He cleared his throat. "And give her my sympathy and Keiko's." Jeff left, still shaking his head.

Rob checked on the search for Harley Hoover. No results so far. He decided to run home to eat—and find Lucy's phone number. He had to know what was going on down there. He'd shrugged into his jacket and was groping for the keys to the pickup when the office phone rang. Inside call.

"Llama-Man!" Ellen Koop, the prosecutor.

Rob had to smile. "You're thinking of Jake Sorenson, Ellen. How are the critters?"

"Doing well. Happy as clams—well, happy as llamas, which isn't very. Are you going to interview those arson suspects this afternoon? I might sit in."

He explained the situation, and for good measure, his forthcoming trip to Portland Airport. She sent Meg her sympathy.

They talked for a while about the urgent need for more material evidence, and thanks to Leon, the likelihood of finding tracks left by the motorcycle's tires. After getting yet another search warrant for the Jackman house—specifically including the garage—Forensics had confiscated the cycle that morning as well as the riding gear, which was found scattered throughout Marybeth's formerly immaculate bandbox.

"It's only been five days since she was killed, and with the holiday..." There was no need for Ellen to complete the sentence.

They were both silent a moment, contemplating the effect of holidays on the processing of evidence, not to mention surveillance of vacant houses. Rob gathered his wits. "What can you tell me about statutory rape?"

"Whoa!"

"Change of subject." He repeated what Tessa Muller had told him about state law. "Is that true?"

"I'm afraid so."

"That's moronic."

"Worse, it's a legal trap. The age of consent has been sixteen forever—I think since the nineteenth century."

"The other law is more recent?"

"Aimed at teachers and coaches, priests, and the occasional scout leader or youth minister. I think the legislation was well-intentioned. Kids are always developing crushes on their teachers, and teachers sometimes take advantage. College teachers more often than K–12, in my experience, though most college students are over eighteen. In that case, seduction can be prosecuted as sexual harassment, but it's not considered rape."

Rob described what he knew of the relationship between Aidan Pascoe and Carla Jackman.

Ellen snorted. "Well, Pascoe could be prosecuted, though I'd hate like hell to try. If I did, you can bet the jury would give him a slap on the wrist. He's not in a position of authority over Carla, after all, not a teacher or an employer. It's just a case of good old-fashioned lust, and apparently it's mutual. Nobody's suggested he's beating her or otherwise coercing her, have they?"

"Not that I know of," Rob murmured. Not even her father.

"If he had a record as a sexual predator, all bets would be off, but he's a pretty ordinary kid, right?"

"Shy, if anything, or so I'm told."

"Well, there you are. What's this about?"

"I'm not sure, Ellen. I need to think about it. Aidan has no criminal record as an adult."

"I could probably ask around, see if anybody in Juvie heard of anything when he was underage." Juvenile records were erased when the subject turned eighteen.

"Please do. I suspect he'll come up clean, but something is off. Marybeth Jackman was vicious but not stupid. From what Muller said, she sounded confident."

"I'll look into it. Give Meg my best." She hung up.

Rob stared at the phone. After a moment, his brain started working, and he dialed Jake Sorenson's extension, knowing full well Jake was still in Hood River.

Jake had army connections, having served as an MP. Rob had already put in a formal request for information on Harley and Aidan and the units they had served with. The likeliest sites for their basic training were Fort Leonard Wood, Missouri, or Fort Sill, Oklahoma. Nothing closer.

He left Jake a message, asking for gossip. He worded the request with care because Jake was a little touchy, but gossip was what Rob wanted. Why, at a time when the army was desperate for personnel, had these two young men been released, Harley, at least, with an honorable discharge?

Rob had some army connections himself. His father's lieutenant was now a paunchy brigadier posted to the Pentagon, and General Whitcomb always said, "Anything for Charlie Neill's son." If need be, Rob would call him on it, but not yet. He wanted to see what Jake could do first.

When he got home he looked up Lucy's number, constructed a sandwich of elderly turkey and slightly dry bread, and took up the phone. He was out of luck. Lucy's message informed him she would be at "the lab." He didn't know whether that meant one of the two freshman-level labs she taught or one of the graduate-level labs she was taking. She was a formidable intelligence, and Stanford was grooming her for great things. But she was, he presumed, on the way home from LA. Perhaps she'd forgotten to change her message.

He had only met her once, the previous summer when she breezed through Portland on her way to a conference in Canada. Lucy was smart, and she was also cheerful and funny. Meg flew south to see her every couple of months. He thought Meg had done an outstanding job of parenting. Which reminded him he hadn't heard from Willow, who ought to be back on campus. He sent his daughter an e-mail to let her know of Meg's bereavement and refrained from cross-examination about the ski holiday at Timberline. He also tried Meg's number again without response.

Back at his office, he found that Jake had brought Carla and Aidan home to Latouche County, so he called Linda's desk, though he was conscious that he still had not gone to see Jack Redfern, and he and Linda went down together to the basement room where formal interrogations were conducted.

"We're waiting for Carla's father," Linda said.

"I figured. Let's take a look at Pascoe. Hell, I forgot. Ellen Koop wants to sit in." He called Ellen, but she'd already gone home for the day. Banker's hours?

"You want to do the interview, sir?" Linda was always a little too polite.

"No, go ahead. I'll horn in if I think of something, but it's your case."

She nodded and polished her glasses on a little blue cloth as the guard ushered Aidan Pascoe in.

He shambled. He was not a bad-looking kid when you got past the shaved skull, the tattoos on his neck and forearms, and the piercings. The latter were probably post-army. He was about six feet tall and beginning to fill in around the shoulders and neck, but he had a pouty mouth, the scars of acne, and big spaniel eyes.

His hands twitched in nervous spasms as Linda greeted him by name, introduced herself and Rob, and asked whether he objected to the recorder. He shook his head no.

"Sit down, Aidan," Linda said pleasantly. She activated the recorder and went through the routine of date and time, and the roster of those present. She offered him the opportunity to call a lawyer, and he shook his head again. "Please answer yes or no."

"No," he croaked.

"Thank you. Would you like something to drink, a Coke or coffee?"

"No. Fuck, I just want to know why I'm here. Is that too much to ask?"

"We want to ask you some questions."

"What about?"

"Do you own a Honda motorcycle?" She rattled off the model and license numbers and the year.

"Yes. So what? We were driving Carla's mother's car. It's Carla's now. Her mother died. We didn't steal it." The Camry sat, impounded, in Hood River.

"I asked you about the Honda cycle."

"Yes. I own it."

"Where were you Sunday morning between one and six A.M.?"

He made a strangled sound, cleared his throat. "Asleep."

"Where?"

"At Carla's house in Klalo."

"And you were with Carla Jackman?"

"Yeah. In the same bed." His voice was truculent. "In Carla's mother's bed, if it's any of your business. It's a big one, plenty big for games, and the old lady won't be needing it, will she?" He laughed, *haw-haw*, a forced noise like the villain's laugh in a western movie, or Dick Cheney shooting pheasants, but he blushed.

"Can anyone else verify you were there? Did you call friends on the landline or make a racket when you came in or when you left?"

"No." He shifted on the hard-backed chair.

"I'm sorry to say I don't believe you."

"It's true. She...Carla had permission to go home. The police released the house, except for the deck. We didn't go onto the deck."

"You may have entered the house when the police left. That I don't doubt, though you were probably there earlier than one o'clock in the morning."

"Maybe."

Linda waited for him to elaborate. He didn't. "But later, around three or three-fifteen A.M., you got on your cycle with Miss Jackman riding behind you, drove to Two Falls, parked your bike in an alley there, and threw an incendiary device, a Molotov cocktail, at the house where Chief Thomas of the Klalos lives with her husband, Jack Redfern. You and Miss Jackman returned to the motorcycle, revved the engine, laughing as you did so, and rode off." Linda spoke with deliberation and confidence, as if they could prove what she said was true.

As she spoke, Pascoe stared at her, mouth slightly agape. The color drained from his face slowly, and the spaniel eyes shifted from Linda to Rob and back. When she fell silent, he continued to stare as if hypnotized.

"No," he whispered at last. "No! It's not true. You're trying to frame me. I want a lawyer. Now." The last was a shout, almost a scream.

"Convince me I'm wrong, Aidan." Linda smiled at him. "Tell me again where you were Saturday night and early Sunday morning."

He shook his head. No.

Someone rapped at the door. Rob stood and opened it. Deputy Perkins, grinning, handed him a note. Rob read it and gave it to Linda. The forensics crew had taken a cast of tracks in the alley outside Leon Redfern's bedroom. They matched the treads of the bike's tires.

Linda was looking at Rob, eyebrows raised. He nodded.

"Aidan Pascoe," she said. "You are under arrest and will be charged with arson in the first degree...." And on she went, making the charge clear, Mirandizing him properly, and offering to call an attorney from the pro bono list. Rob was proud of her.

He watched the young man. Aidan stiffened and turned even paler. Rob thought he might faint. But he didn't. Maybe there was more to him than met the eye.

He said, "I want to see a lawyer."

Eventually the guard reappeared, and Aidan shambled from the room with the prospect of a defense attorney in view. No revelations had occurred.

Rob checked his watch. After three. He'd have to keep an eye on the time. The last two days the weather had been calm and overcast. The radio was promising wind and snow. Everything he needed for the trip to the airport was already in the pickup—chains, a box of kitty litter, a short-handled shovel, even a Thermos of coffee. He'd also kept in mind that Meg was going to feel the cold and had probably not taken a warm jacket. He could set out straight from the court-house.

He gave himself a mental shake. "Shall we talk to Carla Jackman?"

Linda nodded. She looked pleased, even smug. The incriminating tire treads pretty much cinched her case, though Rob still wanted to know why. Madeline was surely going to want to know why.

Carla entered the room accompanied by a man who had to be her father. She was tiny, as small as Meg. The county's orange jumpsuit did not become her. Rob rose and shook hands with Edwin Jackman, who looked depressed, as well he might.

Rob turned to Carla. "Miss Jackman, I'm Robert Neill. Under-sheriff. I'm sorry for your loss."

She stared from slightly protuberant green eyes and gave a high-pitched giggle. She didn't extend her hand.

"Carla." Her father's eyes, behind fashionable rimless glasses, pleaded with Rob.

Rob introduced Linda and indicated that the Jackmans should sit.

"Where's Aidan?" Carla had a piping little-girl voice.

"In custody," Linda said. "Waiting for his lawyer."

"Lawyer? He doesn't have a lawyer."

"He will," Linda murmured.

Jackman cleared his throat. "Has he been charged?"

Linda nodded. "With arson."

He gaped and turned to his daughter. "What is this? I thought it was a matter of underage drinking."

You poor sap, Rob thought.

Carla gave a high-pitched giggle but said nothing.

Forty-five long minutes later, Carla was released into her father's custody, having kept to her silence. Rob wondered why the man hadn't summoned a lawyer for her. Perhaps he was in denial. He was not a forceful character.

He was taking her to her mother's house, where he said he would stay with her and bring her to the courthouse at nine Tuesday morn-ing. By that time, Rob trusted that Forensics would have produced sufficient evidence from the cycle and leathers to make a double ar-rest satisfactory to the prosecutor. Rob made sure his forensics people would also check for evidence that the cycle had been at Trout Farm. Now that Aidan was in custody and Carla available, it should be easy to do DNA comparisons from the samples of organic evidence taken at the vandalism scene.

It was past four-thirty by then. He set out for Portland Airport using the Hood River Bridge again. I-84 was usually faster than Highway 14. It had already begun to snow.

Chapter 14

SHE SPOTTED ROB as soon as she rounded the corner and headed toward the security apparatus that barred the main corridor. The glimpse brought a jolt of relief so strong she almost passed out. She leaned on the handle of her wheeled carry-on, waited for the dizziness to pass, then straightened and plodded on. It seemed a long way.

He was listening to his cell phone, head bent, shoulders hunched in a nylon wind-cheater. As she watched, he flipped the phone closed and stuck it in his pocket. He wore hiking boots, jeans, and an old ski sweater under the jacket, and his sandy hair flopped on his forehead, but Meg thought as she plodded along how good he was to look at.

He was one of those men who are nothing to write home about at twenty, but look great at forty and fabulous at sixty. Somehow she didn't think *she* would fit that pattern. She and Rob were both over forty, Rob pushing fifty. Right now I'll bet he looks younger than I do, she thought through the fog of weariness. By the time I'm fifty, people will wonder what he sees in the old bag. It was an index of her desolation that the thought did not provoke in her the slightest urge to laugh.

For thirty-some hours she had not slept. She had spent the last interminable hours standing in lines at the airport or flying. Before that, there was the hospital and her mother's death. The emotional numbness that hit Meg somewhere over Sacramento had come as a blessed relief, but she hadn't been able to sleep on the plane, and she did not do well without sleep.

He had seen her. He watched her come, frowning, and stood like a boulder while other passengers from her flight streamed around him. When she stumbled past the last uniformed guard, Rob pulled her to him and held her. She was trembling. He held her until the shaking stopped, then gathered her paraphernalia with one arm, put the other around her waist, and guided her to the nearest empty seat in the waiting area.

He knelt in front of her. "It's snowing."

She ducked her head yes. She'd noticed. Dimly.

He began untying her shoelaces. "They're going to close I-84, so we'll have to take Highway 14." He removed one sneaker and began on the other. "I figured that might happen, so I brought you boots and a parka." In case they had to spend the night in a ditch.

Meg was wearing her Universal Flying Costume, a track suit that permitted her to sit for hours without pinching vital organs. It was not very warm. The temperature in Los Angeles had been in the high sixties. She watched with detachment as he inserted her feet into the suede ankle boots. They were lined with sheepskin.

He squished her sneakers into her carry-on. "Do you want to stay in a motel?"

She shook her head no.

"Home, then. I thought so." He huddled the parka around her shoulders, stood, and folded the book bag that had held her gear. He poked the bag into her floppy purse. "You didn't check anything?"

"No," she croaked.

"Good. Do you want to eat dinner here?"

"No."

"Okay. Sit with the luggage, and I'll be right back." He strode off, light-footed as a twenty-year-old.

Meg stared into space and let the airport noise take over, anything to avoid thought. The public address system announced a Denver flight. A family with half a dozen small children reunited with happy shrieks two yards from where she was sitting. The P.A. announced that

Portland International Airport permitted smoking only in designated outdoor areas and thanked her for her cooperation. It announced another flight in English, Spanish, and what sounded like Japanese. Northwest Airlines flew the great circle to Japan, via Alaska. Meg let her mind drift north.

A music box in a nearby shop played "The Little Drummer Boy." A child wailed. Somebody sneezed. Due to added security, passengers were warned that unattended luggage left in slovenly heaps would be blown up in the middle of the north-south runway. No mercy would be shown. The muscle tension that had held Meg upright began to loosen, and her head drooped.

"Time to go." Rob shook her shoulder.

"Mmmm."

"Come on, love. Give it a try." He boosted her to her feet and helped her put her arms in the sleeves of her jacket. She caught the scent of bakery goods. "This way."

By the time they had stumbled across the exposed sky-bridge to the parking structure and Rob had started the pickup, Meg was awake enough to think about Highway 14, her least-favorite thoroughfare.

"Won't they close it, too?" Her breath puffed out in a cloud of white. She was shivering.

"They sand it at the first sign of trouble." Rob made his way down the ramp and out to the toll station. He'd remembered to pay for parking, so the truck slid onto the eastbound access road without pause. "If it's impassable, I'll turn around, and we can stay at a motel in Vancouver. Want some music?"

He handed her the zipped CD case, meaning *he* wanted music. Fine with her. She didn't want to talk. She inserted Bach and let the elegant impersonality of the music quiet her mind.

They caught the last of the homeward-bound rush hour traffic on the Glen Jackson Bridge, which crossed the Columbia east of Vancouver. The drivers were just rediscovering snow. Cars slid and wallowed. One spun out as Meg watched.

At Camas, the traffic evaporated to the *Goldberg Variations*, freeway lights disappeared, and the road narrowed to two lanes. Snow drove from the south, straight across their eastward path in not-quite whiteout density. Wind gusted. Rob held the truck steady, but Meg could see the strain in his hunched shoulders and clenched hands.

The bakery scent was strong. Her stomach rumbled. "Do you want something to eat?"

"Not yet." He dimmed for an oncoming truck. "Help yourself. I got sausage rolls and a couple of chocolate croissants. There's a Thermos of coffee behind the seat." He wheeled the pickup gently around a wide curve with a two-hundred-foot drop-off to the right. Wind and snow pushed the pickup toward the other lane. "I bet they didn't feed you on the plane."

"Sugared peanuts."

He inched past a two-trailer semi the driver had parked half on a turn-out, half on the road. The driver was affixing chains. Meg wondered whether Rob should put chains on the pickup.

She pulled the Thermos from behind the seat and poured a cup of tepid coffee. "Tell me what's happening."

"I will, if you don't mind random pauses while I grit my teeth." He gripped the wheel and peered out the windshield. The snow blew thicker and faster.

Meg turned the music off. "Tell me."

He gave her a succinct, if hair-raising, summary of everything that had happened during her absence. It was almost too much to take in.

"If Carla and her boyfriend tried to burn Jack and Maddie out, then they probably trashed the farmhouse, too."

"I think so."

Meg took a croissant from the bag and began to eat. Her coffee was cold. "I don't see why."

"Me either." He swore under his breath as an idiot with brights on came at them at high speed. Rob held the pickup steady.

"And Harley's still missing."

"Yes." He didn't elaborate. Visibility was almost zero. Rob leaned forward, squinting. He turned on the high beams, then dimmed them. He slowed, and slowed again.

Meg chewed. Bittersweet chocolate, flaky pastry. She couldn't remember whether she'd eaten lunch.

A gust of snow-laden wind smacked the truck. Rob grunted and kept the pickup in the right lane with difficulty. They were passing the turnout for Beacon Rock, the core of an ancient volcano that towered beside the highway.

"How does this business of statutory rape come in?" Meg popped the last bite into her mouth.

"If you mean how did it affect our crime wave, I have no idea. I need to have another session with Madam Muller. Good thing you exiled her to Azimuth, but it's a little hard on the patrons there."

"I was too kind. I should have sent her to Flume."

"There's no branch library in Flume." A tiny logging town, Flume lay to the north, practically at the base of Mount Saint Helens.

"It's bookmobile territory," Meg agreed. "How's Annie?"

"She didn't want to tattle on her co-workers, but she's been having a hard time. Something else going on there."

The car ahead of them, a junker with a very short driver, crept ahead, going perhaps thirty. Rob slowed. Behind him, an impatient van flashed its lights and roared around the vehicles, narrowly missing an oncoming truck.

Meg choked on a bite of the second croissant, but the truck driver was too smart to slam on his brakes. He did hit the horn. The junker slowed even more as the sound Dopplered down. Half a mile further on, a passing lane appeared and Rob used it, sliding by the dim driver with a pitying look. Meg admired his patience.

The snow was beginning to ease up, though the wind continued to blast erratically. At least the edges of the road were now visible. Meg thought she caught a glimpse of whitecaps on the river. They passed Bonneville Dam, a fandango of light and drooping power lines in velvety blackness. Meg brushed the crumbs of the second croissant from her lap.

The sanding crew must have stopped its work, because the road was suddenly slicker. Rob slowed and drove like an ice-skater. The trick was not to jerk the wheel, he had taught her. A body in motion continued in motion in the way that it was going until you jerked the wheel. Then you had an uncontrolled spin.

They slid along the river forever, close to it now with only riprap on the bank between the pickup and the murky depths. There were five tunnels in this stretch of the road. As they entered the third, its lights went out.

"Oops. Power failure." Rob's headlights probed inky darkness. Beyond the tunnel, snowflakes scrawled graffiti on the night. "Do you want to talk?"

"No!"

He must have caught the edge of panic in her voice. After a long silence, he said, "You don't ever *have* to talk to me about anything, Meg, certainly not about your mother, but if you want to talk, I can listen." His tone was matter-of-fact, and he drove on without looking at her. Her panic leaked away.

Except for the headlights, it was still black out on both sides of the river. Rob kept the pickup moving at about thirty until the road kinked at a derelict lumber mill. Just like that, Meg knew exactly where they were, even in the disorienting darkness. Almost home.

He negotiated the two ninety-degree turns without incident but turned off on a ramp that led to a small park. The park served wind surfers in summer. The pickup came to a stop, slewing a little in the empty lot. He set the brake and left the engine running.

He laid his forehead on his clenched hands for a moment then pushed himself upright. "I'd better eat something. Hand me a croissant, will you?"

"I ate both of them." Meg burst into tears.

"Hey!" He took her face in both hands and kissed her on the forehead and both eyelids. His hands were warm and rough with calluses from all that karate. "Hey, I can do sausage."

Meg said something incoherent about her greed and rummaged in the bakery sack. She watched him eat a sausage roll in two efficient bites. "I love you."

He brushed crumbs and smiled at her, but his face was tired in the green light from the dashboard. "I love you, too. Isn't that a piece of luck? Shall we go home?"

She nodded. "N-not Bluff Road." She didn't want to pass the murder scene.

"Corky closes it before the first flake of snow hits the ground."

They reached Meg's house by way of the relatively flat grid of streets. By that time, power had been restored in town. Snowflakes still drifted. A couple of inches had accumulated. Rob left the pickup in her driveway and helped her into the house, then went back out for her belongings. It was almost ten-thirty. The trip from the airport was supposed to take two hours maximum, even in heavy traffic. They had left for home before seven.

Meg collapsed onto a chair at the kitchen table and let the familiar warmth comfort her. The kitchen was her favorite room in a house she loved too much. Rob had offered her Hazel Guthrie's almost-mansion, and she had said no without hesitation. So he had moved in with her and left the big house next door empty. For the first time, she wondered whether she had been fair to him.

Her faults and failures swept over her, and she sat without moving. If Jeff Fong had come and charged her with murder, she might have confessed.

Rob bumbled back, dropped his load on the new floor tiles, and came over to her in a burst of cold air, kicking the door shut behind him. She braced herself for sympathy.

"I'll haul your bag upstairs and listen to my messages." He kissed the top of her head, pulled her parka off, and hung it beside his own on a wall hook by the door. "You could pour us both a scotch." And he was off.

This display of tough love stirred her enough so she got up and used the downstairs bathroom. Her bladder was grateful. And she poured each of them three fingers of Laphroaig. Straight. Then she sat down again and didn't move. She didn't fall asleep as she had at the airport, just sat and counted her sins.

Although Rob made a certain amount of noise while he was upstairs, she didn't hear him come down, probably because he'd taken his boots off. He padded barefoot to the stove, turned on a front burner, and sliced some bread. He was rummaging in the refrigerator for eggs before Meg stirred.

"I could do that."

"You could, but I might as well." He cracked four eggs into a bowl, stirred them with a fork, and dolloped butter into a small skillet. Only when he had popped the bread into the toaster did he come to the table for his whisky.

"I'm not hungry." Meg heard the whine in her voice.

"Probably not after two croissants, but I am."

That was unanswerable. She eyed him with the beginning of resentment.

He raised his glass to her. "*Sláinte.*"

She mumbled a response and sipped her drink. A tiny sip. It slid down, generating warmth as it went.

Rob cooked the scrambled eggs. When the toast popped up, he buttered it efficiently, turned the eggs onto two plates, set the plates on the table, and took his chair. "*Bon appétit.*" He wielded the salt and pepper on his own gleaming mound of eggs, then handed the shakers to her. "Cutlery." Knives and forks clattered into place.

Meg watched him lace into his dinner. After a moment, she took a bite of toast. Presently, mopping the last of the eggs with the last of her toast, she said, "I heard you talking to somebody. Has anything happened?"

He shoved his empty plate away. "A few test results. Otherwise *nada.* I called Dispatch to let them know I was back."

"Well, that's good, isn't it? I mean, good that there aren't any fresh disasters."

"Just fender-benders. Corky's dealing with them." He rubbed the back of his neck. "I was hoping they'd find Harley Hoover. It's not a good time to be lost in the wilderness." His face was bleak and very tired.

Meg felt something give way in her interior ice-jam. "Rob, I...You have to wonder why I came back so soon."

He met her eyes. His were dark and troubled. "Yes, I wonder, but I don't have to know why."

"I need your..." She wanted to say wisdom but she thought he'd laugh at that. "Advice, I guess."

His frown deepened, and he rubbed the spot between his eyebrows. "For what it's worth, my dear."

She cleared her throat. "They left it too late, or maybe I did. I should have gone down in October."

"You were tied up with the levy campaign."

"I gambled and lost." Meg drew a shaky breath. "I saw my mother several times a year, even after Dad did his grand renunciation act when I got pregnant." She made a face. "It was probably not an act. He probably believes he was right to this day."

Rob took a sip of scotch, watching.

"I never told you about it, because it was so banal. When I got my-self pregnant, as my father inevitably said, my boyfriend Deck—"

"Dick?"

Meg sighed. "His name was Dexter Cunningham. He was a guitar-ist, and he was always called Deck. He has since become an accoun-tant."

Rob's face had taken on a peculiar expression.

"What?"

"I can't believe you fell for a guy named Dexter."

"His name is not the point," Meg snapped. After a moment, she added, "He did offer to pay for an abortion."

Rob's lip curled. "Large-minded of him."

"And, very reluctantly, to marry me. When I saw how reluctantly, I said no to both offers and told him to buzz off. He went his way rejoic-ing." Meg had told this story before, not often, but often enough so she knew the narrative line.

Rob said gently, "Don't make a joke of it, Meg."

She gulped. "Okay. It wasn't a joke." She shut her eyes. Exhaus-tion swept back. "I believe women should have the choice of abortion, but I also believe it involves a serious moral decision. I didn't think I'd be justified, and after I'd talked it over with my mother I was sure I wouldn't. After all, I was healthy, I had a job, I had medical benefits and even maternity leave, and I had friends to help me. So I decided to keep the baby."

"And that was when your father found out?"

"Yes. My innocent mother..." Her throat clogged.

"She told him?"

"She believed it was her duty as a wife. He was outraged. He tried to coerce Deck into marriage until I pointed out that I didn't want to marry him. Then *Dad* offered to pay for an abortion, and never mind that he was always ranting that abortion was murder. In the end, he swore he would not subsidize me or my bastard." She took a large swallow of scotch and choked a little.

Rob's warm hand covered her free hand.

"Hey, it's okay. This was twenty-one years ago. Once I decided to keep the baby, I found I was fascinated by what was happening to my body. Morning sickness wasn't fun, and I thought the ninth month was never going to end, but I was ready to love Lucy by the time she was born."

"Did he...your father suggest you put her up for adoption?"

"So I heard. I wasn't speaking to him, but I was always in touch with my mother and my Aunt Margaret. Mom had scruples about going against Dad's wishes, so I didn't see a lot of her over the years, but she knew what was going on. Mostly I called my aunt when I needed advice, and even a couple of times when I needed help."

Rob cleared his throat. "Your aunt left you her house."

Meg nodded. "I think I was ready to try to reconcile with my father at that point. After all, Lucy turned out just fine. She was in high school by then. But he contested the will, as if Aunt Margaret had no right to make her own decisions. He lost and had to pay court costs, and that made him even angrier. I'm telling you all this so you'll understand my brothers, why they waited too long to let me know how sick my mother was."

"You were in touch with them, too?"

"With Duncan anyway. With the other three, it was a Christmas-card-every-year and family-funerals connection. Dunc and I exchange e-mails and have lunch together every once in awhile. I thought we understood each other." Her throat constricted. "I thought that until Mom died."

"What happened?"

"It was the middle of the night. Duncan and I were with her. Dad had gone home to rest, and so had my oldest brother, James. She just... stopped breathing."

"No resuscitation?"

Meg shook her head, unable to speak. At last she said, "It took awhile to round up my other brothers from the cafeteria. The boys went off in a huddle, and I sat with...with the body, thinking about things and crying. I called Lucy, and she said she'd come. She had a key to my motel room. I told her to check me out and bring my suitcase up so I could change at the hospital, because I felt grubby and grimy. By the time Lucy got there...no, before Lucy got there, Duncan came over to me and explained about what he called the arrangements."

"That was fast."

"They were prepared," Meg said bleakly. "They'd been expecting her to die at any time. The funeral is Wednesday. Duncan told me where it would be and the time, and then..." She broke off and shut her eyes. Rob's hand tightened on hers. "He told me he was glad I'd been there, and everyone would be happy to see me at the funeral, but could I please not bring Lucy because of Dad."

Rob's hand clenched on hers. "For Christ's sake, she was Lucy's grandmother!"

Meg was crying, great whopping relieved sobs. He understood. Well, he would. His grandmother had been important to him.

"I didn't say anything," she gulped, blowing her nose on a paper napkin. "I couldn't. I was too dumbfounded. He patted me on the shoulder and huddled with the other boys. They went off for coffee, and I sat there by my mother's body and got angrier and angrier." Tears gushed. She mopped at them. "Angry for being angry at such a time. I loved my mother. She was weak maybe, but she was a kind woman and good to me when I was growing up. I wanted to mourn her properly."

"Of course you did."

"Finally Lucy stuck her head in the room, so I brought her in and let her say good-bye to her grandmother. She wasn't close to Mom, but they'd met. Mom came to Lucy's high-school graduation."

Rob massaged her hand. "So you had Lucy drive you to the airport?"

"Yes. We stopped in an all-night restaurant and ate breakfast and talked. I told her what had happened. I've always tried to be open with her."

"It's probably why she turned out so well."

Meg blew her nose again. "When we left the hospital, I told the nurse on duty to let my brothers know I'd gone with my daughter. I suppose Duncan and the others think I'm at that grotty motel. And do not," she said fiercely, "suggest that I fly back for the funeral. I will not go where my daughter isn't welcome."

"I think your mother would probably understand." Rob bit his lip. "Hell, I shouldn't have said that. I used to hate it when people tried to tell me what my father would have thought about something. They didn't know. *I* don't know. I guess I'm too tired to think."

It was her turn to pat his hand. "It's okay. I'm more than tired. Let's leave the dishes."

"I'm sorry I never met your mother, Meg." Rob finished his drink and smiled at her. "Your turn to wash."

Chapter 15

He TURNED HER alarm off, and since the sound of the shower almost always woke her up, took his clothes downstairs. When he had
done his morning *kata*, Rob climbed into the huge claw-foot tub in the
downstairs bathroom and used its hand-held shower to get reasonably clean. He'd forgotten his cordless razor, so he padded upstairs
barefoot, found it, and dropped a kiss on Meg's forehead. She didn't
stir. He sneaked back down to finish dressing.

Feeling unnaturally virtuous, he did the dishes and set up the coffeepot for her when he had toasted a frozen bagel and drunk his own
ritual three cups. Then he drove off to work. The snowplows and
sanders had done their job. The schools were opening only an hour
late.

It was after eight when he reached the courthouse annex—late for
him—so he had a pile of e-mail in his office. He dealt with that first.
The most annoying message was the army's response to his urgent request for the service records of Aidan Pascoe and Harley Hoover. His
inquiry was being "processed."

Sorenson was now on nights. Rob made a note to call Jake at home
later and considered phoning the brigadier in D.C. but didn't. There
was time. He was about to wander out for another coffee when his cell
phone rang. Jack Redfern.

"Hey, Rob. Hear you made an arrest."

"Yes. How are your hands?"

"Fine." For once, Jack didn't indulge in a series of polite questions. "Listen, Harley called me."

"He did?" Rob froze, torn between relief and fury.

"Yeah, just now." Jack gave a little wheezing cough. "I should've thought. It turns out he went to Flume, see, to his Grandmother Hoover."

Rob said carefully, "When Madeline reported him missing, she told me she'd called Mrs. Hoover, and that Harley wasn't there."

"He only went to her after it started snowing heavy. He was out on a kind of spirit quest, see, only he didn't figure on the snow, so he come in to his grandmother's late last night." Jack was always reluctant to talk to an outsider about Klalo customs and beliefs.

Rob tried to fill in the blanks without success. First things first. "Can you hold, Jack? I need to call off the search."

"Sure. I'm just sitting here at the old B and B, looking at the snow. Take your time."

Rob canceled the Missing Person bulletin for Harley Hoover, copying to Corky and the whole investigations team. He thought about sending a patrol car out to Flume at once. Instead, he left a message for Todd Welch with the desk sergeant. Todd would be coming on duty in a few minutes. Rob didn't want anybody else taking Hoover into custody.

When Rob picked up the phone again, Jack was still there. "Tell me about Harley."

"Head injury."

"So Meg said. It's a pity." Rob waited.

"He saw some bad shit. In Iraq."

Rob waited some more.

"I take him fishing, see. After a while on the water, he wants to talk. They've got a big river over in Iraq, but not as big as this one, and he don't like deserts." Jack wheezed. "The way I don't like jungles."

When Jack didn't continue, Rob said cautiously, "Does he know the guy we arrested for torching your house?"

"Pascoe? Feels sorry for him. Harley's real softhearted. He was a year ahead of the boy in high school, so he knew him then, and they was both in one of them light armor outfits out of Fort Lewis but not in the same unit. He says Aidan got shafted."

"How so?"

Jack was silent a long moment. Rob heard him wheeze. "Big scandal couple of years ago. Casualties in this village outside Baghdad. Rape and murder of civilians. Sort of like My Lai. It made the TV news, you remember."

"Vaguely."

"When the army got around to investigating, they court-martialed everybody in sight. Captain demoted, lieutenant and a sergeant doing prison time. They dismissed the grunts who was on the patrol from the service, all of them, including Aidan. Well, he was a witness. Nobody claimed he done anything but watch, but he didn't report the incident either."

Incident. What a word. The information fit all too well with what Rob had heard about Aidan. What was it Beth had said, a shapeless personality? Passive and complicit. So what was Aidan doing tearing around the county on a motorcycle, vandalizing property and firebombing double-wide manufactured homes? That sounded way too active. Did showing off for the girlfriend make sense of it?

"Thanks, Jack." Rob drew a breath. "I hope Harley's going to be okay."

"He will be, if you don't toss him in the brig."

"Why would I do that? I just need to talk to him. I'll ask Todd to bring him in. Does Madeline want Harley to go back to Trout Farm when I finish interviewing him?"

"I guess so. I'll have her call you. She's with the insurance guy right now. Oh, and I spoke with Opal, too. She's worried about the bookmobile."

It took Rob a moment to make the connection. Opal was Mrs. Hoover, Harley's grandmother. "What about it?"

"I'm not sure. There's this new church out there. Church of the Ignorant Word."

"You're a bad man. Church of the Inerrant Word."

"That's the one. They don't like the library, and that goes double for the bookmobile. They say it brings the devil into their neighbor-hood."

"I have the feeling he's already there."

Jack laughed at Rob's not very clever gibe, but his cackle ended in a cough. "Annie drives her rig to Flume on Tuesdays, and Opal's oldest granddaughter—Katie Bell, you know Katie—takes her little girl to check out picture books. Only Katie's afraid to take her to the book-mobile today. Katie told Opal those church people are planning some kind of demonstration."

"That doesn't sound good."

"No. Course it snowed a lot. Maybe Annie won't be able to get out there this morning anyways."

Rob thanked Jack again, they hung up, and he called Annie's house, but Bob said she'd already left and that she had her cell phone turned off. When Todd stuck his head in the door, Rob was almost ready with instructions—and almost tempted to go along. But too much business in town demanded his presence, including the interview with Carla Jackman and a fresh talk with Aidan Pascoe. Flume was an hour north of Klalo on a narrow winding road that was subject to slides. Rob didn't want to get trapped way out there.

~

WENDY called.

Meg had slept until almost nine. She woke refreshed, and it was not until her second cup of coffee that misery swept over her. By that time she had showered, dressed, and even phoned Pat Kohler, by de-fault her second-in-command at the library, to say she was back.

Pat expressed condolences, and Meg thanked her, wondering how she'd heard the news. When Pat asked about the funeral, Meg lied. She mumbled something about a memorial service being held later.

The heavy weight of grief pressed down. Meg didn't like to lie, but she liked the idea of explaining her family to an outsider even less. Pat urged her to take a day of bereavement leave, and Meg agreed, feeling will-less. She was sitting, staring into her cup, and wondering what to do with herself when Wendy phoned.

"You've got to warn her!"

Meg recognized the voice without joy. "Warn whom?"

"Annie!"

Meg had had more than enough of that feud. "I have no idea what you're talking about, Wendy. What Annie does or doesn't do is not your business."

"I'm afraid—"

"*I'm* afraid I'm going to hang up if you don't come to the point."

"They're going to attack the bookmobile when it gets to Flume."

Melodrama. Meg took her cup to the sink and poured the luke-warm coffee down the drain. "*They.* They who?"

"Members of that new church, the ones who campaigned against the levy."

Several local churches had done that. With Marybeth's encourage-ment. "And you know this how?"

"One of the women sent me an e-mail."

"When?"

"Sunday after services. The preacher criticized the bookmobile again in his sermon. She said he was inspiring. I'm afraid," she repeat-ed.

"Why didn't you warn Annie when you got the message?"

Meg listened with half an ear as Wendy babbled excuses. Given that she'd hired a lawyer, she was surprisingly open about Marybeth's attempts to undermine the levy. They had included messages of sym-pathy to people who wrote to the local newspaper attacking the mea-sure, including the minister of the Flume church. Stale news.

The news might be old, but Meg had a sudden craving for action. "If you think they're planning some kind of protest, maybe we can de-fuse it. Have you tried phoning Annie this morning...oh, Flume has no cell-phone service. Never mind. I'll see you at my house in fifteen min-utes. We can go in my car."

"Go?"

"To Flume. Get over here. If you participated in Marybeth's little scheme, it's the least you can do. Tell Nina to cover for you." She hung up.

By the time Wendy appeared, only ten minutes late, Meg had donned boots and parka, checked the camera function on her cell phone with the idea of recording details of the protest—faces, slogans, the size of the crowd—and was attempting to put chains on her Accord. It took two tries.

"Hop in." She opened the passenger door.

Wendy wrung her hands. "But I can't..."

"In."

Wendy sat. Her shoes would be a catastrophe if she had to walk in snow, but her coat looked warm enough.

"Buckle up." Meg slammed the door and got in the driver's side. She fastened her own seat belt and put the car in reverse. The engine hummed. Exhaust billowed white on the crisp air. It then occurred to her that she hadn't called Rob to let him know what she planned to do. He hated that.

Foot on the brake, she fumbled her phone from its pocket in her handbag and hit the speed-dial. He had turned his cell off, as he did when he didn't want to be interrupted, so she left a message. She thought he was going to interview Carla and Aidan again.

Time for action. She backed onto the street a little too fast. The chains on the front tires held, but the rear end fishtailed. Wendy squeaked. Meg eased the car into Drive and headed for Highway 14.

The state highway was clear now. It carried east-west traffic to both bridges over the Columbia, so the pavement was gritty and almost bare from heavy commuter use. Meg followed the road five miles west, then turned north on Highway 153, which traced the canyon of the Little Coho, a short swift river favored by salmon and white-water rafters. The road was steep and wound around, sometimes sharply, but it had been sanded, and chains helped. After six or seven miles, it was joined by Alt. 153 from Klalo and headed due north toward Mount Adams.

Wendy was still babbling. The chains made a lot of noise, so Meg concentrated on the road and didn't try to listen. Four years ago, driving on packed snow would have terrified her. Now she was just cautious. There was no traffic for a good ten miles until three vehicles approached, shoppers heading toward town to stock up.

Meg chugged on through winter-bare orchards and vineyards. She caught a glimpse of Mount Adams, her favorite of the three nearby volcanic peaks, before she had to turn onto the last and worst stretch of driving, the paved road to Flume that was not exactly a highway. Beyond lay the invisible presence of Mount Saint Helens.

The road had been built for log trucks in the heyday of the timber industry. Maintenance was spotty. However, the snowplow had made its way through sometime earlier, and a sander had followed it. Snow thrown up by the plow had formed berms on both sides of the road. It was probably too cold for mudslides. She drove with increasing confidence.

Wendy had fallen silent miles back.

Meg cast her a sideways glance. "What's the preacher's name?"

Wendy started. "Brother Josiah."

"Josiah what?"

"Uh, well, his name was Kevin Allday, but when he was born again he took the name of Josiah." Wendy squirmed against the seatbelt. "He's very good-looking."

Handsome is as handsome does, Meg thought darkly. "And you fell under his spell."

"No. I'm not susceptible." Her voice was bleak.

Meg drove on past straggling houses with unplowed driveways. She had come out to Flume twice, once with Annie, but the snow made everything unfamiliar, brightening the dark embrace of the Gifford Pinchot National Forest. There was hardly any downtown to Flume—a post office, a gun shop, a convenience store, a 1930s brick building that had once been a grocery and now housed a thrift shop. She remembered two taverns and three churches, one of them a Catholic mission to which a priest came once a month. About half the Klalos were Catholics, as were most of the Hispanics.

Annie used to park near one of the Protestant churches, which was then vacant. If, as Meg suspected, it was now the Church of the Inerrant Word, she hoped Annie had had the wit to move the bus to another venue. Maybe Annie didn't know about their negative feelings.

"I'm not a dyke. I just don't like men."

Meg didn't comment on Wendy's politically incorrect non sequitur, but her hands twitched, and the car responded by swerving a little. *Front-wheel drive. Follow the turn.* Slowly she eased the car back to the center of the lane.

If Wendy were a lesbian, then her attachment to Marybeth would make sense, except that it was hard to imagine Marybeth in an unconventional relationship, or indeed in any relationship other than master and slave. Or was that the attraction? Meg felt her cheeks go hot. *I am naïve,* she reflected. *Truly naïve.*

"Isn't that...?" Wendy pointed.

They had passed through most of the town, such as it was. Meg glanced right and swerved again. She pulled to the edge of the curbless main street and braked. "What's going on?"

Annie had parked the bookmobile two blocks along the unpaved side street, across from a small plain church—no stained glass windows, no steeple. THE WORD! ALL ARE WELCOME! proclaimed a professionally lettered sign. A clump of people in winter gear trampled the snowy lawn and milled in the unplowed parking lot.

Meg cracked the door, stuck her head out, and heard shouting and whooping. As she watched, a flurry of missiles flew at the bus. "Are they throwing snowballs?"

"Ice soakers." Wendy jumped from the car and grabbed the door as her feet skidded on packed snow.

Meg had grown up in Los Angeles. She knew what a snowball was, a cute fluffy thing children threw at men wearing tall hats, right? "What's an ice soaker?"

"A chunk of ice with a rock in the center."

Thunk, thwap, crack. The cheers doubled and the missiles flew. Meg disentangled herself from the seat belt and climbed out, wondering whether the schools were having a snow day, or were these kids homeschooled? Whatever. Their game had to stop. They were intimidating potential patrons, and Annie must be terrified.

Meg slammed the door and took a long step forward. Her foot slipped, and she fell on her ass. She scrambled to her feet. The shouting intensified, and so did the thuds as ice soakers hit metal and glass.

"Come on! We have to stop this!" She didn't check to see whether Wendy was following. Two anonymous women who appeared to be joining the fun would surely not be attacked.

Meg didn't run. She didn't need a broken hip. She stared at the mob as she plodded forward and tried to think. Her impulse was to tear into the milling protesters, screaming at them to stop. It didn't seem likely that they would. She glanced up and down the street—small, depressed-looking houses on both sides, no signs of life. She quickened her pace, slipped again, and regained her balance. Had she seen a twitching curtain?

She made for the house. It was on her right, the bookmobile side. No one had cleared the walk or driveway. An old car drooped under half a foot of snow. Meg stood on the porch and banged the door. No one answered.

"Please help me," she called and banged again.

Eventually she heard a faint voice say something and the door cracked. "Be quiet, will you? Who are you?"

Meg lowered her voice. "I'm head of the library. They're attacking the bookmobile, and I'm worried about the driver. Can I use your telephone? My cell phone—"

"Cells don't work out here." The door opened. A young woman in a sweatshirt, jeans, and socks cradled a sleeping baby. Meg thought she was Klalo or maybe Hispanic. She looked Meg over, unsmiling. "Come in."

"Thanks."

Without a word the young woman led her into a small cluttered kitchen and indicated a portable telephone on the counter. "Please keep it quiet. I just got her to sleep."

Meg nodded and dialed 911.

It took a while to clarify where she was and what was happening, but Jane Schmidt was finally able to assure Meg that Todd Welch was in the area and would come to her assistance. "Can you stay on the line?"

"No. I need to check on Annie Baldwin. They've already broken one of the windows on the bus."

"If they're throwing things, you'd better not go near it."

"I have to try. I'm going to hang up now, Jane, and please don't phone back here if you can help it. There's a sleeping baby."

When Meg hung up, the woman with the child gave her a wan smile. "Thanks. She's teething. Cried for hours."

"It's hard, isn't it? A sheriff's car is on its way. Thank you, Mrs...."

"I'm Judy Hoover. I like the bookmobile. Annie brings me stuff to read while my old man's working nights. I finished my GED with the books she brought out here. Don't let those racist clowns have their way."

"I won't, Judy. Thanks again." Meg made her way back to the door and slipped out, trying to close it quietly. Racist?

Outside the noise level had not diminished. A *smash, crackle, pop* suggested another broken window. Cheering followed a fusillade of ice balls. Meg pulled her phone from her purse, turned it on, and activated the camera. She wished she'd sprung for video.

She crossed the street, careful of ruts in the packed snow, and walked toward the church half a block away. She could see Wendy talking to a tall man in a hooded parka. Clouds of breath rose between them. Brother Josiah? Meg took a picture of them, heads together, but the man's face wasn't clear.

She turned her attention to the manic snow-ballers. They were mostly young, middle-school and high-school–aged, and all of the ones Meg could see were white. Several chunky women behind them chanted, "Witch bitch, witch bitch, witch bitch," and jigged up and down.

Meg focused on the women and took more pictures. Others were shouting words that didn't register. She wanted faces, twisted with glee or hatred, mouths open to shout. She got shots of a hatless young man as he hefted an ice soaker in one bare red hand, wound up, and let fly. The kid had a great arm. His missile flew straight at the side door of the bookmobile.

Meg peered. The door was open, and she thought she saw a booted foot on the bottom step. The foot didn't move.

"No!" she shrieked, horrified. "Stop it, you maniacs. She's hurt. You've hurt her!" As if they would care. As if they could hear.

Heedless, she stuffed her phone into her purse and ran and skidded to the bus. She was hit several times, once hard enough to sting, even through the padded parka, but she kept going.

"Annie, Annie! It's me, Meg." As she dived through the door, an ice ball hit the side of her head hard enough to stun her. She fell across Annie's legs, and somebody screamed. Herself?

Dazed, Meg crawled up the shallow steps beside the bookmobile driver. She heard a soft sound, half moan, half sob. She kicked at the door until it shut. The shouting outside receded a little, but thumps resounded as ice soakers hit the old bus. Her left hand, braced on the top step, squished liquid—blood. Annie was bleeding.

Meg sat on the step by her wounded friend and stroked Annie's face, which was streaked with tears and drying blood. "Annie, come on, Annie. Wake up, it's okay." But it wasn't. Though her skin was warm, Annie didn't respond.

Another ice soaker hit the latch, and the segmented bus door popped open again. Meg heard the yelp of a siren in the far distance.

When Todd got there, he could call for EMTs from the nearest fire station, wherever that was. She gave Annie's still face another pat, stood on wobbly legs, and retrieved her telephone/camera from her handbag. As she set the purse on top of a bookshelf, a round of ice soakers hit the bus. Meg was scared. Beyond scared, she was furious.

She took a couple of shots of Annie lying there bleeding. The bus was dim. Annie didn't stir. Meg made her way past the low shelves of books to the nearest unbroken window, cleared mist from the glass with her sleeve, and took photographs of the protesters. From this vantage she could see the attackers better than from the edge of the church lawn.

Younger kids were dipping snowballs into a bucket of water to supply ice soakers to the warriors—three larger boys, including the pitcher with the great moves. Behind this trio of activists, a dozen or so girls were making and tossing ordinary snowballs, all the while yelling shrill cries of "Witch bitch." A cadre of older women stood behind them, close to Wendy and the tall man in the parka. The women didn't participate in the one-sided snowball fight, but they were laughing and shouting and pointing.

Wendy tugged at the man's arm, talking earnestly, and he shook his head, brushing at her hand. His hood fell back. Meg got a clear shot of his face. He was handsome.

It was then that she heard low voices and scrabbling sounds from the other side of the bus. The bookmobile was surrounded! What if they started to rock it?

Stiff with fright, she skirted the central bookshelf with its bright ranks of picture books for toddlers. She knelt on the padded bench Annie's husband had installed for her older patrons to sit on while they browsed. The window above the bench had fogged. Meg brushed it clear and peered down.

A big man crouched below her, surrounded by six or eight children of middle-school age. They were busy making snowballs—the regular kind, not ice soakers—and had amassed quite a pile. As she watched, another volley of thuds sounded from the other side. The man looked up, spotted her, and grinned.

He put a finger to his mouth. *Shh, be quiet.* It was Harley Hoover. Dazed, Meg sank back onto the bench. Not the cavalry exactly. What was going on? Where was the sheriff's car?

She went back to Annie and sat on the carpeted floor beside her friend's head. Calmer now, Meg felt for a neck pulse and found it, slow and steady. Water pooled on the steps. The blood on the carpet was tacky.

Annie must have slipped on a wet step and hit her head on something, part of the gear mechanism or even the metal edge of the top step. She had bled heavily, but she was breathing, and the wound on her head was oozing only a little. Meg took more photographs. When she spoke to Annie, the injured woman muttered something and groaned. It was best not to move her, Meg decided. She took off her own parka and covered Annie's torso with it.

Shivering and damp in spots from the wet steps, Meg went back to her viewpoint for another try at photography. She had no idea how many photos the tiny card stored, but she intended to create a slide show for the edification of the library board—and the sheriff's department, if it came to a lawsuit. She wanted a record.

As the thought surfaced, she heard Harley give one of his signature shouts. The higher voices of his troops answered, cheering. She cleared the unbroken window again with her sleeve, raised her telephone/camera, and started shooting the now two-sided Battle of the Bookmobile.

Harley's kids had the advantage of surprise, though the enemy had probably spotted some of them sneaking in behind the bus. As she found out later, the two smallest children remained behind, making ammunition and pitching the snowballs out to the ground behind and in front of the bus. The six largest children, abundantly armed, swarmed around, three at each end of the bus, and began hurling snowballs directly at the big boys who were pitching ice soakers from the church lot.

The church girls shrieked. Two of them continued to throw snowballs, but the rest ran behind the adults. The chanting women stopped their jig. All of this was by way of distraction. While snowballs flew from both directions, Harley charged straight at the three antagonists. He bellowed. The major-league pitcher backed away, stumbled on the water bucket, and fell. When Harley reached them, the other boys sort of flew through the air.

Harley's momentum carried him straight at Brother Josiah. Wendy ran and lost a shoe. The preacher held his hands up, defensive, but Harley dived for his knees, and the man fell on the snowy lawn. Meg clicked away.

At that point she became aware of an ululating siren, flashing lights, the squeal of brakes, and an amplified voice ordering everyone to calm down and stop throwing things. Todd Welch's four-wheel-drive Jeep was followed by an ambulance. Somebody else must have seen Annie fall and called 911.

Todd emerged from the sheriff's vehicle without haste, nor was he fazed when a snowball knocked his hat off. He didn't bother to draw his handgun. He raised the bullhorn again and ordered everyone to calm down and stay where they were while the ambulance crew did its work. A uniformed deputy—Henry Perkins, Meg thought—emerged even more slowly from the passenger side, all six blond feet of him.

Meg didn't stop to parley. Coatless, she jumped down the steps of the bus and ran for the ambulance, slipping and sliding. She wasn't the only one to disobey Todd's orders. About half the church militant took off running. Harley sat by the preacher in the snow and laughed.

Chapter 16

"HE'S BEEN BEATING HER. Take your jacket off, Carla."

"No."

"Take it off. Go on, Carla. You asked me for my help. If you want it, you're going to have to cooperate for once in your life." Edwin Jackman had brought his daughter in at nine on the dot, a man of his word. Rob noted that.

Father and daughter stared at each other. Carla stuck her jaw out, a parody of stubborn resolution. Jackman glared back. He didn't budge.

After a still moment, she shrugged out of her black-striped jacket. She wore a lacy pinkish top, transparent, revealing barely perceptible breasts. To Rob's untutored eye, the blouse looked like some nine-teenth-century undergarment. The sleeves were no more than tiny caps of fabric. Her arms were bare. He saw no tattoos.

Jeff Fong sucked in his breath. Bruises ringed the girl's biceps on both arms. The marks had turned green and slid downward, as bruises will.

"Nasty," Ellen Koop said in a clinical voice.

Rob's stomach knotted. "Nasty but not new."

Linda Ramos said, "When did he do that?"

The interrogation room, which always seemed large for three, steamed with crammed humanity—seven people counting the guard. All of them stared at Carla. Despite or perhaps because of the sexy lace top, she looked about twelve. Her cheeks were flushed, her eyes downcast.

"When, Carla?" Linda, sharper.

Carla's mouth thinned to a line. She shook her head no. Her short hair flopped. She was not going to talk.

Rob looked at Jackman. "Do we have your permission to take photographs?"

"Yes, and I damned well want him charged with assault." Edwin Jackman shook with suppressed fury.

Carla shook her head. No and no and no.

Ellen cleared her throat as if to speak but didn't. Jeff was frowning. Rob caught his eye, and Jeff nodded.

Rob stood. "Mr. Jackman, I'm going to send for a medic and a staff photographer. While I'm doing that, you might reconsider calling your lawyer. I think it's past time. Ellen?"

The prosecutor sighed. "Oh, yes. No doubt about it."

It was nearly eleven before Carla's bruises had been examined and photographed from all angles, and the lawyer, who drove out from Camas, had arrived to take his clients off for consultation.

Ellen left to see a man about a dog—literally. A pit bull had got loose and destroyed a neighbor's cat. The dog's self-righteous owner was howling his way to a serious charge. Before she took off, she advised Rob to wait and charge Carla with arson the next day. Both of them were conscious of the girl's upcoming birthday.

Her father, and Rob assumed, the lawyer would press for immediate arraignment, and Rob couldn't fault their logic. Carla had a blameless record, clean as a whistle. If she were tried as a juvenile who had been bullied into crime by a man with a record of brutality, she might plead guilty to arson and get away with community service, or if she pleaded innocent, be sprung by a sympathetic jury. Otherwise, she would do jail time. Ellen could probably charge her as an adult. Eleven-year-olds had been charged as adults in other states.

They broke for lunch. Linda would interview Aidan again afterwards, or not, as his attorney decided. Rob told her and Jeff about

Aidan's disastrous service record, but both of them thought they should wait for official confirmation from the army before raising the subject with lawyers present. If true, it would give weight to Mary-beth's threat to charge Aidan with statutory rape. At least, he must have feared it would, and his fear was a solid motive for murder. Harley would have to be questioned on that point, too—and others.

Linda was going to concentrate on the arson, and on the possible, indeed probable, vandalism. DNA samples had been taken to compare with the plentiful evidence from Trout Farm. Until results of the tests came in, that investigation would hang fire.

Jeff left for the library, looking as grim as Rob felt. Rob ducked into his office, checked his phone messages, and discovered that Meg had gone off to Flume, unattended, with another suspect in the murder of Marybeth Jackman.

He was gritting his teeth over that, and trying to decide whether to radio Todd or let him deal with Flume unadvised, when Jane Schmidt, the dispatcher, interrupted.

"Uh, if you have a minute, Rob, I can fill you in on that snowball fight in Flume."

Snowball fight? Rob went out to Dispatch so Jane could field incoming calls while she talked. He needed a little comic relief.

~

MEG rode to Klalo in the ambulance with Annie, who was still unconscious. Henry Perkins would drive Wendy back in the Accord. Wendy hadn't found her shoe and was inclined to resent Harley's successful tactics. She said she had tried to persuade Brother Josiah to call off the war. Meg didn't listen.

Todd assured Meg the bookmobile would be driven or towed to town—to the library lot, she insisted. The remarkably cheerful Harley Hoover would ride in with Todd. The children who had helped Harley rout the ice-soaker assailants were his nephews, nieces, and cousins. Mrs. Hoover, the matriarch, had sent them to defend the bookmobile, and she'd sent Harley, Meg supposed, to see that the kids kept out of serious trouble.

All the way in, when she wasn't brooding over Annie, Meg worried about whether she ought to accuse Brother Josiah of assault, or fomenting a riot, or a hate crime. Poor innocent Annie Baldwin was neither a witch nor a bitch—nor a harlot, another delicate Christian epithet flung at her. In context, the words they used were almost certainly hate speech.

Meg was sure Brother Josiah would laugh the whole episode off as a friendly neighborhood snowball fight, despite the fact that patrons had not been able to approach the bookmobile. She assumed Annie's injury was accidental, but that didn't excuse the attempt to scare her to death, or the failure to help her after she fell. And Meg thought of Judy Hoover, who just wanted Annie to bring her a good read. Judy had a right to it. Well, there was more than one way to skin a cat, or so Meg had heard. She hoped her photographs would print.

Between surges of chaotic thought, Meg touched Annie's hand. Annie groaned. When the EMT intervened, Meg retired to her corner. Her own head ached. The medics had told her they didn't think she was concussed. She did have a goose egg. They'd fixed an ice pack for her, and she held it to her head until her hand went numb with cold. She declined aspirin.

Rob was waiting in the hospital's Emergency entrance when the ambulance arrived. So was Bob Baldwin, with more reason. The EMTs removed both of their patients from the ambulance efficiently, Annie on a gurney, Meg in a wheelchair, despite her protests.

Bob ran to Annie with something between a shout and a sob. Meg thought she heard Annie murmur his name, but Rob was at her side saying something and gripping her own hand.

"Get me out of here," Meg roared. "I have work to do!"

"But your head—"

"My head's fine. I got hit with an ice soaker. I only rode in the ambulance to be with Annie."

The silent EMT wheeled Meg's chair through the automatic door without pause, and then the waiting began.

Annie was seen to immediately, to Meg's relief. Because of the snowstorm, Emergency Services were dealing with bumps and bruises (people falling on the ice), heart attacks (people shoveling snow), and cases of whiplash (people driving SUVs). A bored nurse committed triage, and Meg found herself at the end of the line.

As they settled in to wait, Meg seething, Rob said, "What do *you* know about ice soakers, my little desert flower?"

She gave him a terse definition.

"I'm impressed. Tell me what happened."

She gave him a narrative that started terse. By the time she got to the charge of the Stryker brigade, Meg was hard put not to break up laughing, despite her exasperation and her anxiety about Annie. She was proud of Rob. He did not even smile, but his eyes lit with unholy amusement.

"And you have pictures of the, er, action?"

"As many as the memory card holds."

"Let me guess where your Machiavellian imagination is leading you."

"I am going to spin this story like a wind turbine. That bigoted bully will not know what hit him." Her fists pounded the arms of the wheelchair. "Get me out of here!"

Rob leaned down and kissed her on the lips. "Let's see what I can do."

Twenty minutes later, after she'd told a harassed physician's assistant how many fingers he was holding up and signed half a dozen waivers, Meg left, a free woman.

Rob took her home under protest. She wanted to go straight to the library to inspect—and photograph—the bookmobile. He assured her that Todd had already photographed it *in situ*, that the very rocks that had smitten the bus were numbered, and that the tow truck had probably not yet reached the library anyway.

"C'mon. It's past time for lunch."

"I couldn't swallow a morsel."

"Sure you could. Also you could take a shower and change clothes. Your jacket has blood all over it, and your face is smeared with good volcanic dirt."

Meg digested that. "Maybe I ought to go in to the library covered with Annie's blood."

"Oh, hey."

"Maybe I should call Channel Six and give an interview covered with Annie's blood."

"My sweet Megalith, you abandoned the victim role when you insisted on leaving the hospital."

"What did you call me?"

"Sweet." Rob finally cracked up. He chuckled the rest of the way home. Until he saw Beth's car at the curb.

The sheriff of Latouche County was standing in Meg's driveway in conversation with Henry Perkins, who waited by the Accord with the keys in his hand but not the garage door opener.

Rob groaned.

"You forgot to call her."

"For forty-some hours."

Meg scrabbled in her handbag, found the opener, and dropped down from the pickup. She hadn't realized it was Beth she wanted, but it was. She gave Henry a smile and handed him the opener. Beth embraced her, somewhat impeded by the casserole she was carrying, and they all went into the house. Meg cried.

~

BETH was too focused on Meg's grief and on the bizarre snowball fight to ream Rob out over their casserole lunch, and too kind to do it in front of Henry, but she did give Rob a cogent piece of advice. "Call the stepmother."

So he did. Unfortunately Mrs. Jackman wasn't home. He left a message.

Comforted by the thought that he was leaving Meg in good hands, he drove Henry back to the courthouse and found Todd waiting in his office with Harley Hoover.

Rob shook hands with both of them and thanked Harley for his timely intervention in the snowball fight. Harley grinned but didn't say anything. "And please thank the kids, too," Rob added. "I understand it was your grandmother's idea. She must know that town inside out."

Harley's grin widened. "She doesn't miss much."

Todd laughed. "I used to think she knew everything, and I was sure she knew everything I'd done wrong."

Harley sobered. "That Christian bozo, he threatened to sue me."

"Tell him to go right ahead. I have the feeling he may be facing a lawsuit himself. Meg took photos of the whole shooting match—so to speak."

"No kidding. With her cell phone?"

"Yes. She's ready to swear you just stumbled into Brother Allday when you, er, intervened. I left Meg and the sheriff gloating over Meg's computer and printing up the best shots."

"I've got to get me one of those phones. Mine takes text messages and plays FreeCell, but that's about it."

Rob's cell phone was a telephone pure and simple, at least he thought it was. Todd took *his* phone out to show off the latest pictures of his six-month-old daughter. It was all a little too friendly.

Better friendly than hostile. It did not escape Rob's attention that Harley had undergone a major personality adjustment. He was in high spirits, relaxed and cheerful. There was no shouting.

Todd said that one of Harley's nephews would drive his Corolla to Trout Farm later on, a minor problem solved.

Harley had already called Jack Redfern again. "He said you wanted to talk to me about Aidan."

"Jack told me you felt sorry for him."

Harley nodded, eyes lowered. "Yeah. There was this incident in Iraq."

Rob held his breath.

"It involved friends of his and an officer. Don't get me wrong. It was a bad thing. Aidan should have reported it right off, but he was scared. They, the army, booted him out for not reporting, but, Jesus, they were *friends*, guys he trained with. It really tore him apart." Harley was almost shouting but not quite. He stopped, as if he'd heard himself, and bit his lip.

Rob wanted to press him for details of the "incident," though there had to be other ways of getting the information. *I'm a lousy detective,* he thought, *but what if I get what I want and push Harley back into the pit of despair he just climbed out of?*

He met Harley's eyes, which were dark and anxious, sighed, and backed off. "Aidan wanted to stay in the army?"

"Yeah. He's weird. He thought he was going to be career military. Me, I was relieved to get out. I mean, I feel guilty because of my friends. They've still got months to go on that tour in Afghanistan. I got off easy."

Not so easy. Rob's throat felt tight.

Harley shivered. "The thing is, I'm glad to be home. Aidan's not. He can't figure out what to do with himself." He flushed, as if he were embarrassed by what he'd just said. "I mean, I've been a little confused, too, but Jack and Maddie are helping me, and there's a lot I can do, isn't there?"

"I think so."

"Fishing with Jack. He's teaching me the river. And I've got educa- tion benefits. I was thinking maybe law enforcement." He blinked at Rob. "I mean, Todd likes it."

"But that's Todd."

Todd said, "Hey!"

Harley grinned and rubbed the back of his neck. "You think I could do it?"

Rob cleared his throat and hoped he was not giving false encour- agement. "Well, we're not hiring right now because of the economy, but sooner or later somebody will retire or quit. Take classes at the community college, Harley, see if you like it. Maybe there's something else, something you'll like better, who knows? Meanwhile, Todd can keep you up to date about openings in the department. We do have a veterans' preference."

"No lie?" Harley looked pleased.

"We do. Now, about Aidan. He came out to the farm to see you, right?"

Harley's face went blank.

"Before the firebombing incident." *Incident.* That word again.

Harley scowled. "That really stinks. He could have hurt Maddie and Jack. Did hurt Jack. Maybe I felt sorry for Aidan, but if he did that..."

"They were there. Both of them. They were seen. And we have a tire print from the motorcycle."

"Well, it stinks. He should tell that little slut to get lost." His voice rose toward a shout. Again, he seemed to hear himself. After a pause, he added, quieter, "She's poison."

"Do you mean Carla Jackman?" Rob asked, to make sure.

"Yeah, the Jackman woman that was killed, her daughter. You asked me about the biker at the farm. Aidan didn't come out to see me. Carla did. I told her to fuck off. She'd already done enough damage."

"At the farm? She admitted the vandalism?"

"No." Harley frowned. "But I don't see who else it could've been. Her and Aidan moved the furniture out, so they knew where Maddie told Mrs. Jackman to leave the key. After they'd turned the rental van in, they must've come back and wrecked the place."

"Aidan and Carla."

"Yeah, but you can bet it wasn't Aidan's idea. Aidan doesn't have ideas. He's just a dumb shit who does what he's told."

That fit with what Beth had said to Rob.

Harley went on, "Carla thinks she owns the farm, or her mom does."

"Did," Rob corrected. His mind was racing. "Okay, thanks, Harley. That's very helpful. Let's go through it again. Try to remember what she said to you at the farm."

Harley tried. Rob would have to ask Meg and Madeline if either of them had seen anything that might indicate the biker was Carla. Harley was sure of that but vague on details. Unfortunately, Carla's hair was short and would have been hidden under the helmet, and Meg and Madeline had been upstairs looking down.

Harley did give a lively and detailed account of the snowball fight. When he left with Todd, he was in good humor. Rob was sweating.

He went for a walk—a short one, given the state of the sidewalks—and thought about Harley. He also thought about Carla. When he got back, he called Phyllis Jackman, the stepmother. This time she answered. With her permission, Rob recorded the conversation.

She sounded nervous at first but soon calmed down. She tried but could not remember whether Carla had taken a solo ride on the motorcycle the day Harley said she had visited the farm. Mrs. Jackman might never have known. Carla didn't live with her father.

On the other hand, Mrs. Jackman verified that Carla could and did drive the motorcycle, because Edwin had been horrified at the idea of his child riding it around the countryside. Carla had apparently been doing so since she got her driver's license, driver's ed being one high school class she did well in.

Phyllis Jackman continued to hold to her view of Aidan Pascoe as the source of all evil where Carla was concerned, except for the girl's underlying hostility to her father's second family, which Mrs. Jackman laid at Marybeth's door.

"But Carla didn't act out until she met that boy."

"Hmmm," Rob said.

"I never could figure out her relationship with her mother. Sometimes it seemed as if she hated Marybeth. Other times it was almost as if Carla felt protective."

"Protective?"

"As if people were persecuting her mother, and it was up to Carla to save her. Nonsense, of course. The whole business about the Trout farmstead had Carla up and down for months. I was relieved when Marybeth decided to drop the lawsuit, and so was Edwin, but it made Carla mad. She said the farm belonged to the Trout family, not to those Indians, and she accused her mother of wimping out. Marybeth was... formidable. Carla always claimed to be defying her, but I'm not sure she did, face to face. Maybe it was just talk. Fern Trout left Marybeth a lot of money, you know."

Rob waited. He wanted more.

She cleared her throat. "Look, there was never any sign that Marybeth so much as laid a hand on that girl. If she had, Edwin would have sued for custody, but not without proof. Marybeth had a tongue like a laser, and a trick of putting you in the wrong if you disagreed with her. It would have been hard to live with, *was* hard to live with, Ed said."

"So any abuse would have been verbal?"

"That's right." Phyllis sounded relieved that he understood her. She changed the subject. "Is it true you're going to charge Carla with arson?" Her voice trembled.

"Yes. Tomorrow."

"Oh God, her birthday."

"That's right. She'll be eighteen."

"Ed was going to take her out to buy a used car. But of course now she has her mother's Camry." A long silence. "I wish I could help."

Help whom? Carla? Her husband? The Latouche County Sheriff's Department? That was unlikely.

"Tell me about Thanksgiving," Rob said in what he hoped was a cozy, chatty voice.

"I don't know what you mean. We had turkey."

Everybody had turkey. "Did Carla come to you the night before? How did she get to Camas?"

"Oh, er, well, Ed drove over to pick her up on Thanksgiving morning. He left here around ten, and they were late getting back, so I had to set everything up for dinner and keep the boys under control by myself. I remember that. The gravy boiled over and the potatoes scorched. They—Ed and Carla—were almost an hour late. I was mad, though I tried to keep it pleasant. Carla didn't talk to me, but she never does. Just sat there like a lump. She was all dressed up. I remember that because it was so unusual. No tattoos in sight. She'd washed the dye out of her hair, you know, the streaks of purple."

"Did she seem upset?"

"No. Just sort of bored. Ed bustled around. We ate and watched some TV, and then the police...you called and Ed had to tell her her mother was dead. That was awful. She, Carla, laughed and cried, and screamed at me to leave her alone when I tried to comfort her. It scared the boys. I finally gave her a tranquilizer and put her to bed. What else could I do? I took one myself when I finally got the boys down for the night. Ed didn't sleep."

Rob turned that over in his mind. "You mean he got up and went out?"

"Oh, no. He was in bed all night. I woke up a couple of times, and there he was, staring at the ceiling. I asked if he was okay, and he told me to go back to sleep, said he was just thinking."

Rob let the conversation dwindle to a natural close. Phyllis Jackman had given him a lot to think about.

Chapter 17

ANNIE'S FALL HAD fractured her skull. It was a hairline crack, not a depressed fracture, but it was a serious injury, and she had not yet regained full consciousness.

It was a lesson for Meg to hear Beth pry that information out of the hospital. The sheriff also reached Bob Baldwin on his cell phone while Annie was undergoing an MRI. Beth listened to him, all sympathy, and handed him over to Meg, who was able to assure him that no, Annie would not be fired, and yes, she had enough sick leave for a long convalescence, and if she didn't have enough, everyone at the library would contribute sick days to her. He should just concentrate on comforting his wife. Meg would take care of everything else, unless Bob wanted to help her buy a new bookmobile.

That was a last-minute improvisation but not a bad idea. Who would know better what was needed? Bob was too distracted to do more than express vague interest, so she left him to think about it.

Meg thought about it. Maybe what was needed was a stretch Humvee. No, not a good idea. The library might be besieged, but she was not about to succumb to siege mentality. The free and open circulation of ideas was protected by the First Amendment to the Constitution. Wasn't it?

She wished she could control her errant thoughts. The real issue

was Annie and Annie's suffering family. Then there was her own suffering family. Her mind slid sideways to her mother and her daughter
and her brother Duncan.

Beth listened to her incoherent ramblings as another pot of coffee brewed. Meg's kitchen windows steamed over. It was snowing
again.

Beth poured refills. "Annie is Jake Sorenson's sister. Has anyone
called him?"

"Oh my God." Meg speed-dialed Rob, who had indeed called his
deputy. Jake was at the hospital with Bob—and Pepper. There was
still no word of Jake's sick daughter. Meg's stomach roiled. Families.
Family problems. When she assured Rob she was all right and had
disconnected, she turned back to Beth.

"I'm not handling this very well."

"You have a lot on your mind."

"Tell me what to do!"

"I won't do any such thing. I'm glad you took a day off. Use it to
think. I can call Ellen Koop for an opinion on the legal situation, if you
like. Your photos will help a lot. It looks as if Bob should sue Brother Whatsisname for reckless endangerment—he saw Annie fall and
didn't help her. But it's up to Bob to press charges."

"Annie's my employee."

"And you did your best to protect her."

Meg snorted.

"Hold a rally."

"What?"

"Your real job is to protect bookmobile service. In order to do that,
you need public support. You have contacts. Send out a press release.
Hold a rally in the parking lot tomorrow evening after people get off
work."

"But what should I say?" It didn't escape Meg's attention that Beth
was telling her what to do. It was a great relief.

"Do not attack religion. Brother Boom has a right to bad-mouth
the bookmobile and bully his congregation. He can dance with rattle-
snakes if he wants to. He does not have a right to prevent other people, people who disagree with him, from using the full services of the

public library. What other people read is not his business, and his supporters should not be encouraged to express their brotherly love by slandering and assaulting Annie Baldwin."

"A rally? I'm not a damned cheerleader."

Beth laughed. "Sis-boom-bah." She left for the courthouse, taking a sheaf of freshly printed photographs and the empty casserole dish with her.

Meg called Pat Kohler. They talked a long time. Then Meg sat down to create a press release.

~

ROB had a good and blessedly short talk with Madeline Thomas, who was ready to mount a parade for Harley through the streets of Flume. Or better yet, Klalo.

Rob discouraged that, but gently. He thought Harley wouldn't like it.

"He's modest to a fault," Maddie admitted with real regret. "What's Meg going to do about the bookmobile?"

"Replace it, I guess." It was still drivable, but that was about all, according to the tow-truck people. They'd taped plastic on the broken windows so the books wouldn't be ruined.

"What's she going to do about the *attack* on the bookmobile?"

"Why don't you call her, Maddie? She's at home." He felt guilty for making the suggestion, but Meg had a lot of respect for the chief's political savvy. So did Rob. Between them, Beth and Maddie ought to be able to keep Meg's counterattack within the bounds of reason. Nothing would have compelled him to say that out loud.

By the time Madeline hung up, Rob had made up his mind what to do while he waited for test results, and word from the army, and all the other things that were pending. He set up a review session with the investigations team for four-thirty. Then he called Jeff, who was at the library puzzling over Marybeth's coded journals and was beginning to doubt their relevance. Rob suggested another look at the Jackman deck, the scene of the real crime, the murder.

As far as he knew, the deck was taped off. He called Edwin Jackman at Marybeth's house to warn him they were bringing the county's evidence team. Rob didn't think he could justify the cost of calling the state lab in again, especially since he wanted to know what was not at the scene, not what was.

Jackman didn't object. He sounded despondent. Carla had locked herself in her room with her CD player, earbuds in, and wasn't responding to paternal queries. He thought she might be texting friends.

At least she wasn't texting Pascoe, Rob reflected. Aidan's cell phone had been confiscated. Rob spared a moment to consider the cloud of digital buzz that was probably floating over Klalo like a thunderhead. OMG.

~

JEFF was waiting in front of the house when Rob got there, but the evidence van hadn't yet arrived. Edwin Jackman welcomed them at the door and shook hands with both men. He'd apparently met Jeff earlier. "Are you going to want to question Carla again?"

"Not now," Rob said. "I'd like to talk to you, though, while the evidence team works on the deck."

"Me?" Jackman blinked at him. "Will I need a lawyer?"

"I don't know, Mr. Jackman. If you mean, do I consider you a murder suspect, the answer is no."

"Well then, I'll make a pot of coffee, and we can talk." He bustled off to the kitchen. Carla was nowhere to be seen. In her room, Rob supposed.

The van arrived and the techs trouped through the house looking unenthusiastic. A sharp wind blew from the southwest. The deck lay under an inch or two of wet snow with a bare patch near the French door that led from the dining room—heat leak. The light pole with its infrared lamp pointed a finger at the sky.

Rob gave instructions, and the techs cheered up.

"No prints, huh?" Jeff rubbed his arms.

"The state crew took prints. I want two things. Samples of the moisture on the surface of the deck and another look for fibers on the bench and railing where she must have gone over. We'll have to give up on scuff-marks. Let's hope the state lab got something last Thursday."

"If you say so."

"Humor me," Rob said. "I'm double-checking."

Jeff rolled his eyes and went out to supervise.

A Formica-topped bar lay between the dining room and the kitchen as in most houses of that era. Jackman set two mugs on the bar and poured coffee, though the pot had not finished burbling. He spilled a little, and wiped the drops with a sponge. "God forbid I should sully Marybeth's kitchen. She was a neat-freak."

Rob sat on a bar stool. "Was that why you split up?"

Jackman gave a bark of laughter. "I never knew why we split up. 'Irreconcilable differences' is the term, I believe. She filed for divorce without warning when Carla was seven. Never explained, wouldn't agree to counseling. When I recovered from the shock, I was enormously relieved. I've felt guilty ever since."

"Guilty?"

"I leapt at the chance to escape. And I left Carla to her mother's tender care." He made a face. "One of Marybeth's gripes was that I lost my job when the mill closed. It took me a year to find another one, and that wasn't quick enough to suit her. The loss of status really rankled—imagine an unemployed bum for a husband—and I think she just didn't like to have me underfoot. I figure I got off easy. When I did get a job, she demanded more child support, so I upped the ante without protest. Cheap at the price. My second marriage has been a revelation. Phyllis is a human being."

Rob wondered what he was supposed to say to that. Congratulations? He took a sip of bitter coffee.

"Look," Jackman said as man to man, "Carla isn't a bad kid. She has a lot of suppressed anger—at her mother and at me—and she's acting out. This arson thing..."

"What about it?"

He sat and slurped coffee. "I blame the scum boyfriend."

"Her acting out was a little hard on Chief Thomas and her husband." Rob wondered how Jackman would explain the vandalism. "I'd like you to take me over the events of Thanksgiving Day."

Jackman looked pained. "Again?"

"The morning specifically. You drove over to pick Carla up. When did you get here?"

"Around eleven, a little before."

"Did you see Marybeth?" He would have preferred to say Ms. Jack-man but that might have been confusing.

"No, but then I never did when I picked Carla up. Marybeth always avoided me. She was in her office."

"You know that for a fact?"

"I didn't see her," Jackman said patiently. "Carla said she was in her office, and that was where she usually went when she wanted to hide out."

"Okay. Did you go into the house?"

"Never. I hadn't been through the front door since we divorced. I still feel uncomfortable here. I sat in the car with the heater on and listened to NPR."

"Was Carla ready to go?"

"No. She'd just stepped out of the shower. Her hair was still wet, and she was wrapped up in a bath towel when she answered the door. I wasn't surprised. She's a late sleeper. She told me she'd be right out."

"And was she?"

"I waited in the car. It seemed like a long time, but you know how hard it is to wait when you're impatient. It was fifteen or twenty minutes, tops. Carla got dressed. I liked her outfit. She'd washed the purple streaks out of her hair. I appreciated that. Phyllis doesn't like the Goth look or whatever it's called. Carla came out with her duffel, called good-bye to her mother, and closed the door. She hopped in the car, and we took off. We were late for dinner when we got to Camas, and Phyllis was miffed, but Carla was on her best behavior."

"You were in the car with her for, what, an hour?"

"It was less than an hour. I drove a bit over the limit."

"Was Carla in a good mood?"

"She was fine. We talked about where she could go to college. I wanted to send her away from her mother. Her test scores are pretty high even if her grades aren't, so I thought one of the private colleges would be willing to admit her. I did my undergraduate work at Wil-lamette. Reed is out of the question with Carla's grades, but there's George Fox and Pacific U. and Pacific Lutheran up in Tacoma. I'm willing to foot the bill—or part of it."

"Expensive," Rob said politely. He was footing the bill for Willow to attend Lewis and Clark, not a modest sum. "There's the University of Portland—good school of education." Peggy Petrakis *née* McCormick, the sheriff's younger daughter, had attended the University of Portland.

"Teaching wouldn't appeal to Carla, and besides it's a Catholic school, isn't it?"

"I don't think there's a religious test to get in."

"I am hoping Carla will take an interest in science."

Fat chance, Rob thought.

"She said she'd enroll in classes at the community college and live at home. I told her I thought she should get away from home, so we talked about an apartment in Vancouver or Gresham." There were good community colleges in both towns. "Or she could try for Washington State." WSU had a campus in Vancouver.

"You had a father–daughter conversation, and Carla was in a good mood," Rob prompted.

Jackman drank coffee. "She was quiet, maybe still sleepy. She said she'd been out the night before with Pascoe. I guess I did most of the talking."

"You didn't invite Pascoe to join you for Thanksgiving?"

"I suggested it earlier when I called to arrange to pick her up, but Carla just laughed. He went to his mother in Hood River, I guess."

"You didn't see him here that morning?" Rob persisted.

"No." Jackman looked bewildered.

"Thank you, sir. That's helpful." Rob got up and headed out to the porch.

"When will all this be over?"

It was not going to be over for a long time. "We'll release the deck today. I appreciate your cooperation."

Rob braced himself against the cold. His chilly crew had almost finished. "Find anything?"

Jeff snorted, puffing white steam like an anemic dragon. "Nope. Took your samples." He walked over to the area where earlier forensic ventures had found a partially erased scuff-mark and a thread of fabric, possibly from Marybeth's dress. "I just don't get it. The killer grabbed her and shook her, then threw her over the railing. How come there's no sign of the struggle?"

"Weather," Rob murmured. He thought he knew why.

Jeff shook his head. "Even so."

"Did they look for shoe prints on the bench?"

"Like the victim was standing on it?" Jeff's eyebrows shot up.

"There was no sign on the body that she'd been shoved against the bench, only those narrow bruises on her calves." Rob joined Jeff at the place on the deck from which Marybeth had to have fallen. "If she stood on the bench, it would have been easy to topple her over."

Bench and railing enclosed three edges of the deck with the house the fourth side. Rob could see how the setup had triggered Meg's acrophobia. The railing, which formed a backrest for the bench, was less than waist-high to a woman of Marybeth's stature standing on the deck. If she'd been up on the bench, the railing would have hit her calves.

He caught movement to his left and turned to look. Someone was watching them from the deck of the place next door, not the Waltz house, the one on the other side. The house had been empty over the holiday.

Rob pointed. "Let's go." He and Jeff raced out, banging the front door behind them. They rang the bell, and a sixtyish woman in slacks and a ski sweater answered. "Yes? Please be quiet, my husband's taking a nap."

Rob took out his wallet and showed his badge. "I'm Robert Neill."

"You're the undersheriff, aren't you? Nice to meet you. Are you investigating the murder? Laura Waltz called when she saw our car drive in. She told me about it."

"Were you here at all the morning of Thanksgiving?"

"Yes, but we didn't see anything. The murder probably happened after we left for our daughter's ski cabin. We went skiing at Hoodoo with the kids, and my husband wrenched his knee, poor fellow. We were stuck there in that tiny house for days with our delightful grandchildren."

Rob smiled.

She twinkled at him. "He doesn't trust me to drive him, never mind that I've been driving forty years and never had a moving violation, which is more than he can say, the old blowhard. Last night the baby had colic. This morning Greg gave up and let me chauffeur him home. Come in. I'm Cynthia Pratt."

Rob and Jeff ducked into the hallway, and Rob introduced Jeff.

She shook his hand. "You're Keiko's husband, right? I volunteer at the hospital now I'm retired. How's your son? Does he still play soccer?"

Jeff beamed, and he gave her a rundown on his twelve-year-old's autumn triumphs. Jeff's wife was a physician's assistant.

Mrs. Pratt led them into a comfortable living room with a view that angled southeast. From the room they could not see the Jackman deck, which sat back perhaps five yards and faced south. Mrs. Pratt offered coffee, and Jeff accepted.

Rob said, "Would you mind if I went out onto your deck for a look? We caught a glimpse of you from the deck over there a few minutes ago, and I want to understand the line of sight."

Mrs. Pratt poured coffee and brought it to Jeff. "Feel free. Laura said the little Goth girl, what's her name, Carla?"

"Yes."

"Laura said Carla is living there with her boyfriend. How is she doing? I always felt sorry for the poor little thing. Marybeth was so... exacting. We built a fence so she wouldn't have to look at our dande-lions."

"A difficult neighbor?"

"You might say so. When I figured out what she was like, I avoid-ed her. So did Laura. Marybeth kept the yard in perfect condition, and there was never any noise nuisance or anything like that, so we couldn't really complain, but it would've been nice to have a more con-genial neighbor. We didn't see much of her or Carla."

Rob moved to the door that led out to the deck. "You said Mary-beth was exacting. Can you tell me what you mean by that? It helps to have a clear idea of the victim's personality."

"Well, she was obsessively tidy, for one thing." Mrs. Pratt laughed. "She had that poor child out scrubbing the deck the morning of the murder—with suds and hot water, for heaven's sake. Typical. She'd just hosed it down a few days before for that little reception. That would've been clean enough for most people, but not Marybeth. I expect she was worse than that inside the house. She must have been hard to live with."

Rob turned back and drew a long breath. "The morning of the murder? What time?"

"About nine-thirty or ten. We left early, a little after ten. Laura said Marybeth had invited a librarian friend for dinner, but that Carla was spending the holiday with her father in Camas. Imagine making the child go out into the cold to wash the deck. I waved to Carla, but I don't think she saw me. She had her head down scrubbing."

"You're sure it was Carla, and not her mother?"

Mrs. Pratt laughed again. "Oh, yes—purple hair, you know. It was Carla."

"Thank you." Rob's throat felt dry.

He slid out the door, stood on the Pratts' deck, and looked back at the other house. A blocky conifer, probably spruce, obscured the view of the basalt cliff and the scree at its base where Marybeth Jackman had met her death, but the deck was mostly visible. The techs had disappeared. Rob lurched back to the door into the house.

Jeff abandoned his coffee cup and stood when he saw Rob's face. "She did it?"

"I think so," Rob croaked. "Come on."

Cynthia Pratt stared from one man to the other.

"I'm sorry, Mrs. Pratt. You'll have to excuse us." Rob headed out, Jeff at his heels. "I'll explain later."

Jackman was watching the techs drive off when Rob and Jeff returned. His parting smile faded.

"I want to speak to Carla." Rob didn't quite shout.

Jackman shrugged. "Good luck. She's been ignoring me since we got home." He led the way down a hall toward the bedrooms and rapped hard at a pristine undecorated door. No response. He rattled the knob. The door was locked. "You see?" He stepped aside.

Rob bent to look at the door handle. It had an ordinary indoor lock. He took out his pocket knife and used the blade. When he pressed and jiggled, the lock eventually gave way and the door opened. The room was empty. It was also spotless. A stuffed bear stared at him from the bed.

He checked the window, but there was no sign that Carla had left by that means. She must have twisted the button to set the door lock behind her and slipped out of the room into the hall sometime when her father was elsewhere, in the bathroom or the kitchen. A door at the end of the hall led outside.

Rob turned to Jackman, who was staring around, spluttering incoherent sounds of distress. "When did you see her?"

"Lunch. Late breakfast really. I made waffles for her. And I could hear her shuffling around in her room after that. I talked to her through the door, and she told me to go away."

"When?"

"Where is she?"

"Mr. Jackman, *when* did she talk to you?"

"About half an hour before you called."

Rob checked his watch. It was almost four. Carla had an hour-and-a-half head start at least, probably two hours. "Where's your car?"

"In the garage?"

"Let's check."

"I would have heard the garage door roll up if she'd taken the car."

Jeff had already gone back to the inside door to the garage, which led off the entry hall. "Car's still there."

Rob caught up with him and peered over his shoulder. The garage, impeccably clean with shining tools that hung from white walls, contained only Jackman's winter-grubby Taurus. Pascoe's motorcycle was in the Latouche County car pound and Marybeth's Camry in Hood River. Rob turned to Jackman. "Other vehicles?"

"No, well, Carla's mountain bike. Oh, it's gone."

She could have wheeled it out the garage's small side door. "All right. She can't go far on that, not with the side streets unplowed. Who's her best friend?"

"Aidan Pascoe."

"Besides Pascoe," Rob snapped.

"I don't know, I really don't know."

"She was in your custody on a serious charge. If you helped your daughter escape, you're looking at jail time."

"But I didn't...I wouldn't...God, I just wanted to help her," Jackman wailed.

Rob whipped out his cell phone and called Dispatch. He told Jane to put out an APB for Carla Fern Jackman, age seventeen, who was wanted for murder.

Chapter 18

WHEN SHE WAS satisfied with her press release and the photographs she had chosen to attach to it, Meg sent it off to all her media contacts, including the weekly papers, and *The Oregonian*, *The Columbian*, the country-and-western station across the river that broadcast local news, CNN, and the Portland TV channels. That left her with nothing much to do but mourn, so she went online to catch up on the library forums and chat groups she'd been neglecting. She was halfway through a listserv digest that dealt with freedom-of-information issues when her brain caught up with her mouse. Of course.

She amended the press release, removed the photos, and sent the message to every library website whose members might be interested, with a link to the Latouche Regional Library site. Then she put together a slide show with explanatory comments for the library board. No, not just for them. For all patrons of the library.

When she was satisfied with the show, she put it on the website and sent out an e-mail to a select list of other people she thought might also find it interesting. It was surprising how little she had to say besides "Look."

While she didn't think it was true that any old picture was worth a thousand words, there was no doubt in her mind that her photos were eloquent. Once she had adjusted the contrast, the best ones showed

Annie lying unconscious on the steps of the bookmobile, but Meg kept those back. For the purposes of the slide show, she called up a bland portrait from the website personnel page and saved the victim shots for the sheriff's department.

While it didn't seem right to expose Annie's suffering to public view, her injury *was* part of the story. Meg was torn. It was past time to talk to Bob Baldwin.

She prepared prints of selected photographs, including the vivid ones of Annie bleeding and unconscious. When she got to the hospital, she found Bob pacing in the otherwise empty waiting room near Intensive Care while nurses tended to his wife's needs. Jake and Pepper had gone home.

"Is she conscious?"

"Sort of." Bob looked miserable. "Sleeping. They say she'll be all right, but she's so still and pale. Not like Annie."

"I feel awful. I should have taken better care of her, but I didn't hear about the protest until it was almost too late."

"I don't understand why anybody'd want to hurt Annie."

Neither did Meg. "They intended to hurt the bookmobile, and they did. Do you want to see my photographs of what happened?"

"You took pictures?"

"Yes. It wasn't safe for me to move Annie with a head injury involved, and I knew the police and the ambulance were on the way, so I decided to record what was going on." She sat on a stiff couch and patted the seat beside her.

Bob sat and shuffled through the color prints, silent until he came to the first shot of Annie lying there bleeding. He let out a strangled shout and jumped to his feet. The folder slid to the floor, and photographs slewed out onto the carpet. "I'll kill them, I'll kill the fuckers."

"Hey, Bob! Bob, calm down. Listen, the sheriff's department has copies. They know who was involved. Let the police take care of it." Meg was gabbling. She reached out to touch his hand, but he jerked away from her.

"What's his name, the preacher? Christ, some preacher, standing there with that grin on his face. They hit her, they hit my Annie." His fists opened and closed.

"Listen to me, Bob. They didn't hit her. Snow from the ice soakers melted on the steps, and she slipped when she stood up to see what was going on. That has to be what happened. It was an accident."

"Did they stop? Did they try to help her?"

"No." And they went on calling her names, even after she fell.

"Okay in here?" A nurse's aide stuck his head in the door.

"Fine," Meg said. The aide disappeared.

They stared at each other, Bob red in the face and panting, Meg scared. She was glad she hadn't included the shots of Annie in her website show. She wanted to conjure a rally, not a lynch mob.

Meg talked. She mentioned civil lawsuits. She repeated what Beth had suggested. She tut-tutted and soothed and uttered platitudes, and it must have worked because Bob calmed down enough to resume his seat.

Meg picked up the photographs and stuffed the folder into her purse with a better understanding of the term inflammatory. "I'm sorry I upset you, Bob. I just wanted you to know there's a record of what happened. We're going to hold a bookmobile rally tomorrow." Probably the last thing he was interested in. Meg told him what she planned to do. She wasn't sure he was even listening.

"I'm going to make her quit driving that thing," he said in an exhausted voice.

"Oh, my dear, no. You can't. Annie does a wonderful job, and she loves doing it. She *is* the bookmobile. We just have to see to it that it's safe for her."

"How are you going to do that?"

"I'm not sure yet, but when I am I'll let you know. Give Annie my best, and tell her not to worry."

"Yeah."

She left him sitting there, staring at the carpet. She went straight to the library and the somewhat awkward embrace of Pat Kohler. As children's librarians go, Pat was not cuddly, though she was wearing a bright green holiday sweater and her reindeer pin. Meg showed her the photos and told her Bob's reaction.

Pat scowled. "It all goes back to Marybeth."

"I suppose so, though the Church of the Inerrant Word was fertile ground. I wonder how many other vicious projects she set in motion?"

Pat looked uncomfortable.

"Tell me."

"She was trying to get you fired."

"Well, I know that. Anything recent?"

"Just her alliance with the 'unco' guid and the rigidly righteous.'" It was a rare children's librarian who could quote Robert Burns on cue. "Some of whom are on the library board."

"Ah, fornication," Meg murmured.

Pat blushed.

"What would *you* do?"

"Get married."

"Allow myself to be bullied into it?"

"Rob doesn't bully you."

"No."

"He wants to marry you?"

"Yes."

"Why punish him because Marybeth was a scumbag?"

Meg heaved a sigh. Why indeed? "Let's go look at the bookmobile. Is it snowing again?"

"Not at the moment."

As they made their way out into the cold, Meg noticed library employees and some of the patrons watching them. Maybe she should wear a scarlet *F*.

The tow truck had parked the bookmobile with its nose pointing south toward the river. The door was visible from the street, not the library. The driver's side of the bus was unmarked, of course, so the contrast with the other side was striking when Meg came around the back for a look. Two windows had been broken out and three cracked into starbursts. Dents dimpled the surface, and one panel of the door hung drunkenly. So did the side-view mirror.

Someone had left a bunch of chrysanthemums on the snow near the steps and a hand-lettered sign that said GET WELL SOON, ANNIE. As Meg and Pat watched, a girl of about ten darted up with another bouquet. A woman watched her from the sidewalk. She saw the two librarians and smiled.

Meg walked over to her. "I'm Margaret McLean. I'm head of the library."

The woman said her own name and jerked her head at her daughter. "She's home-schooled. Annie brought her great books every week."

"You live out of town?"

"Yes. Out by Two Falls. We drove in as soon as we heard about it on the radio."

"We're opening a branch library near Two Falls."

"Um, oh, that's nice. But we like the bookmobile." The woman hesitated. "A big library's confusing. The bookmobile is just the right size. I can tell what's there and, like, guide Emily in her choices. And Annie is always so friendly. How is she?"

Meg told the woman what she knew and described the upcoming rally. "We'd be glad if you came."

"Oh, I don't know. A crowd. Lots of strangers."

"People who care about Annie and the bookmobile."

"I...yes. I'll try to come. Emily!"

The girl came back to her mother, disconsolate. "I can't get my book."

"Which one was it?" Pat asked.

"*Artemis Fowl.*"

"Let me see if I can find it." Pat made for the door.

Meg opened her mouth to say wait, then shut it. The heck with it. The girl wanted her book.

Two minutes later, Emily and her mother left with their choice of reading material and big smiles. Pat and Meg looked at each other.

"Let's close it," Meg said, "and cancel Annie's rounds. I want people to know what it will be like without the bookmobile."

Pat thought that over and nodded. "Okay. That door is not just open, it's damaged."

"Not surprising." Meg described the last ice-soaker barrage, which had been aimed at the door.

Pat listened, but her mind was on the rally. "We'll need a banner."

"And a big portrait of Annie." A shrine. Not a bad idea.

"I'll remove the books before they're soaked. Leave it to me and my aides."

So Meg did. She went home and cooked, but every time she thought about Annie she boiled with fury.

~

JEFF drove the department car back to the courthouse while Rob toyed with the radio and tried to think things through. He'd already made several calls.

"We need the names of Carla's girlfriends," Jeff ventured after a few silent minutes.

"I know where she is."

"Where!" Jeff had stopped at the light at the south end of Oak Street. The light changed, but Jeff just sat.

"Aidan's apartment. He has that studio over the pizza place on Spruce, doesn't he? She must have a key."

"You're sure?"

"Of course not. I'm not sure of anything, but where else would she go on a bicycle? She doesn't have a lot of friends."

A horn honked. Jeff jerked the car into motion.

"Drive," Rob snapped. "I need to talk to Aidan and get his keys." The keys were in the evidence room, but Rob might need Aidan's permission to use them. So far there had been no reason to search his apartment.

"He's not talking." The car moved slowly.

"He will."

"Shouldn't we...?"

"Put the SWAT team in place?" They didn't have a SWAT team, not being the LAPD. "I asked Hug to station a car on the street." Wade Hug was the town's chief of police.

"She'll see it."

"Probably."

"She'll slip out the back way."

"The back way is a fire escape on the alley. Hug's car can watch both the front and the side entrances." *Somewhat impeded by the people going in and out of the pizza joint. Christ, that will have to be evacuated, the whole block will have to be.* Rob visualized the area, but didn't recall other gathering places. *Insurance agency, dry cleaner, hobby shop—is that open late for kids buying games?* He glanced at his watch. Four forty-two. Most of the businesses closed at five.

"So you think she'll lie low?"

"I hope so." He also hoped Carla wouldn't think too much. They had a suicide watch on Aidan.

He needed to call Beth. Phone, not radio.

She was in her office working on the county budget. "No overtime," she said. "Don't ask."

In some ways working with Beth was like working with her late husband. *"Plus ça change,"* Rob said with what he knew was an atrocious accent. "We've got a situation."

"Tell me."

He gave her a crisp summary as Jeff pulled into the annex parking lot. Rob got out of the car with due attention to the rutted snow underfoot. Jeff jumped out and fell down. "Hurt yourself?"

Jeff shook himself off with dignity.

"Jeff fell," Rob said. "So what do you think, Beth?"

"Appeal to Aidan's better nature."

"He's in love with the girl?"

"Sounds like it to me."

"I hope to hell there's no weapon in that apartment."

"Of course there's a weapon. Steak knife. Scissors."

"A gun," Rob interrupted before she could suggest rat poison.

"Ask Aidan. One thing." She hesitated. "Go carefully, Rob. If she killed her mother—"

"If!"

"If," she said firmly. "Even if she didn't, Carla's frightened, and she sounds like a volatile personality. But you do have other viable suspects. The two librarians sound like unpleasant people. Me, I favor Aidan. Motive, means, opportunity."

"No sign he was there on Thanksgiving. Mr. Jackman didn't see him that morning."

Rob heard Beth shrug. "I agree that you have to bring Carla in. Evacuate everybody, and close the street. I don't want anyone hurt, but you ought to go in armed." She knew he would go in himself, and she knew his preference for unarmed negotiation. "In fact, that's an order."

Rob grunted. He would be armed because that was department policy. He didn't have to like it.

He made his way to the sidewalk, which had been shoveled and sprinkled with grit. The county did not use salt when it could be avoided. "Should I call the father?" *Jesus, of course I should.* Carla was technically still a minor. "I don't want him rushing over there and screwing things up."

"Why not get everything in place, and then call him?"

"Okay. Thanks."

"For nothing. Be careful, Robert. I'm not ready to be a real sheriff yet."

That was an ongoing joke between them. Rob laughed a perfunctory laugh and hung up. Beth had been a real sheriff from the moment she took office. He'd never had any doubt about that.

Since he'd called a meeting of the investigations team for four-thirty, life was almost simple. Everybody was already at the courthouse annex. He assigned Jeff the task of evacuating the area around the apartment, with Henry and a couple of other uniforms to assist, since the murder was Jeff's case. Linda was going off-duty at six, so he left her to respond to calls about the APB and shuffle paper.

Jake had come, though he was on nights. He looked to be at the end of his tether. His daughter was still at OHSU undergoing tests, but at least his ex-wife's sister had agreed to take care of Pepper. Jake had been to the hospital and said that Annie was sleeping normally now, a good sign.

Rob said, "Will you bring Jackman over when we're ready to talk to Carla?"

Jake nodded and the lines around his mouth eased a little. Glad to be doing something, Rob surmised.

He let Todd, who was in fine form, tell them about the events in Flume, which he did with an inborn talent for narrative that reminded Rob of his Aunt Maddie.

Jeff dashed off to begin the evacuation. Rob wanted it done as undramatically as possible. He thought Jeff relished the challenge. He probably also resented not being the one who would try to talk Carla out of the apartment, but Rob had never yet placed one of his team in that kind of situation. They didn't happen often. In fact, it was more than four years since the last time.

Rob knew the buck stopped with him. That being the case, he was going to do the talking himself. He—and Edwin Jackman. But that was assuming a lot. Doubt nibbled. Maybe he was wasting time. Maybe Carla wasn't even there.

He called Aidan's youthful lawyer, Mark Larsen, who aspired to Ellen's prosecutor role but understood the plight of defendants without funds and did a good job for them. With a little more experience, Mark might even do a great job.

Half an hour later, Rob, Mark, and Aidan sat in the interrogation room together, and Aidan was talking. He wanted to protect Carla and kept insisting she couldn't have killed her mother, but he thought she could well be in his apartment. She had a key of her own. Though Rob was aware of every tick of the institutional clock on the wall, he kept quiet and listened.

Aidan and Carla had been playing house for more than a year, he gathered, and enjoying it. Aidan waxed almost lyrical. She cooked for him. He wasn't used to that. He'd grown up in his father's house on fast food and dry cereal. She'd fixed the apartment up and made him keep it clean. He liked that, too. He liked everything about Carla. They'd been happy. They were going to run off to Elko, the nearest town of any size in Nevada, and get married just as soon as she turned eighteen. Her mother couldn't stop them. He'd find a job and so would Carla. Nobody could stop them.

Rob felt almost paralyzed with sadness, since he was going to do the stopping. He let Aidan talk a while longer. Then he said, "Does she have a gun?"

Aidan choked on his dying fantasy.

"A gun," Rob prodded. "If you want me to bring her out of there in one piece, you should tell me the truth."

"Er, well, yes. We found it when we cleared out the farmhouse. It was in the old lady's bedside table. Carla wanted it, and I didn't see why not. It wasn't much use."

"What do you mean?"

"Well, it was just one of those ladies' guns, a .22 with a fancy grip, probably an antique. Carla thought it was cute. We tried it out at the old quarry."

"You stole it."

Sullen resentment hardened Aidan's jaw. "Her mother didn't know about it. She was downstairs packing up the china. And now the gun belongs to Carla anyway."

"It's a revolver?"

"Yeah. Six shots."

"Do *you* have a gun?"

"No." Unhesitating, unequivocal.

Rob thought of Beth. "Other weapons?" *Boomerang? Atlatl? Mace?*

Aidan stared at him, blank.

Rob shoved a piece of paper and a pencil at him. "Draw me a floor plan of your apartment." There was a second flat in the building, but Rob thought it had a separate entrance.

With some coaxing, Aidan complied.

Rob stood up. "All right. Thank you, Aidan, counselor."

"I want to know..."

"I'll let you know what happens. You don't have a landline telephone in there, do you, Aidan?"

"No."

Rob left with Aidan's keys from the evidence locker. The situation was not good, but it could have been worse. He donned a Kevlar vest upstairs in his office and checked his ugly olive-drab Glock 17. It was weeks since he'd taken it to the shooting range.

Jake was waiting for him, talking to Sergeant Howell.

"You can go fetch Jackman. Bring him to the barrier." The street was blocked off between Fifth and Seventh. "Make sure he's dressed for cold weather. I'm not taking him in until I can be fairly sure of his safety."

Jake nodded and went off. Rob went back to his office and stood for a while, eyes closed, thinking things through.

"You ready to go?" Todd Welch leaned on the door frame.

Rob turned. "Haven't you gone home yet?"

"I thought I'd stick around."

"Beth says no overtime."

"Consider it a donation."

Rob had to smile. "Okay, let's go."

Todd drove a 4x4, one of the newer department cars. About two minutes later, he parked it behind the city car at the improvised street barricade, and Rob got out.

Jeff trotted up, grinning. "We found her bike around the corner. At least it matches the description. She locked it to a parking meter."

"So she's in there."

"After we cleared out the pizza place, Henry thought he heard a toilet flush upstairs. There's no lights on up there though, no curtains twitching or anything."

So Carla was thinking, but not very clearly. "Did you try her cell phone?"

"Uh, no. I don't have the number with me." He looked chagrined.

Rob whipped out his phone and called. Carla's cell was not in service. "She has to know it has a GPS."

"The father?"

"Jake went for him."

Chief Hug came up at that point, which called for interdepartmental diplomacy, since Rob's crew was on his territory. The chief was sixty-five, paunchy, crabby, and a good man. He wouldn't interfere— Carla was wanted on a county warrant. Rob thanked him and filled him in.

Jake drove up—without his lights flashing, Rob was glad to see. The sidewalks were empty of pedestrian traffic, though a small crowd of the curious had gathered behind the cop cars at each end of the barricaded street. It was snowing again. Flakes drifted lazily in the light from the street lamps. Time to do something.

Chapter 19

"SHOULD I CALL out to her?"

"Quiet." Rob gestured to Jackman to get behind him on the landing.

They were standing at the door to Aidan's apartment with half a dozen armed officers below on the street and a sniper on the snowy roof opposite the pizza place staring at the dark window. They had orders not to act unless Rob told them to, but people got jumpy in this kind of situation. Rob was jumpy. He touched the Glock. *No.* The aroma of mozzarella and oregano floated on the air.

"Carla!" Rob projected his voice but tried to keep the tone pleasant. "It's Robert Neill. I have Aidan's key. He gave it to me. He wants you to talk to us. It's time to clear things up."

He heard a tiny high-pitched giggle. Not good. He thought she was across the room. Not at the door anyway.

"Your father would like to talk to you, too."

A definite giggle. Maybe she was high or drunk. Or just scared.

"He's right here. Carla!"

"Go away!"

"I can't do that." He slid the key into the lock and turned it gently. A click indicated the lock had opened. He gave the door a nudge.

"I'll shoot you if you come in."

So she had the handgun. "Shortsighted of you."

He nudged the door again. It opened far enough to tell him the chain was not engaged. That was strange. He thought of the bike, just around the corner, and the flushed toilet. She was not thinking clearly, not at all.

"Shortsighted! You're a funny man."

"Not very. I want to talk to you about your mother's death."

"I'll kill you, kill you both!" she screeched. "I know you're there, Dad. Don't think I can't do it. Don't think I won't."

Rob clucked his tongue, nudging the door again while she screamed invective. Though the room was dark, he saw her sitting on a futon that was in couch mode—straight across from the door, staring at it. "Put the gun down, Carla."

"Why should I? You've got a gun yourself, don't deny it. Why should I put mine down?"

"Because it can't do any good, and it can harm you."

"I don't care. I want to die. Come on, cop. Blow me away, and I'll return the favor. I killed my mother. There, I admitted it. I'm guilty, right?"

"If you say so, though you have a habit of creating drama when it's not called for. Like your mother."

"I am *not* like my mother!" she screamed.

Wrong approach. "Not much," he agreed, "though she did know how to make a scene. Is that what happened?"

"Why can't you leave me alone?" He thought she was crying.

He slipped into the dark room, eyes on the revolver. In the light from the window, it looked larger than it was because Carla was small—and because she was waving it around. Light glinted from the barrel.

She wiped her face with her sleeve.

He almost jumped her then, but Carla could move fast. She gripped the gun in both hands and trained it on his stomach. Rob held her eyes and tried not to blink.

"What now?" he said softly.

Jackman chose that moment to enter the room and flip the light switch. The gun jerked, and a shot rang out. Carla shrieked.

"Wild shot," Rob shouted, blinking hard. "Don't shoot." He visual-

ized the sniper across the street. Carla went on screaming. When he
didn't hear the tramp of feet on the stairs, Rob's muscles eased a little.
His phone was on, and he knew Jeff was listening.

When he could see, he took a step toward the window, glancing at
Jackman, who had fallen into a surprisingly elegant armchair. Aidan
had said she'd fixed the place up. "Did she hit you?"

"N-no." He didn't sound certain.

Carla was still shrieking and waving the gun. Rob wondered why
she didn't stand up.

Her voice trailed off in a silence that rang. Now that he could see
her clearly, he decided her face was even paler than usual under the
tear blotches. Her jeans were stained dark at the knees.

"Are you all right?"

"I fell off the fucking bicycle."

"Then we need to get you medical attention."

"I told you, I want to die." She sounded hoarse and exhausted.

"Well, I can't oblige you."

"Oh, you are so-o-o cool." Sarcasm dripped.

"No, I'm not. I'm sweating like a pig, and I don't trust my bowels, if
that gives you satisfaction, but I'm not going to blow you away. I want
to talk to you."

"So you can gloat?"

"I don't do that either."

"I want to die."

"You said that. Why? You say you killed your mother. I believe you.
And afterwards you scrubbed away the evidence of the scuffle. That
was smart, though somebody might have seen you." Did see you.

"The neighbors?" She gave a snort. "They never see beyond their
noses. I bet they don't even see the mountain." She meant Mount Hood.
"I had plenty of time. I scrubbed the deck. I vacuumed the carpet. I
threw my clothes and the cleaning rags into the washer for a ten-
minute rinse and tossed them in the dryer. Then I shoved the fucking
Thanksgiving dinner into the oven and set the timer. I figured Wendy
would find her, and by that time I'd be safe in Camas. And it worked,
didn't it?"

"You had us running in circles," Rob murmured, watching her. She was in pain. "Why did you have to kill her, Carla? You had *her* running in circles."

"I thought I did." She sounded disconsolate.

He forced a chuckle. "Threatening to get a tongue stud. Describing biker weddings at Stonehenge in graphic detail. Don't tell me you couldn't twist that woman like a pretzel."

She stared at him. "How do you know about that?"

"I listened to what people said about you. I thought you were smart. Killing your mother a few days before your eighteenth birthday wasn't smart, though, so I figure she must have done something awful that morning, something that made you lose it."

"Well, I did lose it. I killed her. So why don't you just shoot me and get it over with? I can't shoot myself. I tried."

"Carla," Jackman moaned.

"A lot you care." Her contempt slashed like a whip.

Jackman put his head in his hands.

Rob said slowly, "The only thing I can think of is that she must have threatened Aidan."

Tears slid down her face. "Shoot me. Please. I read about the penalty for murder in this state. Lethal injection." Her voice shook with horror.

"If you read about it, you must know that it's very seldom used. You're not a serial killer, and you didn't commit aggravated murder."

She snorted again. "Aggravated murder!"

"It's a stupid term, sure enough. Your mother's death doesn't fall into that category. I was thinking myself that it was manslaughter. Maybe even justifiable homicide or self-defense, depending on the circumstances. You can see why I need to talk to you."

"It wasn't self-defense."

"Carla!" Jackman's voice rang sharp.

"Mr. Jackman," Rob said, "shut *up*."

"Don't talk to my father like that!" The gun barrel waved.

Rob drew a breath. "I apologize."

Jackman didn't say anything. Carla sniffed.

"You were saying it wasn't self-defense. What was it?"

"Vengeance."

"Come on, Carla. You were defending Aidan, weren't you? She

threatened to charge him with rape, and you were afraid we'd believe he molested you."

"You can't know that," Carla whispered.

"Both the sheriff and the county prosecutor agree that Aidan's background in Iraq might have given weight to the charge. You were right to take your mother's threat seriously."

"He couldn't have borne it. It was so unfair." Her voice rose in a wail on the last word.

"Well, I don't know. Technically, since you're under eighteen—"

"Even consensual sex would be considered rape," she interrupted, sounding like a book. "Since he's so much older than I am."

"Right." Four years seemed like a lot at seventeen.

"I'm a virgin."

Jackman raised his head and stared at her. So did Rob.

Her mouth twisted. "I told my mother that, but she wouldn't listen. She never listened."

When neither man said anything, she gave a harsh laugh. "Do I have to spell it out? We didn't fuck. Aidan is impotent. I read up on that, too. It's a result of post-traumatic stress. God knows we tried."

"Then you're just—" Friends, Rob was going to say. He felt dizzy.

She interrupted him, mouth trembling. "He can't get it up."

"So you could have defended him in a court of law, but you didn't want to humiliate him."

"A court of law? I sure as God didn't want to tell that to some judge. I didn't even want to tell it to my mother." Her eyes brimmed tears. "*Especially* not to my mother. When she explained to me what she was going to do to Aidan the Monday after Thanksgiving, I did tell her. And you know what? She was glad! She didn't care about me. Oh no. What she cared about was being able to watch Aidan suffer."

"My dear," Jackman said.

She turned toward him, the gun waving wildly. "She grabbed me by both arms and shook me. Got that, Dad? It wasn't Aidan who assaulted me, it was my mother. And she was smiling, smiling and spitting, the way she does on sibilant sounds. So I killed her."

"How?" Rob didn't like the way she was looking at her father. Edwin Jackman had shrunk back in the chair.

Carla turned to focus on Rob. "You thought Aidan did it, didn't you? It was me. I chased her through the house and out onto the deck. When she scrambled up onto the bench to get away from me, I climbed up and grabbed *her* by the arms. I shook her and spat in her face. Then I threw her over the cliff. There. Are you happy?"

"No. But I'm convinced." Rob spoke quietly. He felt like an over-wound spring.

Carla looked at the gun, her finger white on the trigger. She raised the barrel.

"No!" Rob lunged for the revolver, so she shot him.

The gun flew in an arc of light, and Carla screamed. Rob couldn't breathe, though he wanted to answer Jeff Fong. Jeff was shouting something—a question. Rob opened his mouth, but he could not breathe.

~

MEG had a lot of food to cook. She'd stopped at the supermarket on the way home from the library and found a stewing hen, so she tossed the chicken into her big kettle, along with an onion, celery, tarragon, a bit of salt, and a pot of water. While it came to a slow boil, she made pastry and stowed it in the fridge to chill. The cookie supply was run-ning low, too.

Because she was tired of her incredibly healthy oatmeal-raisin cookies, she made pecan sandies. That involved a lot of hearty pulsing with the Cuisinart, a satisfying noise. The sandies were refrigerator cookies, so she chunked that dough in the cooler, too, and chopped vegetables. She had blanched the veg and made a large bowl of *béchamel* by the time she ran out of steam.

She took a break then to check her phone and e-mail. Her brother Duncan had called her cell and left a message about the funeral that repeated the time. He sounded distracted and clearly thought Meg was still in California. She visualized Lucy and suppressed the im-pulse to return his call. Seven journalists had left messages. She wasn't ready to deal with them one-on-one, so she took down the names and numbers and zapped the messages.

She hadn't emptied her e-mail box since she got home from Cali-fornia. She exterminated the obvious spam and looked at what was left. Journalists again and three library board members. She composed a boilerplate message for the board members describing the upcoming rally, and when she'd sent that one off, she decided to do the same thing for the journalists. It took awhile. She felt tired but not sleepy, so she indulged in another hot shower and went back downstairs to flense the boiled chicken.

Deboning the cooked bird was satisfying in her mood of repressed rage. By the time she tossed the skeleton, she had a heap of meat sufficient for three meals for two people, and that pleased her. Time to stock the freezer. The chicken broth had cooled, but it was cloudy.

Ordinarily Meg didn't give a damn about cloudy broth, but today she took pains to clarify it, a process that involved cheesecloth and egg whites and a lot of fussing. She was left with four quarts of perfect broth. The addition of a cup of decent riesling even made it taste good. She reserved a bit and froze the rest, properly labeled, along with packets of the meat, also labeled. She was in an exacting mood, doing everything absolutely right. She wondered why. Her mother would have wondered why.

The thought of her mother made Meg want to weep, but she'd cried too much. There was no point in self-indulgence. She made up four perfect individual chicken pot pies with fancy-dancy pastry decorations, brushed them with egg white, and set them in the fridge, because they didn't take long to bake, and it was too early to expect Rob home for dinner. She double-checked her watch. There was time to bake the cookies.

They came out so beautifully she wanted to prohibit anyone from eating them—each an impeccable golden oval with a perfectly centered pecan half. She took out her cell phone and photographed them. Proving what?

I am so fucking domestic, she told herself, *I'd take a fucking blue ribbon at the fucking state fair.* Her mind drifted sideways. Maybe she should serve her cookies to the library board. *Naw. Let them eat Fig Newtons. There was that F-sound again. Fornication. I am not punishing Rob,* she told herself. *I'm not. No.*

Bleary-eyed, she checked her watch. Rob would be home soon. She turned the oven to the right temperature and set the pot pies on a baking sheet so her oven wouldn't end up resembling the landscape of Iceland. When the oven was hot, she placed the sheet in it and set the timer.

She went back to her computer, carrying the timer with her, because if she stayed in the kitchen to make salad she might chop off all her fingers.

The library website had a message board and a blogspot. Each of the professional librarians was assigned blog duty on a rotating basis, with the rest of the staff welcome to blog when the spirit moved them. Sometimes the discussions got heated. More often they got esoteric, with somebody riding a hobbyhorse around the pasture while the readers dropped off. Marybeth had done that. Her style didn't command much interest. Meg didn't censor the blogs as long as the authors kept their musings clean, spell-checked, and focused on books—or at least on library issues.

She went onto the website with nothing in mind but to kill time. Almost at once she caught on that the subject of the day was the bookmobile. By the time she'd scrolled through the last of the messages, she was so stunned she almost didn't hear the oven timer.

She went to the kitchen in a daze. The pies were perfection itself, but she no longer cared. She set them on a rack to cool and put the cookies away in her cookie jar. *The heck with salad.* She went back to her computer. While she was in the kitchen, five more messages had come in, and they were not from local people. Her Internet venture was bearing fruit. On impulse she looked at the Foundation site.

One of her least-favorite jobs as head of the system was to seek donations. The Foundation site, her invention, offered browsers an opportunity to contribute to the library, either to the general operating fund, to the book fund specifically, or for other earmarked causes such as technical databases, audio books, and computer games. There was one *F*-word she had not so far had to deal with. She had not been Fired, probably because she surprised herself and the board by being good at garnering large gifts. Marybeth had hated that.

The Klalo donation of the Trout farmhouse was unusually generous but not unprecedented. Even so, large contributions were rare and blotted up a lot of Meg's time and energy. What seemed to be happening now was a rash of small donations from all over the country, some from Canada and the U.K.; almost all of them were earmarked for the bookmobile, and the strangest thing was that she hadn't solicited them. She would have to delegate a volunteer to create thank-you messages and send out tax receipts.

She was about to call Pat and gloat when Lucy rang up. Lucy was sad, Meg a strange mixture of sad, angry, and delighted. They talked for a long while. By the time they hung up, Lucy sounded like her usual ebullient self, and Meg felt steadier, which was a good thing. She had just turned back to the computer when Madeline Thomas called.

"Meg, are you all right? I couldn't get through."

"Do you mean, am I over my mother's death, or am I in tune with my inner librarian? No and yes."

Madeline didn't laugh. "I tried to call Rob. The dispatcher said he'd been shot."

Meg's heart seized. She stared at the phone as if it were a rattlesnake.

Madeline apologized for being the one to break the news and assured Meg she'd get off the line if Meg would promise to let her know what had happened.

Meg promised. She didn't even try to call 911—the line would be jammed. Her hand shook so hard she had to hit the speed-dial twice for Beth's number. Beth's line was busy, but she returned Meg's call almost at once. Must have call waiting.

"You heard?"

Meg's throat was dry. She tried to paraphrase what Maddie had told her and failed.

Beth said, "Yes, he was shot, but he was wearing body armor, thank God. It was a glancing blow, a heavy impact at close range. It knocked the wind out of him, broke a couple of ribs, and gave him a big bruise. He'll be okay, but you need to get over there and take him home."

"I'm on my way!" Meg shouted.

Beth said something else, but Meg didn't stop to listen. She was halfway to her garage before she noticed it was snowing, and she didn't have a coat on.

Chapter 20

"YOU HIS WIFE?"

Meg hesitated a nanosecond and lied. She was lying a lot lately. "Yes."

"He's in X-ray. You can wait for him out here or in the cubicle." The oblivious receptionist gave her a room number and pressed the button to open the security door that led from the lobby to Emergency.

As Meg ran down the short corridor to the central holding area, two aides pushing an unconscious patient on a gurney sprinted past her. The PA crackled.

Patients who came by ambulance entered through automatic doors on the far side of the big square room. Patients' cubicles ringed the rampart of counters at the center that protected nurses, aides and orderlies, doctors, and computer jockeys from the melée. EMTs in uniform lounged in and out.

Meg squinted. She couldn't remember how the room numbers went. Then she spotted Todd in conference with Linda and one of the other deputies, and she knew where to go. Linda gave her a hug. Todd patted her on the shoulder. The uniformed deputy disappeared.

"Rob's all right?"

They exchanged looks.

"Well, he's not bleeding or anything," Todd said. "I mean not externally. They were afraid of clots."

"Three broken ribs," Linda said. "Right now they're checking to be sure the breastbone is not broken, too." She touched her sternum. "And they're worried about, you know, internal bleeding. She was near him."

"She?"

Another exchange of glances. Todd said, "Carla Jackman shot him with a dinky .22. She didn't use hollow-point ammo. Good thing."

Meg gaped.

"Hey, sit down." Todd pulled a chair for her.

Meg sat. "You'd better start from the beginning. I do not know anything, not a thing."

By the second telling, she began to sort it out. At least she sorted what the two deputies knew. She was dumbfounded. Carla? She would have bet on Aidan as the killer, with Wendy a close second. "So where's Jeff?"

Todd said, "He took Carla to the jail as soon as the doctor said it was okay." The county jail lay between the courthouse and the annex. "To book her. She was hysterical."

Linda sniffed. She probably didn't like that term any better than Meg did, but there was that high-pitched giggle. Meg shivered.

"Well, she *was* hysterical," he repeated. "Crying and laughing and stuff. Jeff said she was raising the gun to shoot herself, so Rob tried to knock it out of her hand. He did knock it across the room, but she fired first. Maybe it was a hair-trigger. She'd already fired a wild shot." After a moment, he added, "Her father went to the jail with her, called the lawyer."

"Bad seed," Meg muttered, but her heart wasn't in it. *I should have shit-canned Marybeth the year I came. I knew what she was. My cowardice almost got Rob killed.*

She closed her eyes and felt easy tears roll down her cheeks. Todd made a strangled noise, and Linda murmured soothing words in two languages.

"Ready to go?"

Meg jumped to her feet.

Rob scowled at her, eyebrows twitching. "Here I thought you'd be glad to see me vertical." He was leaning on a walker. A cross-looking orderly stood behind him with a wheelchair.

"Oh, Rob, oh, I am glad."

"No you don't, I'm not huggable, believe me." He fended her off and smiled a little. "And whatever you do, don't make me laugh. Let's go home."

And they did. He was standing because bending hurt. The cross orderly inserted him into the car. Fastening the seat belt would have hurt too, so Rob didn't. Meg drove carefully.

It was almost ten. She offered to fix a bed on the hideaway couch in the living room, but Rob said he could make it upstairs as long as he didn't have to twist. Though he was doped to the eyeballs and both of them were exhausted, neither was sleepy. Meg warmed the pot pies. They ate, Rob a lot. They went to bed.

And lay there radiating warmth. At last Meg began to talk. When she remembered the unforeseen donations to the bookmobile, she even cheered up, though she stopped short of making him laugh. After that, he talked a little about Carla, but not about the shooting. He was sorry for her.

Meg felt less tender. After all, Carla had pulled the trigger. Meg didn't say so, but she was thinking, *Like mother, like daughter.*

The phrase struck her like a bolt. Tomorrow her mother would be buried, and she would not be there. She asked Rob whether he thought she was a bad daughter. He didn't answer, because he had fallen asleep. When she stopped feeling neglected, Meg fell asleep, too, but she didn't sleep well.

~

JUDGE Rosen presided over the preliminary hearing. Ellen Koop intended to charge Carla with second-degree homicide and first-degree arson, both as an adult. Rob thought it was a good decision in the legal sense, though he couldn't rid himself of the feeling that Carla was a victim. She looked tiny and fragile in her orange jumpsuit. She wasn't required to plead at that point, and she didn't cry. Bail would be argued the next day. Carla did not look back when the guard took her off.

To his surprise, Edwin Jackman came up with his hand extended as the crowd of journalists and onlookers dispersed. Rob shook it.

Jackman said, "I'm grateful, Neill. You saved Carla's life. I'd like you to meet my wife. Phyllis, this is the undersheriff."

A pleasantly plump woman in her early forties smiled at Rob. "I'd recognize your voice."

"And I yours." He thought about thanking both of them for being helpful, but that might be misconstrued, so he said he hoped Carla's lawyer would give satisfaction, excused himself, and went over to Linda and Jeff. Beth was talking to Madeline, Jack, and Harley. Meg hadn't come, though half the library staff had. Tessa wept, and Wendy patted her shoulder. The children's librarian looked on with a stony face.

Rob was worried about Meg. The hearing had started half an hour after her mother's funeral was scheduled to begin. She'd elected to stay home for a private time, a time to mourn. He hoped she wasn't waiting for her brothers to call her.

He listened with half his attention as his crew prepared to dig into the DNA test results from Trout Farm. He thought his people would do a good job, but he didn't want to be there. He spotted Henry near the courtroom exit and asked the young deputy to drive him home.

Henry not only agreed, he brought the car right to the courthouse steps. Rob managed to get in without falling and breaking the rest of his ribs. He felt sore as a boil.

"Uh, you heard about Jake?"

"What?"

"He called in this morning. His little girl, she has some kind of anemia. It's serious, but it's not cancer, not leukemia. Jake went to Portland." Henry beamed as if he'd known Jake for his whole life instead of six months.

"That's great news." It was. Rob felt a layer of anxiety peel off. *Like a very large onion, a Walla Walla Sweet.* He had to smile at his own dopiness. Henry shot him a puzzled look, so Rob composed his face and asked a semi-intelligent question. Henry told him the details of Jake's call.

Meg was not in the kitchen. Rob stood listening until he heard the soft *clack-clack* of her keyboard. In her office. He filled a water glass and took another pain pill. Then he went to find her. To his relief, though she looked sad, her agitation had eased.

"Hello, love," she said. "I'm glad I stayed here. I was able to think about her for the first time since I flew home. Without distraction, I mean. All four of my brothers called and left messages, but I kept both phones off the hook the whole time." She drew a breath. "I don't *have* to answer."

"I'm glad, Meg." Another layer of the onion peeled away. He told her his absurd simile and provoked a smile, and then he told her about Jake's good news, and that delighted her. They drifted back to the kitchen for coffee and Meg's sculptural cookies.

"Do you think Carla will plead guilty in the long run?"

Rob picked the pecan half off his cookie and munched it. "I don't know. For the sake of the county budget, I suppose I hope so."

"She confessed."

"A confession can always be retracted. She was under a lot of stress."

"Ha!" Meg said darkly, but she didn't pursue whatever vengeful thought had intruded. "Are you coming to my rally?"

Rob groaned.

She looked stricken. "I'd forgotten the ribs."

"I hadn't. I just took a pill that's going to knock me out for a couple of hours." He checked his watch. "When is the love feast scheduled?"

"Love feast!"

"A Methodist term, I believe. My command of religious jargon is shaky at best."

"Well, I hope the Methodists turn out. We need all the help we can get." She looked pensive. "Seven-thirty, Rob. And I'll have to go over to the library earlier."

"Uh-huh." His mind had turned down a rocky path. "I'd better call Wade Hug. It's his jurisdiction."

"What do you mean?"

"Better safe than sorry." He took out his cell. "Maybe the Inerrant Word guerrillas will mount a counter-demonstration."

Meg's turn to groan.

But hyper-efficient Pat Kohler had already warned Chief Hug, and all was well. Meg retired to her office again, and Rob creaked upstairs to lie down.

~

THE first van came across from Oregon, from The Dalles. Meg wasn't expecting it, but she knew some of the librarians, so she went over and shook hands. They asked about Annie, looking serious and sympathetic, but she could see they were in high spirits, and they had signs, big signs.

The biggest said THE DALLES PUBLIC LIBRARY, but the others were more inventive. One showed a glass full of milk. It said GOT BOOKS? Another said READING MAKETH A FULL MAN, over a picture of a paunchy gent with a big grin. There were more, smaller and hand-lettered, along the lines of SUPPORT YOUR BOOKMOBILE. The Dalles contingent joined the small crowd of townspeople who had showed up early. Some of them were holding unlit candles, and others had their own signs. One just said READ!

Pat had set things up, even to the cop car lurking discreetly on the street outside the parking lot. She must have gone to Kinko's with a picture of Annie, because the "shrine" photo was poster-sized and blurry. It sat on the steps of the bus where Annie had fallen, and the banner above it said ANNIE BALDWIN'S BOOKMOBILE. A low platform stretched left along the dinged side of the vehicle. Pat had removed the plastic film from the windows so everyone could see they were broken, even in the dim pink glow of the parking lot lights.

The heap of votive flowers had grown. Some of them were artificial, some bouquets from the supermarket with green tissue paper around them, some single blossoms, roses and daisies, all with cards or small hand-lettered signs. GET WELL SOON, ANNIE and ANNIE BALDWIN, OUR HERO. Two poinsettias and a tiny Christmas tree sat in pots. And there were stuffed animals, too, probably from little kids. As Meg watched, several people sidled up with more flowers.

Library board members, most of them elderly, had called to approve the rally and wish Meg well, but none were coming. In a way, that was a relief. Beth and the mayor of Klalo lurked at the edge of the crowd.

Pat pinned a tiny microphone to Meg's collar and gave her a big smile. "Go for it, Meg."

Meg didn't know what *it* was, but she was willing to try. "Does this thing work?" she started to say, and her voice rang out. She turned the mike off quickly. "Lord. Is there a program?"

Pat handed her a sheet of paper with bulleted headings just as Madeline Thomas's pickup pulled into the lot and disgorged Maddie and a large elderly lady in full ceremonial regalia. If Maddie looked good in elkskin robe and headband, this woman looked magnificent. It had to be Opal Hoover, Harley's grandmother. Meg didn't see Harley.

She stuffed the program into her pocket and hurried over to the two women. She was able to trot without falling because somebody had plowed the lot and spread grit. Half a dozen young Klalos, probably high school students, beat her to it, and swarmed the two women, laughing and chattering. Mrs. Hoover administered pats and hugs. Madeline gave Meg a big wink.

"I'll get some chairs." Pat dashed toward the main entrance. The library, supervised by Nina and a couple of stern-looking volunteers, was still open for access to the rest rooms in the basement.

By the time Meg had greeted Mrs. Hoover and escorted her and Maddie through the crowd, there were folding chairs in place on the platform Pat had conjured from the high school. An anxious-looking man in a dark suit sat in one of the chairs. As Meg, Maddie, and Mrs. Hoover approached, he rose and introduced himself as Peter Nussbaum. He was the head minister at Trinity Lutheran Church, there for the invocation. Much hand-shaking.

Somebody was singing "Kumbaya," not a surprising choice if not particularly apt. Voices joined, hesitating at first. As Meg watched another van draw up, the words percolated through to her. "Someone's reading, Lord, Kumbaya."

She smiled. Lucy's father had played that song over and over with the three chords he knew. At the time Meg had thought it was wonderful. It was one of the few songs anybody could sing, cats and dogs even, and it still sounded good.

The second van parked neatly. Eight people bubbled from it, one waving a sign that said MULTNOMAH COUNTY LIBRARY. Oregon was coming through for Annie in a big way. Meg felt a prickle of excitement alongside her surprise. She didn't know these librarians, but she smiled and shook hands, and they joined the expectant crowd, which was now singing "We Shall Not Be Moved." Meg thought of Harley and wondered if they were going to sing "Ain't Gonna Study War No More," too. They probably didn't know that one.

More people, people of all ages and both sexes, came in from the community—and from outside Klalo, too, in spite of the weather. Most of them had candles. A few cars drove past. One driver honked. The candle flames flickered, illuminating faces like medieval saints. Fortunately, the wind had died down, though it was still snowing a little. She thought she saw a video camera.

Then another van came. It was from Vancouver with a big sign that said FORT VANCOUVER REGIONAL LIBRARY and gave the names of all the branches served by that big system. She did know the Vancouver people. She went to them and told them how touched she was that they'd driven all the way up on Highway 14 for the rally. They said it was all right, they'd used the freeway on the Oregon side. Meg laughed.

And then it was time, past time, so she went up to the platform and took the program from her parka pocket. She looked out at the sea of faces and the flickering candles, and her throat closed. Meg spoke in public a lot and didn't suffer from stage fright, but this was different.

"Hello," she mumbled.

"Turn on the mike," Pat hissed.

"Oh, sorry." Meg touched the switch and cleared her throat with a resounding boom. "Your honor, Sheriff McCormick, ladies and gentlemen. Welcome to our patrons from Klalo, a lot of whom I recognize, and especially to those of you who drove in from the country, from places Annie Baldwin serves every week."

There was a ragged cheer at the mention of Annie's name.

"In case you don't know, people, we have visitors from other libraries here tonight, and we welcome them too, because the attack on our bookmobile is not just a local problem. I want to tell you what happened in Flume yesterday, but first I hope you'll welcome Pastor Peter Nussbaum of Trinity Lutheran Church who has volunteered to give us some words of inspiration. Pastor Nussbaum."

The anxious man stepped forward. "Thank you, Ms. McLean." He was not a large man but he had a large voice.

Meg realized she'd forgotten to introduce herself. Sheepish, she stepped aside and left the limelight to the minister.

"I'll try to inspire you," he said. "Let me tell you about Annie."

A ripple of applause spread through the crowd.

"Annie Sorenson Baldwin." He intoned the name as if it were an in-vocation in itself. "Annie was baptised in our church, confirmed there, married there. Both of her children were baptised at Trinity. I've been in Klalo twenty years myself, so I know Annie. She is the key woman on our telephone tree. She takes food to the sick and the bereaved. She comforts the dying. She teaches in our Sunday School every week. She is a good woman, and I need not tell you the worth of a good woman. It is above rubies. Some day, God willing, Annie will be an elder of the church."

The crowd stirred, restless.

Pastor Nussbaum fixed them with a glittering eye. "Yesterday morning, people claiming to be Christians attacked Annie. They threw stones at her. They called her names. They did not know her, or they wouldn't have done that. I'd sooner chop off my right hand than harm Annie Sorenson Baldwin."

He drew a breath and roared, "And I tell them, as Christian to Christian, 'Let he who is without sin cast the first stone.'"

A burst of applause. *Oh thank you,* Meg thought. *I wish I'd said that.*

When the clapping faded, he went on, quieter, "I just came from the hospital. Annie's skull is fractured, and she's still sleeping, but her doctors are optimistic. I am going to pause now. I hope you will send Annie your good thoughts. I am going to pray for her." He bowed his head.

So did Meg. Opal Hoover nodded as if in approval.

When Pastor Nussbaum raised his head, indicating that the time for prayer was over, Meg stepped back to center stage.

"I'm Meg McLean, the head librarian. Before I launch into my re-port, I'd like to introduce people to you. The sheriff is here and our mayor." Beth gave a little wave. Ripple of applause.

"On the platform with me is Mrs. Opal Hoover. Mrs. Hoover is an elder of the Forest Band of the Klalo Nation. She lives in Flume, and when she heard of the demonstration against the bookmobile, she saw to it that there would be defenders as well as protesters yesterday morning. Her grandson, Harley Hoover, put a stop to the attack. By that time, I was inside the bookmobile myself, and I can tell you I was glad to see Harley and his young helpers. Please welcome Mrs. Hoover."

The applause was warm and sustained. To Meg's surprise Mrs. Hoover stood and stepped forward. "People who live in Flume like the forest," she said in a high clear voice that held only a hint of old age. "We gather berries and mushrooms in their seasons. We see bear and deer and elk every day. Eagles soar above our streams. Raven sees us. We watch the mountain, and the mountain watches us." She meant Mount Saint Helens. Hair rose on Meg's nape. She was listening to a true storyteller.

"Flume is a good place to live, a good place for children. My children and grandchildren and great-grandchildren come there to learn the forest. But we live in the world, too, and Annie Baldwin brings a part of the world to us every week. That's good for Flume. Annie likes the children, and they like her. They tell her stories, and she listens and gives them books with pictures." Her eyes twinkled. "And she has a nice place for elders like me to sit and rest our feet while *we* tell her stories."

The audience smiled and chuckled.

"I brought our principal chief here tonight to honor Annie. Tomorrow, in Flume, we will dance for Annie." She gave a brisk nod and tottered back to her chair.

Cheers from the young people who had greeted Mrs. Hoover led the applause. Meg clapped, too, eyes prickling.

As she stepped forward again to introduce Maddie, something flashed past Meg's head and hit the bookmobile with a whack. Pat shouted. Nussbaum jumped to his feet. Another missile flew but it fell short of the bus.

"Please, everyone. Please." Meg had no idea what she meant. She was damned if she was going to drop onto her belly, though that was probably what she should do.

The crowd milled and yelled. Signs swayed. Toward the back, near the hedge that separated the parking lot from the sidewalk, a scrum of dark forms tussled and heaved. She thought she saw Beth. As Meg watched, a uniformed policeman leaped from the city car and ran across the street toward the action.

"Please be calm." Meg pitched her voice so that, thanks to the microphone, it filled the area. "Now you know what the attack was like. That was an ice soaker that just hit the bus. I'm from a hotter place than Flume, so I had to be told that an ice soaker is a ball of ice with a rock in the middle. They make a lot of noise when they hit metal. One of them hit me on the side of the head yesterday, which may explain why I'm not very articulate tonight." She was chattering to override the turmoil. She peered. "Ah, I see that things are calming down. If I may have your attention..."

People had stopped screeching and jumping around, but they were still talking in high excited voices. Meg waited. The cop waved at her and shouted something. Everybody watched as he and two other men led two kids in parkas across to the patrol car. Beth followed them.

"That was invigorating. May I have your attention, please?" Meg repeated the refrain until the audience was quiet. "Thank you. Our second guest needs no introduction to most of you. Madeline Thomas is hereditary chief of the Two Falls Band and principal chief of the Klalos. She is also a longtime Friend of the Library. Ladies and gentlemen, Chief Thomas."

Madeline smiled at the applause. "Thank you. I'm a Friend of the Library, because the library has been a friend to me. Last year the Klalo Nation received a bequest from Miss Fern Trout. She left us her family's farm, an orchard outside Two Falls. Margaret McLean and I have conferred, and the upshot is that the Klalos will donate the farmhouse to the library district, to serve as the new Two Falls Branch Library." There was a stir of interest and a scattering of applause. Madeline raised a calming hand.

Meg felt a moment of intense annoyance. Maddie should have warned her. All the same, she trusted the chief's instincts. Maddie was taking advantage of a dramatic moment to underline the tribe's generosity and probably to convince rivals and disaffected tribe members that she'd made a good decision. She'd also made an end run around the holdouts on the library board.

"...and that will free up money from the levy to replace the old bookmobile," she was saying. "The farmhouse is our gift not just to the library, but to the people of Latouche County. We in Two Falls, all of us, not just the Klalos, need the new library, but the bookmobile serves the whole library region. We need it, and we need Annie Baldwin to drive it. Thank you all."

Warm applause followed, with cheers from the Hoover contingent. Out on the street, the police car pulled away, and a county car replaced it. Beth walked back to the parking lot. Meg breathed a sigh of relief.

She thanked Madeline and talked a bit about the pictures on the website and the donations coming in to the Foundation from faraway places. Then she launched into her account of the attack on the bookmobile. She kept it as crisp and factual as she could.

"It was a frightening experience," she said when she reached the point at which Todd and the ambulance arrived, "and I've thought a lot about it. I want to share those thoughts with you. First, Annie had already fallen by the time I reached the bus, and when I got to her she was unconscious. The people standing on church property could see her. They were right across the street."

Silence.

"They continued to throw snowballs and rocks at the bus, they went on calling Annie names, and they made no effort to help her. I had already called 911, and I think someone else had, too, but the people standing there chanting and throwing things hadn't."

She let the silence ring. It had a rhythm of its own.

"The second thing I want to mention is that nobody else was coming to the bookmobile. In fact, other than the church people, Wendy Resnik, Harley Hoover, and his young helpers, I saw nobody out on that street at all. So I think it's safe to say that people in Flume who would have used the bookmobile were afraid to go to it. People without cars, young mothers with toddlers, elderly people."

Silence. The candles flickered. One of them guttered.

Meg drew an amplified breath. "The third thing I want to mention is the names this...congregation was using against Annie."

The crowd stirred.

"Harlot and bitch are merely despicable slanders, but witch is something else."

At that point there were groans and murmurs but no one interrupted her.

"You probably know that some religious groups object to the portrayal of witches in movies and books. Works like *Harry Potter*, or I suppose, *Macbeth*. I'm not a great believer in witches myself. The term means whatever an unscrupulous person wants it to mean. Mostly it means 'this is a woman I don't like.'"

Nods and murmurs of agreement.

"Boycotting books and films, picketing, preaching, discussing black magic—all of those are perfectly legitimate things to do. At the same time, I want to remind you that women in this country were put to death because their neighbors imagined they were practicing witchcraft. I also want to mention that the preferred method of executing witches in the Old Testament is to stone them to death."

There was a collective moan.

"They were throwing rocks at Annie Baldwin!" Meg heard herself shout. Just like Harley Hoover. She bit her lip and took a calming breath. She needed to finish before she lost control.

"People in rural Latouche County, and in every rural area of this country, have a right to read what they want to read without being intimidated by liars and slanderers—by bullies who orchestrate violence and hide under the tattered cloak of piety. Thank you for coming tonight to honor a brave woman, and please, please support Annie's bookmobile."

She was only half-aware of applause and shouts of encouragement. A reporter came up, and Meg said something vague to him. Beth waved and slipped away. The mayor had gone. Mrs. Hoover smiled and patted Meg's arm. Meg shook a lot of hands. Eventually everyone including Meg went home.

Chapter 21

IT WASN'T UNTIL she had parked the Accord in her garage that Meg started to shake. A light shone in the kitchen. She made it to the back door, fumbled her key into the lock, and wobbled inside. The house was warm but silent. Rob had not come to the rally. She supposed he must be asleep, though it was not yet ten.

She rejected scotch in favor of chamomile tea, slopped water into the kettle and set it to boil, warmed the teapot, and finally, when the shaking stopped, hung her parka on its hook by the door. As she did, she heard creaking sounds above, but she had brewed her tea and sat down to sip it before Rob appeared, almost at her elbow.

She jumped. Tea spilled into her saucer.

"I didn't mean to startle you." He wore the *gi* and was barefoot, his ghost persona.

"You didn't come to the rally." She hadn't meant to sound accusatory.

"No." He sat, grimacing. "Hug called me. Said you had an incident."

"Somebody threw a snowball."

"Ice soaker."

"Whatever. They took two kids into custody."

"From the church. I e-mailed your photos to Wade. He recognized

217

the boys from the crowd in Flume. Handgun in their pickup. Unregistered." He was speaking in bursts. "Keeping them overnight."

"Are you okay?"

"Trying to cut the medication."

"Why?"

"I needed to think. Tell me how it went."

Meg collected her wits. As she told him about the rally, the good feelings it had generated came back with a renewal of energy. By the time she wound down, she almost felt up to posting an account of the rally to the nice people who were sending money from Saskatoon and Hampstead and Sydney.

She offered Rob tea, which he refused, and warmed her own. "The best thing was all those librarians showing up. Oh, and Mrs. Hoover. She's terrific."

"I bet Maddie was front and center."

"Well, yes." Meg grinned. "*Toujours* the politician. I wish I had the instinct."

Rob didn't smile. "Your brother called."

Meg set her cup down. "Duncan?"

"Yes. We talked."

"I suppose he's upset."

"Yes. I explained why you came home."

Meg turned that over in her mind. "Thank you, I think."

A muscle jumped at the hinge of his jaw. "Can I ask you something?"

"Of course."

"Why the hell did I have to explain to your brother who I am?" He didn't shout, but he might as well have.

Meg went cold. "What do you mean?"

He fell silent, obviously wrestling with his temper. At last he said with evident care, "We've been together four years, you and I. Duncan is the brother you communicate with. Isn't it a little strange that he didn't have a clue? He thought I was a neighbor, or a passing Jehovah's Witness, or the goddamn doctor making a housecall."

"Duncan and I don't talk about anything but family." The moment Meg said that, she knew she couldn't have said anything stupider or more hurtful. She bit her lip so hard she tasted blood.

Rob stared at her.

Tears welled in her eyes.

He closed his. "And please don't cry. I can't deal with that now. In fact, I can't deal with anything right now. Good night, Meg." He shoved himself to his feet, grunting with pain, and walked out of the kitchen.

It was one of the more miserable nights of Meg's existence. When she dragged herself upstairs an hour later, Rob was so heavily asleep he had to have taken a pain pill. She didn't try to wake him. He needed to rest and heal. So she told herself. She was also afraid to wake him.

She lay still beside him for hours, thinking about him and about her mother. She slept a little, waking with a start and sliding back into dream-plagued sleep. At five she got up and went downstairs. It had warmed up during the long night. The rain dissolved snow and ice, cleaning everything.

She took a shower in the tub downstairs and dressed in clothes from the drier. She tried to think about Rob, but her mind ran in circles. At six-thirty, she was posting her version of the rally on the website when she heard him come downstairs. She jumped up and ran to the kitchen.

"Hi."

"Will you help me out of my corset?" He ran a hand through his hair, which stood up.

"What! Oh, the strapping."

"Yeah. Takes too much twisting to get it off. I need a shower." He sounded bleak and distant.

"Okay, but I'll follow you upstairs and do it there." The less time he spent with unstrapped ribs the better.

"Okay." He trudged back up and took off the jacket of the *gi*. He'd slept in it, and it was crumpled and sweaty.

Meg did not want to look at the bruise on his chest, but she gritted her teeth and undid the Velcro straps that held the device in place. Corset was not a bad name for it—it looked Victorian. The bruise was still fresh, black with blue edges, a little off-center, and huge.

Meg gulped. She was not going to cry. "That's horrible."

"Yes." He headed for the shower. "Maybe you can see why I wasn't about to fire the Glock at a hundred-and-ten-pound girl who was not wearing body armor. Thanks."

"What do you want for breakfast?"

"Coffee." He turned back, wincing, and smiled a little. "*Toujours* Meg." That was more like Rob.

She expelled a relieved breath. "Pancakes."

"I'm not hungry."

"No, but you will be." She practically ran downstairs, grateful for something to do. She heard the shower running, and thought she heard his cell phone ring. When he came down, the pancake batter was ready, and she had fried bacon and warmed the maple syrup.

"Coffee smells good." He wore a clean *gi*. He saw her looking at it. "Easiest thing to get in and out of." He laid the rib protector on the table and took off the jacket. "Maybe I'll wear the *gi* to work."

Meg fumbled around but got the straps tight enough eventually. He was sweating by the time she finished. He sat in stages, eyes shut.

She set coffee in front of him and turned to the griddle. "Did you take a pain pill?" She poured batter onto the hot surface.

"Yes, ma'am." He picked up his mug.

She watched bubbles form in the batter and flipped the first cake.

"I'm sorry, Meg. I should not have rained on your parade last night."

"You meant what you said."

"Yes, but I didn't need to say it then."

She slipped the pancake onto a warming plate and poured more batter. "When I said Duncan and I only talk about family, I meant that he updates me on my parents and brothers, and on everybody's offspring. He asks polite questions about Lucy. I tell him her accomplishments. I never tell him anything else about her, not her bad jokes or that speeding ticket she got or her latest boyfriend. That would be too much information. We say a word or two about our work. That's it. We don't even talk politics. Both of us are making an effort, but it is an effort."

"I see. I misunderstood."

Meg flipped the second pancake. "I *confided* in Aunt Margaret. I confide in you. I don't confide in Duncan."

"Why not? He seems like a nice guy."

"He is. I just don't trust him. With reason," she added, bitter, thinking of the last week.

Rob ate his pancake very slowly. He didn't touch the bacon. Neither of them said anything for a while. Meg warmed both coffees.

At last Rob said, "When my father was killed, I felt sad and angry, but when my mother died, I felt like a worthless piece of shit."

"Rob!"

"Hush. I do have a point. Would you say that you left LA feeling like a piece of shit?"

"Yes."

"Before he shipped out, Dad took me aside and told me to be brave and take care of my mother."

"How *could* he?"

"Come on, Meg. It's the kind of thing men in precarious occupations have always told their sons. Daughters, too, for all I know."

"What happened?" Meg whispered but she knew.

"My mother went haywire when he was killed. She cried and yelled and drank too much. After a while she partied nonstop. She was still young. I guess she was trying not to grow up. Or denying that things had changed. She ran her car off the road when she was drunk, and I thought I'd failed her. My father didn't mean to do that to me. What he said was just a platitude."

"I'm sorry."

"Yeah. Me, too. It probably cost me my marriage."

Meg stared at him.

His eyes were somber. "After my grandfather died, I decided I had to move up here, no matter what, to take care of my grandmother."

"But..."

"I probably didn't have to. Gran was surprised. She had good caregivers and lots of friends. I could have come up and visited every month, talked with her on the phone each night, that kind of thing. But I quit my job and told my wife we were moving north."

"And she refused?"

"Of course she refused. All her friends were down there. She was a stay-at-home mom, and her house meant a lot to her. Her family was there. And she hates rain."

Meg said in a small voice, "Do you wish you were still married to her?"

His mouth eased in a smile. "No. She'd drive me nuts. And vice versa. Also, pardon me, but I don't like Southern California. I just wish I hadn't been so damned compulsive. I hurt her unnecessarily. And Willow, too."

"Willow's okay."

"I hope so." He swallowed coffee. "I've gone way around the block to get a simple point across. My dad didn't really think an eight-year-old could take care of a grown woman—or should. He was probably just telling me to behave myself."

"I see." Meg didn't.

"Your brother didn't really think the sight of his illegitimate grand-daughter would give your father a heart attack. What he thought was that your father would create a scene, ruin the funeral for your mother's children, and hurt Lucy's feelings."

Meg turned that over in her mind. "I'm not sure I believe it."

Rob shrugged and winced at the incautious move. "I could be wrong. Duncan was a little incoherent. Whatever he meant, though, you should talk it over with him. Not now when you're still raw. Later. Call him for Christmas."

Meg thought about it—and about Rob. She almost opened her mouth and said, "Marry me." It would not have been good timing. Instead, she told him how her inadvertent fund-raising progressed. There would be enough for a down payment on a bus if the cash flow continued.

After eight, journalists started calling her. They had called before the rally, and she had left messages for them. Now they sounded urgent in the deadline-in-the-offing way of newshawks. She gave a couple of telephone interviews from her home office, decided it was only a matter of time before a video crew showed up at the library, and went upstairs to dress like a respectable librarian. She had only herself to blame.

Rob was on the phone—his phone.

She dressed quietly, watching him. He stood still, head bent. After a while, he leaned against the wall as if he needed support. He didn't say much. At last, he flipped the phone cover down.

"What?" Meg said.

"That was Beth. Aidan Pascoe tried to kill himself early this morning."

Meg's breath escaped in a moan.

"I'm going to the hospital." He could not drive the pickup with the bruise and broken ribs. It had a manual transmission.

"I'll drive you."

"Beth is sending Henry Perkins." He said the deputy's name with surprising venom.

She stared at him, bewildered, but he didn't explain. She helped him into jeans and a button-up shirt and jacket. She even put his shoes on. He was silent all the while, vibrating with what she understood was anger. They went downstairs together.

Rob didn't sit. He stood at the door to the back porch and stared out at the rain. When Henry beeped the horn to announce his arrival, Rob turned the knob.

"Rob—"

"I'll call your cell." He was out the door.

She had the feeling she had missed something in his account of the events in Aidan's apartment. "Okay," she said quietly. "I'll be at the library." He probably didn't hear.

~

"DISPATCHER said to pick you up, sir?" Perkins sounded uneasy.

Rob took his time fitting himself into the patrol car. It was one of the old low-slung cruisers, so he had to do some bending and twisting.

"Seat belt, sir?"

"No. Go slow. To the hospital."

"Sir?" He sounded surprised.

The radio crackled. Henry responded appropriately with his number and destination.

Rob looked at his profile. Big, handsome, blond kid, straight out of Klalo High School and the community college law enforcement program. High scores. Popular with the other uniforms. Corky thought well of him.

"Where were you while I was negotiating with Carla Jackman?"

"Huh? Ah, down on the street, sir."

"At Jeff Fong's elbow, right?"

"Well, sort of, yeah. The other guys stood over by the dry cleaners. Jeff said he wanted a runner, in case...you know."

"In case he needed to race upstairs and shoot up the apartment."

"Yessir."

"Do you know the meaning of the word discretion?"

"Like being discreet?" The car crept along Oak.

"I take it you could hear what I was saying to Carla."

"Well, most of it."

"And what she was saying to me."

"Her I heard. She was screaming." His mouth twisted in a smirk. The car lurched, and the movement jabbed Rob in the side.

"Take it slow." Rob took a long breath—not a deep one. He wasn't into gulps of air these days. "Jeff is an experienced detective. He knows better than to blab what he hears at a crime scene to all and sundry. Do *you* know better, Perkins?"

"I just thought it was funny."

"What was funny?"

"You know, about Pascoe. I know him, sir. We were in the same classes in high school. He's a dork."

"And being a dork is a capital crime?" It was a rhetorical question, and Henry had the wit not to answer. The car oozed along toward the hospital. "Do you have a personal computer?"

"Sure."

"So you get those come-ons about women who can't get enough of men with very long dicks."

"Sir!"

"Hell, my *grandmother* got them."

"It's just spam."

"And the ads aimed at my age group."

"Viagra?"

"Right. Impotence. The big fear. More spam, Perkins. More crap. All of it feeds into and preys on the fear of impotence. As you heard Carla say, Aidan is suffering from post-traumatic stress, with one of the commoner consequences. If you'd thought more about traumatic stress and less about impotence, maybe you wouldn't have found Aidan's situation so fucking funny you had to share the joke with your friends."

Henry didn't reply. His jaw set.

"And of course, they shared it with their friends and girlfriends.

It was too good not to repeat. They had lots of time to circulate your joke. By midnight last night, it was a big yuck at the Latouche County Jail. I suppose you've heard."

"What? That people are talking?"

"Aidan tried to hang himself this morning."

Henry said nothing, but his hands clenched on the wheel. The car lurched again. Rob swore.

The hospital had moved Annie Baldwin out of Intensive Care to another floor. She was conscious but slept a great deal, or so Beth said when Rob dragged the reluctant Henry up to the room where Aidan lay with tubes and wires keeping him alive.

"Still no family?" Rob asked.

"His mother's here. I sent her down to the cafeteria to eat something." Beth turned to Henry with a smile that told Rob she didn't know of Henry's little indiscretion.

Henry nodded and shuffled his feet. He wasn't looking at his victim.

Rob took in Aidan's blank face and bruised throat. *My victim? No, but not exclusively Henry's either.* "What unspeakable moron supplied the kid with sheets?" Aidan had torn them and braided a noose.

"Now, Rob."

"I had him on suicide watch."

"I know, my dear. You did what you could."

He digested that. Cold comfort.

"He's comatose," Beth said. "Not, they think, brain-dead. At least not yet. Bring Carla to him."

"Do you think she'll come?"

"Ask her."

Rob rousted out Edwin Jackman and a sleepy Linda Ramos to accompany him. That took time. He knew the responsibility for telling Carla was his, but misery loves company.

He thought Carla had probably heard something, though women prisoners were kept on a different floor from the men, and he was right. One look at her swollen red eyes told him that she knew what had happened.

He said, "I'm sorry, Carla."

Instead of screeching at him, she just nodded. "And I'm sorry I shot you. I didn't mean to."

"I know."

She was sitting, her shoulders sagging, on a bunk in a cell meant for two. She turned to her father. "What do I have to do now?"

Jackman said, "I'm sorry, too."

She fired up. "No, you're not. You think Aidan is scum on the sole of your shoe."

"I think he's an unhappy young man. He needs your help."

"My help." Her laugh was bitter. "When I did this to him?" She looked from her father to Rob. "Do you think I'm dumb? If I hadn't told you, he wouldn't have tried to hang himself."

Rob said, "There's plenty of room for blame."

"What do you mean?"

"One of my deputies overheard you and had to tell his buddies."

"Not Sergeant Fong?"

"No." Rob drew a breath and felt the jab in his ribs. "He, the deputy, will be reprimanded."

She snorted. "Big man. I'll bet he's a jock."

"He played football for Klalo High School."

"I know the type. They always win, don't they? The jocks and the bullies."

"Not always. I, uh, took him up to look at what he'd done. We'll see how he reacts to that."

"He'll probably turn it into a joke."

"He may." Rob met her eyes. "Or maybe he'll grow up a little."

After a long moment, she looked down at her hands, which were clenched in her lap. "Happy birthday to me." Carla was not stupid. "What do I have to do?"

"You don't have to do anything, but I think you care what happens to Aidan. He's in a coma. The sheriff, who is pretty smart, thinks you ought to talk to him."

"About what?" Her voice rose.

"About whatever it was the two of you enjoyed doing together." Pissing on books, throwing Molotov cocktails. Rob steered his thoughts to other channels. "His mother is here."

"Oh, *she'll* be a big help."

"Maybe she will," Rob snapped, losing patience. "At least she's trying."

"The thing is—"

"What?" Edwin Jackman interposed.

"I don't want to marry Aidan, Dad." Her tongue touched her lips, as if they were dry. "I like him. I feel sorry for him. But I don't want to tie myself to him."

Linda Ramos drew an audible breath. Jackman looked bewildered, as well he might. Aidan was comatose, near death. He and Carla were both charged with crimes that meant serious jail time. Marriage had to be the least of his worries.

Rob thought of Meg's objections to marriage and felt as if he were drowning in irony. He reached for practicality as for a life preserver. "All you need to do is talk, Carla. Talk about the weather. It's raining. Talk about music or politics or the price of gas."

Her eyebrows shot up.

Rob groped. "About riding the motorcycle and fixing up the apartment and cooking something for him besides popcorn. Aidan is surrounded by machines going *beep*. Let him hear a human voice."

To his dismay her eyes flooded with tears, but she sniffed and squared her shoulders. "Yes. All right, I will." She wiped her nose on her sleeve. "Thank you."

Chapter 22

ROB DIDN'T CALL.

Meg was so busy she didn't notice until afternoon. She'd made a quick visit to Annie at the hospital before going on to the library, but Annie was asleep and Bob drowsing, so Meg didn't stay long. Bob knew nothing about Aidan Pascoe's condition, and the nurses on that floor wouldn't say anything, just that Aidan was in Intensive Care. So Meg went to the library to face the media.

The half dozen reporters made her task easy. There was an unspoken consensus that an attack on the library was an attack on the press, so their questions weren't hostile, and her account of the international response to the bookmobile's plight perked them up. News to them.

So she gave her brief press conference and later, when the watery sun was at its best, did an on-camera interview for Channel Ten, standing by the battered side of the bus. Pat had removed the platform. The dents and broken windows showed up vividly, but she hadn't removed the shrine. Sodden flowers and stuffed bunnies and bears had their own mute eloquence. Meg felt only slightly nauseated when the reporters heard of a breaking story, wheeled like sandpipers in a metaphorical clump, and vanished.

She called together the staffers on duty, gave them a report on Annie's condition, thanked them for their support of the rally, and

announced that she was appointing Pat to Marybeth's position as second-in-command, with an assistant so Pat could carry on as children's
librarian. Pat would have Marybeth's office. Also, straight-faced, Meg
thanked Wendy for warning her of the attack on the bookmobile and
accompanying her to Flume. Not for a moment did Meg think her staff
couldn't figure out what had happened. They had all known Marybeth, and they knew Wendy.

She called Madeline at the B&B, but Jack told her his wife was out
in Flume—dancing. So Meg went back to the hospital, and this time
Annie was awake.

Bob had gone off somewhere. Annie still looked sleepy. She gave
Meg a shy smile.

Meg told her about the rally and the interlibrary and international
responses to her plight. That the Klalos were dancing for her seemed
to interest her more. She wanted to know what it meant. Meg did her
best, and tried to question Annie about the attack, too, but the subject
clearly upset her. Meg thought she had known it was coming.

Meg left when Bob returned, hoping she hadn't worn Annie out.
Annie seemed dissociated from the bookmobile. She showed no interest in a new vehicle. She wanted the old one fixed, she said.

Meg didn't argue with her. She hugged Annie, assured her that she
had plenty of sick leave, and took off for home. It was nearly six, so
Meg stopped by the only Chinese restaurant in Latouche County and
picked up dinner. Jeff Fong had given the restaurant one star, meaning
it was tolerable but nowhere near as good as the real thing. Rob liked
it, though, and Meg was not in a cooking mood.

While she waited for her order, she called Rob, but his phone was
still taking messages, so she said, "Chinese okay? Love you," and hung
up, puzzled and a little worried. She called the hospital, but she was
not a relative, so they wouldn't give her information about Aidan.

Surely Rob had not been at the hospital all day. She tormented
herself for a few minutes with the possibility that a clot had broken
loose, and he had suffered a stroke. The restaurant cashier called her
number. She paid up and carried the sack of aromatic cartons out to
the car. Everything was still hot when she got home. It was stone cold
by the time Rob arrived around eight.

When she heard him, she jumped up from her computer and got to the kitchen as he grabbed at a chair back to steady himself.

"Rob!"

"Hi, Meg. Long day." He opened his eyes. "I need a shower."

"What!"

"Believe me. Will you come up and liberate me from this torture device?" He meant the corset.

So she did. She heated food while he took the world's longest shower. He trailed downstairs in a clean ghost costume, and she re-strapped the ribs, muttering to herself about heroes in fiction who always recovered within twenty-four hours from bullet wounds, head injuries, major surgery, and the loss of loved ones. The man had three broken ribs.

"Can we eat? I think I forgot lunch." He put himself into a chair and sat there, slumped against the chair back.

Without thinking, Meg poured each of them a whisky.

Rob took a pain pill with his first swallow of scotch.

"For God's sake."

"It's okay. You can carry me upstairs when I pass out."

Meg glowered at him and dished up. They ate in silence, Rob with a fork, an index of his exhaustion. He usually insisted on chopsticks with Asian food.

Meg toyed with a morsel of moo shu chicken. Rob ploughed through fried rice, princess shrimp, and the moo shu, apparently without tasting anything. He was hungry, right enough.

Waiting was hard. When she thought he was slowing down, she said, "What happened?"

"Aidan died." His mouth twisted. "To be exact, his mother pulled the plug."

"Oh, no!"

Rob's fork clattered onto the plate.

"I mean, the poor woman."

He picked up his glass and swallowed scotch.

"Did Carla—"

"Carla talked to him. She gave it her best shot. Aidan didn't respond. He was brain-dead. Flat-lined. Gonzo."

"Robert."

"Yeah, I'm unreasonable. I expected them, someone, the doctors at least, to give him a chance." His eyes clenched shut. "Damn it to hell."

Meg instructed herself not to cry. She had been blubbering like a two-year-old for a week. Now was not the time, and she didn't have the right. She had never met Aidan Pascoe. She cleared her throat. "He was a kid who never did have a chance, from the sound of it."

Rob scrubbed at his eyes with both hands. "I came close to strangling Henry Perkins this morning."

"Henry!"

The whole story poured out. Meg could not have said what horrified her most—Henry's conduct or the fact that Rob hadn't told her of it.

She supposed that, for women, infertility would be an equivalent of impotence, and she had known barren women who obsessed about their condition, but there was nothing like the shame and humiliation young men evidently felt when faced with impotence. Especially a young man with a father like Aidan's. That the feeling was stupid and pointless didn't negate it. That other young men would turn on the victim mercilessly seemed shameful to her, and she said so.

Rob didn't argue. He looked too depressed to argue. "What gets me is the fantasies Aidan and Carla constructed, in spite of everything. It turns out the Trout orchard was at the center of their imaginary universe."

The observation came out of left field. Meg could only gape.

Rob thrust a hand through his hair. It stood up in sandy tufts. "After Aidan died—and it took awhile—Carla asked to see her lawyer. She intends to plead guilty to everything. He advised her to wait, but she's determined."

"But why?"

"Because Aidan won't be around to care one way or the other."

"You're going to have to explain."

"When Fern Trout started to fail, Carla had just met Aidan. Marybeth talked a lot about how the family farm would come to her, because she was her aunt's only surviving relative. She trotted Carla out there for inspection, and Carla and Aidan started dreaming about what they'd do with Trout Farm when Fern died."

"What *they'd* do?"

Rob toyed with the empty shot glass. "Carla said her mother didn't really care about the farm and would never have wanted to live way out beyond Two Falls."

"True. So?"

"So Carla thought she could con Marybeth into letting her run the place with Aidan."

"The Marybeth I knew would've subdivided it," Meg said flatly. "I don't know what she told her aunt she'd do, but that's what would have happened."

"It was a fantasy, Meg. It hinged on Marybeth's assumption that she'd inherit the land. I remember Miss Trout. It would have taken her two sessions with Marybeth to see right through her. One, really, but Miss Trout was always fair."

"She gave everybody a second chance?"

"Even me." Rob smiled a little. "Carla said the will was a total surprise and that her mother was very angry."

Meg shivered. "I can imagine."

"She talked to her lawyer about filing suit and blustered a lot. The lawyer—and I have to get the man's name because he deserves a medal—said contesting the will would eat up most of the cash she'd inherited, and that she probably wouldn't win the case, that the will was tight."

"And Marybeth threw in the towel?"

He nodded. "Still blustering. Carla decided to trash the house. She thought her mother would be pleased, that Marybeth might change her mind and file suit after all. Carla really wanted that farm."

Meg thought about it. "When they told her what they'd done, Marybeth probably reamed the kids out." She would have been self-righteous about it.

"So Carla said. I gathered it was a major disillusionment for her." His tone was sardonic.

"She was only seventeen," Meg protested.

"She had seventeen years' experience with Marybeth. And she knew better than to ruin a house that didn't belong to her. Remember all those books."

Meg did remember. "Marybeth was dead by the time they tried to burn Jack and Maddie out."

"Yes. Carla and Aidan were higher than kites when they threw their little bomb. The arson was pure spite. There is a lot of Marybeth in Carla. Which makes for irony, since she can't inherit from her mother if she pleads guilty."

"Good God," Meg said blankly.

"Yeah. In both cases, the arson and the vandalism, the idea was Carla's. Aidan was just following orders." He gave her Harley's assessment of Aidan's character.

"It makes sense."

She thought he was about to say something profound like "Nothing makes sense," but his cell phone rang.

He took it out, looked at it with loathing, and poked the Talk button.

"They what? Who's hurt?" He rolled his eyes and listened. "Call Captain Kononen with my compliments and tell him to handle it. I'm going to bed." He listened some more and signed off, closing the phone with a clack.

"What?"

"Seth Pascoe took a shot at Henry out at Logger Lover." Logger Lover was the local watering hole for cops. "Henry shot back."

"Seth? Aidan's brother?"

"Yes. Henry missed Seth but not the mirror behind the bar. Their friends disarmed them." He set the phone down and looked at Meg. "Nothing makes sense."

～

MEG got to the library late the next day. Thanks to the combination of Chinese food, scotch, and Vicodin, Rob was a late starter, too. Meg drove him to work.

A man by the name of Frank Waltz was waiting in her office. She did not know him, but she thought she had heard his name.

"I am...or was, a neighbor of Marybeth Jackman," Waltz said, rising from the guest chair. "My wife and I were shocked to hear that young Carla has confessed to her mother's murder."

"I think it was more like manslaughter." Meg shook his hand. "Shocking even so. What can I do for you, Mr. Waltz?"

He laughed. "It may be that I can do something for you, Mrs. McLean."

Meg smiled and didn't correct him.

"Annie Baldwin is a member of our church, so we were concerned to hear about her injury and the attack on the bookmobile. I had a look at the damage as I came into the lot this morning. It's superficial, of course, but that's an old rig. School bus at one time?"

"Yes."

"The wife and I have a large RV, big as a Greyhound. We bought it when I retired five years ago. Thought we'd travel around the country in it every winter, but we only took one trip. My kids don't want it. It's a diesel but expensive to run, and they're both whatchacall'em, greenies. Won't touch it." He sounded glum.

Meg could see where he was going and her heart sank. Expensive to run. "Uh, what kind of mileage are we talking about?"

He named a figure that was better than the bus's, even with Bob's tender ministrations. The bus also ran on diesel. "I drove it over here. Want a look at it?"

Meg didn't, but she said yes with what she hoped sounded like enthusiasm.

~

"IT'S a palace." She told Rob that evening in the kitchen. He'd come home early and looked better, though the corset was still in place. The table was set, bread cut, beer poured into glasses that matched. "Why do people buy something like that, something hugely expensive, and not use it? They took one measly trip in it."

Rob was cooking—or, rather, thawing. A frozen vacuum-packed wedge of chili floated in a pot of simmering water. He plucked the edge of the plastic sack, flipped it so the other side would thaw, and blew on his fingertips. "They were buying a dream. Or showing off."

"They seem like nice people."

"The neighbors? They are. Conscientious. Kind. Charitable."

"They want to donate it. He said he can't sell it. Buyers are scared because of oil prices. Everybody's staying home. He was going to give it to Trinity Lutheran, but he said they wouldn't use it. They'd just sell it for ten cents on the dollar. He wants somebody to use it."

"Would it make a good bookmobile?"

"I think so, though we'd have to gut it and put in bookshelves and a wheelchair lift. I'll have to get Bob Baldwin to look it over."

He started to laugh and clutched at his ribs. "Ow. God, that's funny. You pass your levy, Maddie gives you a library in Two Falls, and Waltz hands you a new bookmobile. You'll have all this leftover money, even with the economy down the tubes. Can you donate it to Beth for the sheriff's department?"

"Shut up."

Still chortling, he pulled the chili from the boiling pot, turned the burner off, slopped the package into the sink, got out her kitchen scissors, cut the plastic open, and dolloped the hot chili neatly into two warm bowls. He was a great cook.

"I like this," she said generously as he slid a plate of neat antipasti toward her. "I could get used to it."

"Marry me."

"Okay."

Silence. He stared into her eyes, his suspicious. "Just. Like. That."

"Yup."

ABOUT THE AUTHOR

Sheila Simonson is the author of twelve novels, eight of them mysteries. She taught English and history at the community college level until she retired to write full-time. She is the mother of a grown son and lives with her husband in Vancouver, Washington. She likes to hear from readers, who can visit her website at http://sheila.simonson.googlepages.com.

MORE MYSTERIES
FROM PERSEVERANCE PRESS
🕱 *For the New Golden Age* 🕱

ALBERT A. BELL, JR.
PLINY THE YOUNGER SERIES
Death in the Ashes *(forthcoming)*
ISBN 978-1-56474-532-3

JON L. BREEN
Eye of God
ISBN 978-1-880284-89-6

TAFFY CANNON
ROXANNE PRESCOTT SERIES
Guns and Roses
*Agatha and Macavity awards
nominee, Best Novel*
ISBN 978-1-880284-34-6

Blood Matters
ISBN 978-1-880284-86-5

Open Season on Lawyers
ISBN 978-1-880284-51-3

Paradise Lost
ISBN 978-1-880284-80-3

LAURA CRUM
GAIL MCCARTHY SERIES
Moonblind
ISBN 978-1-880284-90-2

Chasing Cans
ISBN 978-1-880284-94-0

Going, Gone
ISBN 978-1-880284-98-8

Barnstorming
ISBN 978-1-56474-508-8

JEANNE M. DAMS
HILDA JOHANSSON SERIES
Crimson Snow
ISBN 978-1-880284-79-7

Indigo Christmas
ISBN 978-1-880284-95-7

Murder in Burnt Orange
ISBN 978-1-56474-503-3

JANET DAWSON
JERI HOWARD SERIES
Bit Player
Golden Nugget Award nominee
ISBN 978-1-56474-494-4

What You Wish For
ISBN 978-1-56474-518-7

Death Rides the Zephyr
(forthcoming)
ISBN 978-1-56474-530-9

KATHY LYNN EMERSON
LADY APPLETON SERIES
**Face Down Below
the Banqueting House**
ISBN 978-1-880284-71-1

**Face Down Beside
St. Anne's Well**
ISBN 978-1-880284-82-7

Face Down O'er the Border
ISBN 978-1-880284-91-9

ELAINE FLINN
MOLLY DOYLE SERIES
Deadly Vintage
ISBN 978-1-880284-87-2

SARA HOSKINSON FROMMER
JOAN SPENCER SERIES
Her Brother's Keeper
ISBN 978-1-56474-525-5

HAL GLATZER
KATY GREEN SERIES
Too Dead To Swing
ISBN 978-1-880284-53-7

A Fugue in Hell's Kitchen
ISBN 978-1-880284-70-4

The Last Full Measure
ISBN 978-1-880284-84-1

MARGARET GRACE
MINIATURE SERIES
Mix-up in Miniature
ISBN 978-1-56474-510-1

WENDY HORNSBY
MAGGIE MACGOWEN SERIES
In the Guise of Mercy
ISBN 978-1-56474-482-1

The Paramour's Daughter
ISBN 978-1-56474-496-8

The Hanging
ISBN 978-1-56474-526-2

DIANA KILLIAN
POETIC DEATH SERIES
Docketful of Poesy
ISBN 978-1-880284-97-1

JANET LAPIERRE
PORT SILVA SERIES
Baby Mine
ISBN 978-1-880284-32-2

Keepers
*Shamus Award nominee, Best
Paperback Original*
ISBN 978-1-880284-44-5

Death Duties
ISBN 978-1-880284-74-2

Family Business
ISBN 978-1-880284-85-8

Run a Crooked Mile
ISBN 978-1-880284-88-9

HAILEY LIND
ART LOVER'S SERIES
Arsenic and Old Paint
ISBN 978-1-56474-490-6

LEV RAPHAEL
NICK HOFFMAN SERIES
Tropic of Murder
ISBN 978-1-880284-68-1

Hot Rocks
ISBN 978-1-880284-83-4

LORA ROBERTS
BRIDGET MONTROSE SERIES
Another Fine Mess
ISBN 978-1-880284-54-4

SHERLOCK HOLMES SERIES
**The Affair of the
Incognito Tenant**
ISBN 978-1-880284-67-4

REBECCA ROTHENBERG
BOTANICAL SERIES
The Tumbleweed Murders
(completed by Taffy Cannon)
ISBN 978-1-880284-43-8

SHEILA SIMONSON
LATOUCHE COUNTY SERIES
Buffalo Bill's Defunct
*WILLA Award, Best Original
Softcover Fiction*
ISBN 978-1-880284-96-4

An Old Chaos
ISBN 978-1-880284-99-5

Beyond Confusion
ISBN 978-1-56474-519-4

LEA WAIT
SHADOWS ANTIQUES SERIES
**Shadows of a Down East
Summer**
ISBN 978-1-56474-497-5

**Shadows on a Cape Cod
Wedding**
ISBN 978-1-56474-531-6

ERIC WRIGHT
JOE BARLEY SERIES
The Kidnapping of Rosie Dawn
*Barry Award, Best Paperback
Original. Edgar, Ellis, and Anthony
awards nominee*
ISBN 978-1-880284-40-7

NANCY MEANS WRIGHT
MARY WOLLSTONECRAFT SERIES
Midnight Fires
ISBN 978-1-56474-488-3

The Nightmare
ISBN 978-1-56474-509-5

*REFERENCE/
MYSTERY WRITING*

KATHY LYNN EMERSON
**How To Write Killer
Historical Mysteries:
The Art and Adventure of
Sleuthing Through the Past**
*Agatha Award, Best Nonfiction.
Anthony and Macavity awards
nominee.*
ISBN 978-1-880284-92-6

CAROLYN WHEAT
**How To Write Killer Fiction:
The Funhouse of Mystery & the
Roller Coaster of Suspense**
ISBN 978-1-880284-62-9